HATTIE BIG SKY

HATTIE BIG SKY

Kirby Larson

DELACORTE PRESS

Published by Delacorte Press
an imprint of Random House Children's Books
a division of Random House, Inc.
New York

Visit us on the Web! www.randomhouse.com/teens
Educators and librarians, for a variety of teaching tools,
visit us at www.randomhouse.com/teachers

The Library of Congress has cataloged the hardcover edition of this work as follows:
Larson, Kirby.
Hattie Big Sky / Kirby Larson.
  p. cm.
Includes bibliographical references.
Summary: After inheriting her uncle's homesteading claim in Montana,
sixteen-year-old orphan Hattie Brooks travels from Iowa in 1917 to make a home
for herself and encounters some unexpected problems related to the war
being fought in Europe.
ISBN 978-0-385-73313-7 (trade) — ISBN 978-0-385-90332-5 (glb)
[1. Self-reliance—Fiction. 2. Frontier and pioneer life—Fiction.
3. Orphans—Fiction. 4. Montana—History—20th century—Fiction.
5. World War, 1914–1918—United States—Fiction.]   I. Title.
PZ7.L32394Hat 2006
  [Fic]—dc22   2005035039

ISBN 978-0-440-23941-3 (tr. pbk.)

Printed in the United States of America
10 9 8 7 6 5 4 3 2
First Trade Paperback Edition

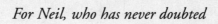

For Neil, who has never doubted

Acknowledgments

My journeys through Montana, literally and in my imagination, were aided by wonderful and generous people. It always amazes me that people will go out of their way for a complete stranger poking around in the past.

I won the editor lottery with Michelle Poploff, Hattie's godmother and biggest fan. Thank you, Michelle. Thanks also to Karen Lampe, the Louise to my Thelma—Billings born and bred and always ready for a road trip; to first readers of this manuscript: Maria Bennett, Kathryn Galbraith, Tricia Gardella, Brenda Guiberson, Sylvie Hossack, Mary Nethery, Dave Patneaude, Ann Whitford Paul, Vivian Sathre, Rhonda Schlafer, and Shelley Seeley; to my mother-in-law, Kelly Larson, for sharing her father's World War I letters; to Marvin Presser, for photos and Wolf Point history; to Mrs. Alma Hall, for opening the Wolf Point Museum just for me; to Nancy Long, who introduced me to the extended Nefzger family through Dick's memoir, *Homesteading in Montana;* to Dea Nefzger

Hostetler, who not only answered my endless questions but played chauffeur and gracious hostess during my stay in Wolf Point; to the good folks at the Montana Historical Society Library, especially Dave Walter and Rich Aarstad; to Dale Robbins, genealogist extraordinaire, who provided a window into Hattie's life; to Tricia and Jack Gardella of Montezuma Angus, who answered a city girl's ranching questions; to Ellen, John, and Dick Baumann and Harold Lyman, who answered a city girl's wheat farming questions; to the Blake family of Blake Nursery in Big Timber, Montana, for answers to wildflower questions; to Marcie Garrity for help with the German translations; to Chris Kiehl for the recording of "The Last Roll Call"; to Janice Hughes of the Selective Service System, who helped me understand the World War I draft process; to Lindsey Korst for Great Northern Railway routes and ideas about Hattie's train journey; to all the homesteaders who took time to write down their reminiscences; and to all the court clerks and librarians who patiently helped me find answers to my many, many questions. Any errors within are my fault alone.

I owe a debt of gratitude to my maternal grandmother, Lois Thomas Wright Brown, for giving me the seed of this story. And I salute the real Hattie Inez Brooks Wright, my step-great-grandmother, and all the men and women like her who tried to carve out places of their own on the Montana prairie and, in doing so, forever carved a place in our hearts and memory.

HATTIE BIG SKY

❧ CHAPTER 1 ❧

December 19, 1917
Arlington, Iowa

Dear Charlie,

Miss Simpson starts every day with a reminder to pray for you—and all the other boys who enlisted. Well, I say we should pray for the Kaiser—he's going to need those prayers once he meets you!

I ran into your mother today at Uncle Holt's store. She said word is you are heading for England soon, France after that. I won't hardly be able to look at the map behind Miss Simpson's desk now; it will only remind me of how far you are from Arlington.

Mr. Whiskers says to tell you he's doing fine. It's been so cold, I've been letting him sleep in my bedroom. If Aunt

1

Ivy knew, she'd pitch a fit. Thank goodness she finally decided I was too big to switch or my legs would be striped for certain.

You should see Aunt Ivy. She's made herself a cunning white envelope of a hat with a bright red cross stitched on the edge. She wears it to all the Red Cross meetings. Guess she wants to make sure everybody knows she's a paid-up member. She's been acting odd lately; even asked me this morning how was I feeling. First time in years she's inquired about my health. Peculiar. Maybe this Red Cross work has softened her heart.

Mildred Powell's knitting her fifth pair of socks; they're not all for you, so don't get swell-headed. She's knitting them for the Red Cross. All the girls at school are. But I suspect the nicest pair she knits will be for you.

You must cut quite the figure in your uniform. A figure eight! (Ha, ha.) Seriously, I am certain you are going to make us all proud.

Aunt Ivy's home from her meeting and calling for me. I'll sign off now but will write again soon.

Your school friend,
Hattie Inez Brooks

I blotted the letter and slipped it in an envelope. Aunt Ivy wouldn't think twice about reading anything she found lying around, even if it was in my own room, on my own desk.

"Hattie," Aunt Ivy called again. "Come down here!"

To be on the safe side, I slipped the envelope under my pillow, still damp from my good cry last night. Not that I was like Mildred Powell, who hadn't stopped boo-hooing since Charlie left. Only Mr. Whiskers and my pillow knew about my tears in the dark over Charlie. I did fret over his safety, but it was pure and sinful selfishness that wet my eyes at night.

In all my sixteen years, Charlie Hawley was one of the nicest things to happen to me. It was him who'd stuck up for me when I first came to live with Aunt Ivy and Uncle Holt, so shy I couldn't get my own name out. He'd walked me to school that very first day and every day after. Charlie was the one who'd brought me Mr. Whiskers, a sorry-looking tomcat who purred his way into my heart. The one who'd taught me how to pitch, and me a southpaw. So maybe I did spend a night now and then dreaming silly girl dreams about him, even though everyone knew he was sweet on Mildred. My bounce-around life had taught me that dreams were dangerous things—they look solid in your mind, but you just try to reach for them. It's like gathering clouds.

The class had voted to see Charlie off at the station. Mildred clung to his arm. His father clapped him on the back so often, I was certain he'd end up bruised. Miss Simpson made a dull speech as she presented Charlie with a gift from the school: a wool stocking cap and some stationery.

"Time to get aboard, son," the conductor called.

Something shifted in my heart as Charlie swung his foot up onto the train steps. I had told myself to hang back—didn't want to be lumped in with someone like Mildred—but I found myself running up to him and slipping something in his hand. "For luck!" I said. He glanced at the object and smiled. With a final wave, he boarded the train.

"Oh, Charlie!" Mildred leaned on Mrs. Hawley and sobbed.

"There, there." Charlie's mother patted Mildred's back.

Mr. Hawley took a bandanna from his pocket and made a big show of wiping his forehead. I pretended not to notice that he dabbed at his eyes, too.

The others made their way slowly down the platform, back to their cars. I stood watching the train a bit longer, picturing Charlie patting the pocket where he'd placed the wishing stone I'd given him. He was the one who'd taught me about those, too. "Look for the black ones," he'd told me. "With the white ring around the middle. If you throw them over your left shoulder and make a wish, it's sure to come true." He threw his wishing rocks with abandon and laughed at me for not tossing even one. My wish wasn't the kind that could be granted by wishing rocks.

And now two months had passed since Charlie stepped on that train. With him gone, life was like a batch of biscuits without the baking powder: flat, flat, flat.

"Hattie!" Aunt Ivy's voice was a warning.

"Yes, ma'am!" I scurried down the stairs.

She was holding court in her brown leather chair. Uncle Holt was settled into the hickory rocker, a stack of newspapers on his lap.

I slipped into the parlor and picked up my project, a pathetic pair of socks I'd started back in October when Charlie enlisted. If the war lasted five more years, they might actually get finished. I held them up, peering through a filigree of dropped stitches. Not even a good chum like Charlie could be expected to wear these.

4

"I had a lovely visit with Iantha Wells today." Aunt Ivy unpinned her Red Cross hat. "You remember Iantha, don't you, Holt?"

"Hmmm." Uncle Holt shook the newspaper into shape.

"I told her what a fine help you were around here, Hattie."

I dropped another stitch. To hear her tell it most days, there was no end to my flaws in the domesticity department.

"I myself never finished high school. Not any sense in it for some girls."

Uncle Holt lowered one corner of the paper. I dropped another stitch. Something was up.

"No sense at all. Not when there's folks like Iantha Wells needing help at her boardinghouse."

There. It was out. Now I knew why she had been so kind to me lately. She'd found a way to get rid of me.

She smoothed her skirt again. "God moves in mysterious ways. We should not question this bounty from Iantha." Though her comments directly affected me, I knew better than to say anything. Yet.

Uncle Holt tamped the Prince Albert tobacco down in his pipe. "There are only a few months left of the school year." He lit it and took a puff before continuing. "Seems to me it makes more sense for Hattie to finish." This wasn't the first time Uncle Holt had taken my side; I resolved to polish his shoes for him that very night in thanks for it.

Aunt Ivy glided on, as if Uncle Holt hadn't spoken. "It was agreed that Hattie would go where she was needed. And she is *needed* at Iantha's."

And not wanted *here,* I added. To myself, of course.

5

Uncle Holt squinted at me through curlicues of cherry-scented smoke. "Do you want to finish school?"

I set my knitting on my lap and considered my answer. For all I loved books, school was a chore. Especially without the diversions Charlie provided. But compared to working for Iantha Wells . . .

"She knows too much already," snapped Aunt Ivy. "Or thinks she does!" This with a glower in my direction. "It's Hattie's soul we must think of. Helping Iantha would foster a spirit of charity in the child, charity and—" Here Aunt Ivy stumbled, as if even she couldn't imagine what working in a boardinghouse could possibly teach someone like me. "And other womanly skills. It's quite the opportunity for a hard-working girl."

Two bright red spots glowed on her cheeks. Not much doubt that she was peeved. And not much doubt as to why. It galled her that Uncle Holt would ask my opinion about anything, let alone my own future. I was simply Hattie Here-and-There, with no right to an opinion.

I'd been orphaned before I'd lost my baby teeth. Pa's story was a familiar one to any miner's family: the coal dust ate up his lungs. I was just two or three when he passed. Aunt Seah took me in when I was five, after Mama died. The doctor said it was pneumonia that took her, but Aunt Seah claimed it was a broken heart. The kindest of my many stops along the way, she gave me the gift of certainty that my parents had loved one another. After Aunt Seah got too old to keep me, I was shuffled from one relative to another—some of them pretty far down on the shirttail. I'd stay to help out with this sick person or that until I'd run out of folks who needed help and didn't mind an extra mouth to feed to get it.

I was thirteen when Aunt Ivy took me in. She's really no aunt at all; Uncle Holt's a distant cousin. She couldn't resist the opportunity to do her Christian duty. Nor could she resist the opportunity to remind me every single day that I had nothing and no one. I should count my blessings, she lectured. Well, I did count them. The first blessing I counted every day was that she and I weren't related by blood.

The room grew so quiet I could hear Uncle Holt's pipe click against his teeth. He blew out a puff of sweet smoke and then spoke. "I suggest we all sleep on it."

Aunt Ivy wouldn't cross Uncle Holt, not in front of me. She flounced in her chair. "Whatever you say, Holt."

He fussed with his pipe and then with the papers on the pipe stand next to his chair. "Where did I put that?"

"Put what, Holt *dear*?" Aunt Ivy's voice could shatter glass.

"Letter. Came for Hattie today." A pile of newspapers cascaded to the floor. For a general-store clerk, Uncle Holt read more than any human being I knew. I was crazy about reading myself, but my taste ran to novels. Uncle Holt favored newspapers. He was the one who'd first warned about war in Europe. Said any fool could see it coming if he paid attention. Me, I hadn't paid attention until Charlie up and enlisted. Guess I know what category that puts me in.

"A letter!" I said. Maybe from Charlie!

"For Hattie?" asked Aunt Ivy.

Uncle Holt ignored her outstretched hand and delivered the envelope directly to me.

7

"Whoever is it from?" Aunt Ivy demanded.

"Someone in Montana." Uncle Holt disappeared behind the *Arlington News,* his signal that he was done with conversation for the evening.

I opened the envelope. There were two letters inside. The first was dated November 11, 1917.

> *Your uncle axed that I get the enclosed to you when he passed. It's the least I could do to repay him for his many kindnesses. If you decide yes, me and my husband Karl will help all we can.*
>
> > *Most sincerely yours, Perilee Johnson Mueller*

Decide yes about what? I unfolded the second letter.

My dear Hattie,

> *You will no doubt have forgotten me. I am your mother's only brother. Had I married and led a proper life, I would have sent for you long ago. I will not sugarcoat things: I have been a scoundrel. But here in Montana, I've made a new life. Wouldn't you know that as soon as I got a claim staked and a place built, the doc here would tell me this cough was going to kill me. You and I have something in common, besides the Wright blood. Neither one of us had a proper home of our own growing up—you orphaned and me leaving home after sixth grade. You will think I have never thought of the niece in Iowa. But this letter will show you I have. If you come out here to Vida, you will find my claim. I trust you've enough of your mother's backbone to meet the*

remaining requirements. If you do—and you have one
year to do it—320 Montana acres are yours.

"Oh!" I grabbed the arm of the settee.

"What is it? Bad news?" Aunt Ivy was at my side, eagerly peering over my shoulder. With a slight stutter, I read aloud the last paragraph of the letter:

> *Being of sound mind, I do hereby leave to Hattie Inez*
> *Brooks my claim and the house and its contents, as well*
> *as one steadfast horse named Plug and a contemptible*
> *cow known as Violet.*
>
> *Signed, Chester Hubert Wright,*
> *Uncle to Hattie Inez Brooks*
>
> *Postscript: H—Bring warm clothes and a cat.*

Aunt Ivy snatched the letters from my hand. I was too stunned to react. Three hundred twenty acres! A home of my own! Montana!

"It's ridiculous," she pronounced. "Besides, I've promised Iantha you will work for her."

"Seems like quite an opportunity for a hardworking young girl." There was a whisper of a wink in Uncle Holt's voice.

"It's insanity!" sputtered Aunt Ivy. "Holt, not another word. Hattie—"

"As you say, Aunt Ivy, God moves in mysterious ways." I took the letters back from her, folded them, and put them in the pocket of my skirt. "If you'll excuse me, I have a letter to write."

Perilee's letter was answered with one line: "I will come."

Telling Charlie took a mite longer. I didn't want him worrying about me while he was over there in France. I believe I struck the right tone in my postscript, after only a dozen tries. *Think of how much more interesting my letters to you will be!* I wrote.

I posted both letters, the one to Charlie and the one to Perilee Mueller. Perilee's return letter arrived promptly and with the promise to meet me at the train depot in Wolf Point and take me the rest of the way to Uncle Chester's claim. Almost as if she could read my mind, she added to Uncle Chester's brief list of instructions:

> *As far as what to bring with you, your uncle has most everything needed for running a house. A sturdy hat to keep the sun and rain off and maybe some bed linens as Chester's are none too choice.*
>
>

Your new neighbor,
Perilee Mueller
>

A smarter girl than me might have wobbled a bit at the thought of heading west to prove up a claim. I had lived on a farm with some cousins for six months and I helped Uncle Holt with his vegetable garden every year, but that was the extent of my agricultural expertise. I pushed all doubts and worries away the moment they crept into my thoughts. All I could see was the chance to leave Aunt Ivy and that feeling of being the one odd sock behind.

Resolute in my decision, I did what any good homesteader must do: I took the four hundred dollars my parents had left me out of the bank and bought warm clothes and a twelve-dollar ticket on the Great Northern Railway. Packing didn't take long. Uncle Holt gave me his old work boots, and Miss Simpson presented me with a copy of *Campbell's 1907 Soil Culture Manual*. Her brother had gone out to Montana himself and assured her this was the text any homesteader must have for farming in eastern prairie country. And, along with a warm embrace, Charlie's mother gave me a sturdy pair of canvas gloves. My last purchase was a wicker travel case for Mr. Whiskers.

Aunt Ivy was still fuming about the whole thing and refused to come to the station. Uncle Holt drove me there in his new Ford Town Car.

"I know you can do the work, Hattie." Uncle Holt unloaded my trunk, then handed me Mr. Whiskers in his case. "But there will be new ways to learn. Don't be too proud to ask for help." He pulled his pipe out of his pocket. "You know what Ivy says. Pride goeth—"

"Before a fall," I finished. My pridefulness was a constant source of sorrow and agitation for Aunt Ivy. She'd worn out many a switch trying to cure me of it.

Uncle Holt busied himself with filling his pipe and tamping down the tobacco. As he lit it, I thought I saw a dampness in his eye.

"Thank you, Uncle Holt." Three years of small kindnesses flashed through my mind. "I—I—" Our gazes caught, and I felt he understood my feelings, even if I couldn't say the words. "I promise to write."

"No piecrust promises, now." He patted my shoulder

awkwardly. "But it would be good to hear from you. Now and again."

"All aboard!" called the porter.

Mr. Whiskers and I boarded the train. Uncle Holt stood at the station and waved. I waved back. Then I settled myself in and faced west.

CHAPTER 2

January 1918
On the Great Northern Railway,
somewhere in North Dakota

Dear Charlie,

The first night on the train I couldn't sleep for my excitement; the third night, I couldn't sleep for the smell and the din. I can hear you saying that my train ride is nothing compared to your travels overseas. That's true as true, but I'm cross, hungry, and grimy, so I will have my fuss. The book Miss Simpson gave me does not hold my interest. It speaks of work, work, work. I'd rather read the railroad pamphlets, which make homesteading sound as easy as rubbing a magic lamp.

I know there is no genie out there, ready to do my

bidding. That is why a hundred questions bubble up inside me. What shall I do first when I arrive? What is entailed in proving up? What if I can't do it? My mind whirrs at the thought of all that must be done. Aunt Ivy would be as pleased as Mr. Whiskers with a mouthful of feathers to know I am in such a muddle. I'm afraid I will have to rely on that painful teacher, Experience, until I get my homestead legs.

I looked up from the letter I was writing to Charlie and turned my attention outward. The view from the grimy railcar window was most discouraging. "The pamphlet says Montana's the land of milk and honey," I wrote, "but you'd never guess from this endless stretch of snow. I'm sure it's different around Uncle Chester's claim."

I wondered again about my uncle. I had heard of him, of course, but not much and had never met him. He called himself a scoundrel—what did that mean? What had taken him to Montana? It seemed to me that Uncle Chester's heart could not have been all that dark if he remembered a niece he scarcely knew in his will. *I trust you've enough of your mother's backbone,* he'd written. I sat up straighter. I had no idea if I had my mother's strength; I knew little more about her than I did about this long-lost uncle. That didn't stop me from imagining her, perhaps even looking down on me now. What would she say? Would she side with Aunt Ivy? Or approve of my decision? I wondered, as I had so many times, if it would've been easier to lose my parents when I was still a baby, with no knowledge of them at all. The memories I had now were frustratingly faint—whispers of the past. From the one photo I had of them, I knew I'd inherited my father's straight nose and my mother's crooked smile. In what other ways they had made their marks upon me, I had no way of knowing. But, surely, agreeing to move to Montana, to Uncle Chester's claim, showed some familial gumption.

"Me-rowr." Mr. Whiskers wiggled in his case.

"You poor puss." I checked Mother's watch, pinned to my bodice. "You'll be a free cat soon." The train would arrive in Wolf Point in less time than it'd take bread dough to rise. I shifted on the seat, trying to discreetly rearrange the folds of my skirt under a very tired rump. The fat man across from me had been snoring loudly, but my movements woke him. I quickly turned my face to the window again.

"It does make a heart glad to see such country, don't it?" he asked.

I mumbled a polite response.

"Where you headed?" He leaned forward, puffing out breath soured with stale tobacco smoke and whiskey.

A washboard-thin cowboy, slouched in the next seat over, chimed in. "She'd be headed to Helena. That's where all the young ladies aim for."

Despite Aunt Ivy's constant warnings not to talk to strangers, here, in the tight community of the Great Northern Railway car, it seemed bad manners not to answer.

"I'm going to my uncle's homestead in Vida," I answered. "Near Circle."

The fat man hooted and slapped his thigh. "Child, that's near nuthin'. Abso-tootly nuthin'." He shook his head.

15

"Honyocker," the cowboy mumbled. He tugged his greasy hat farther down on his head.

"I beg your pardon?"

"Honyocker, hayseed, squatter—it's all the same." The cowboy wielded a wicked-looking knife to pare a chaw of tobacco off the hunk in his hand.

"Fool farmers think they can make a go of it out here." The fat man swiped his forehead with a grimy handkerchief.

"M–m–my uncle has a lovely farm." I adjusted my new hat. "B-Bumper crops this past year." I cringed a little at my lie. But then I didn't know that Uncle Chester hadn't had bumper crops.

"Goldarned railroads." The cowboy spat toward the brass spittoon in the aisle and nearly made it. The sight made my stomach threaten mutiny.

"Bet he got suckered by them railroad pamphlets, didn't he?" The fat man shook his head. "Thought he'd plow up gold coins instead of turnips."

"My uncle's farm is quite . . ." Flustered, I couldn't come up with the word I wanted. "Bountiful."

The fat man exploded with such an exceedingly indelicate phrase that my stomach lurched. "Blast him," he continued. "Him and all them greedy conniving railroad men, making promises Montana can't deliver." His voice pummeled me with its force. Now all the passengers were nodding and murmuring agreement with this dirty cowboy and red-faced fat man. The only one keeping his own counsel was a man in a dark overcoat.

My tongue tingled with choice words for these rude men.

I clutched my lunch basket closer and reminded myself that a lady should also keep her own counsel. Aunt Ivy had branded that message on my bare legs countless times.

"Wolf Point! All out for Wolf Point!" The conductor stuck his head in the car. "Miss, here's your station."

The train slowed, but the fat man's tirade did not. In fact, he reminded me of Reverend Porter at the last tent revival, proud of his three-hour orations. I tried to shut him out as I gathered my things.

". . . starving to death. Ain't got the sense when to quit," he rattled. "If you was my daughter—"

At that moment, the train lurched. I tottered in the aisle, desperate to preserve my balance—and my dignity—as well as a grip on my bags and my cat. A lady can only bear so much. It had been a long, miserable trip. My patience was as frayed as my second-best dress. "Sir, if I were your daughter," I said, looking him full in the face, "I would wait until this train started up again and throw myself in front of it!"

The car fell into stunned silence. Then the cowboy hooted. "Look like she's told you a thang or two, Chet."

Voice quivering, I managed to say, "Good day, gentlemen." As I passed through the doorway, a man's hand grabbed my arm.

"I beg your pardon." I already regretted my outburst. Now I was probably going to be killed for it. Aunt Ivy had warned me a hundred times about the "wild men out West." I looked down and saw that the hand belonged to the quiet man in the dark topcoat.

"Blame their manners on bad whiskey." He tipped his hat.

"May I say, miss, that I have utmost confidence in your success in this hard land."

"Thank you." I willed my legs to stop shaking. They did not obey. "But my uncle does have a going concern."

"I'm sure he does," the man said softly. "Sure he does." He stepped back inside the car.

I made my way to the corridor and off the railroad car on legs weakened by more than fatigue and anger. It didn't help that Charlie's face appeared before me, awakening memories of his kind and tender ways. Awash in self-pity, I even longed for Aunt Ivy. At least I knew what to expect of her. I thought I'd known what to expect of Montana—that here a person could not only have dreams, but could hold them and they wouldn't shatter. Now I wasn't sure.

I turned around, half thinking to jump back on the train. "Good luck, miss." The conductor swung my trunk down. "And welcome to Montana."

❧ CHAPTER 3 ❧

January 3, 1918
Wolf Point, Montana

Dear Uncle Holt,

A few lines before I say my prayers. To say the trip was an adventure would be a bit like saying you enjoy your newspapers! And, after today, I can only guess it is the beginning of adventures, not the end.

The Muellers indeed met me at the station, though not quite at the appointed time. Isn't it fascinating how long a few minutes seem when you are completely alone—except for a valiant tabby companion—at a strange train depot with not a familiar face in sight? You would be proud of me for putting a plan into action when I realized I may have to rely on my own resources.

I shivered and tucked my mittened hands under my arms to warm them. I had no idea how long the trip to Wolf Point would be for Perilee and her family. And in this weather! What if something had happened on the way? What if they couldn't come? What if their horse broke a leg and they had no way to travel? What if—

My hand went to my mother's watch. I could use some of the Wright backbone now. My teeth pounded out a frozen rhythm in the icy air. Standing here on the platform was not a reasonable course of action. I might freeze to death before the Muellers arrived. A sign down the way advertised "Hotel." It was too darn cold to debate much longer. I left my trunk, grabbed my valise and Mr. Whiskers, and started off down the snow-lined street.

I was not ten paces from the train station when I heard a woman's voice. "Yoo-hoo! Yoo-hoo! Might you be Hattie Brooks?"

A few moments late but certainly true to her word, Perilee Mueller did meet me at the station. Her husband brought the wagon to a creaking stop, and she hopped out.

"Oh, I was afraid we were going to be late." She hurried to me. "Mattie couldn't find Mulie."

I'm certain she thought this explanation was clear as crystal, but I couldn't fathom one word of it. I managed a weak smile. "You must be Perilee Mueller." Perilee was what Aunt Ivy would've called plain. Her long nose sat at odds with her round face. Rusty brown hair scrambled every which way on her head, and she walked with an ungraceful limp. No, Perilee would not turn heads. But when she smiled a welcome to me, I thought her an equal to Bebe Daniels, my favorite film star.

She took my valise and looked me up and down. "Yes, I can see the family resemblance."

"Really?" I touched the brim of my hat. "I never met Uncle Chester."

"He was mighty good to me," she said. "We're glad to help you for his sake." She opened her arms as if to enfold me in a hug. I deflected her by holding Mr. Whiskers between us. Her smile flickered uncertainly, then lit up her homely face again. "And for my own. You'll be my nearest neighbor. I'm dying for some woman talk!"

"It's so kind of you to meet me," I said. "And give me a ride to my new home."

"Pish-posh." Perilee waved her plump hand. "It's a badge of honor! New folks are big news here. I'll be a celebrity for a month." She led me over to the wagon and introduced me to the tall, rugged man in the driver's seat. "This is Karl."

"Guten Tag." Karl nodded.

"H-h-hello," I stammered, surprised at his greeting. *"Guten Tag,"* I replied, using the very little German I'd learned in school. Karl smiled, handed Perilee the reins, then strode back the few steps to the platform to get my trunk. He carried it over as if it were full of feathers.

Perilee nudged me into the wagon, climbed up herself, and tucked us under a huge woolen blanket. She pointed back to the wagon bed. "And this here's Chase—he's eight—and Mattie's six—she's our little magpie—and the baby's Fern."

"Hello, children." I counted heads. "But which one's Mulie?"

Mattie held up a rag doll with a distinct bald spot on her black yarn head. "Why, she's right here!" The doll danced a jig in Mattie's mittened hands. "She says she's very pleased to meet you."

There was something so serious in Mattie's tone that I returned the greeting solemnly. "And I am very pleased to meet you, Mulie."

"Hello, Miz Brooks." Chase stuck out his hand. I shook it. "I've been feeding Violet and Plug for you." It took me a moment to recall that Violet and Plug were the animal part of my legacy from Uncle Chester.

"We've got them at our place," explained Perilee. "Chase can bring 'em over soon as you're settled."

At that moment, little Fern began to wail. Karl finished loading my things, and we headed toward the hotel. He let us out in front and rode on to the livery stable. We hurried into the lobby, to get out of the cold.

"Erickson's isn't fancy," said Perilee, "but the food's good. It's too far to head back tonight. We'll start out after breakfast." She managed to unwrap baby Fern from the blankets, help Mattie out of her coat, and scold Chase for peeking in the brass spittoon, all in one breath and motion.

"How long a ride is it?" My heart squirreled in my chest at the thought of my new home, now within reach.

"Oh, we'll be there by suppertime tomorrow." Perilee rounded up her wayward chicks. "I'd better take the children upstairs."

"That's fine," I said. "I have some business in town. I'm to see a Mr. Ebgard." I relinquished Mr. Whiskers' case to Chase. "About the claim and such."

"Can we pet him?" Mattie asked, crouching down to peer into the case.

"When I get back," I said. "He needs to settle in a bit."

"Ebgard's office is a few doors down thataway." Perilee pointed. "Why don't you pop back over to the hotel when you're done? Then I can help you with your shopping."

"Oh, don't trouble yourself." She didn't need one more chick to watch over. "I can manage."

"See you at supper, then." She herded the children upstairs.

Mr. Ebgard was assisting someone else when I arrived, so I settled myself on the one spare chair.

"That looks like everything, Tom," Mr. Ebgard said to the careworn man across from him. "You got the final filing fee?"

Tom counted out bills onto the desk. "Highway robbery." He shook his head. "Thirty-seven dollars and seventy-five cents for paperwork. After I've already paid twenty-two dollars to open the claim!"

"I'm not getting rich off you, Tom," Mr. Ebgard put down his pen. "My commission's only two dollars."

"Not saying nothing against you, Ebgard." Tom laughed and stood up. "But there's not much free about this free homestead land."

Mr. Ebgard shook his hand. "Congratulations, Tom. You are now the proud owner of three hundred twenty Montana acres. Good luck."

Tom tipped his hat to me as he passed by. "Morning, ma'am."

I nodded back.

"May I help you?" Mr. Ebgard held out the recently vacated chair.

"I'm Hattie Inez Brooks." I sat, hoping to appear more mature than I felt. "Niece to Chester Brooks." I showed him Uncle Chester's letter.

"Most unusual." Mr. Ebgard shook his head. "Most unusual."

"Sir?"

"I don't know . . ." He tapped the pen against his moustache. "How old are you?"

"S-seventeen." I squirmed at the fib.

"*How* old?"

"Sixteen."

"Good heavens!" The pen dropped. "What was Chester thinking?"

There didn't seem to be any way for me to answer the question, so I didn't.

"Why on earth did your mother let you come?" he demanded.

"She's dead, sir." I touched Mother's watch, still pinned to my bodice. "My father, too."

"All right, then." Mr. Ebgard seemed strangely approving of these revelations. "Heir. *And* head of household." He swiveled around in his chair and began to rummage through a wooden file cabinet. "Watson, Williams, Wyatt—too far. Here it is. Wright, Chester Hubert." He held the paper closer. "This claim's about thirty miles from here, about three from the nearest town, which is Vida." He smiled. "*Town* is a pretty big word for Vida. You have a way to get out there?"

I nodded. "Karl and Perilee Mueller."

"Good folks. They'll watch over you." He swiveled back to his desk. "Your uncle tell you that you need to cultivate one-eighth of this claim? That's forty acres." He squinted over his glasses at me. "And set four hundred eighty rods of fence?"

My stomach flip-flopped and my mouth went dry as flannel. Forty acres! Uncle Holt's garden was a postage stamp in comparison. And 480 rods of fence? I couldn't even fathom how much that would be. Sounded like enough to build a fence from here back to Arlington. "He did mention the need to fulfill requirements. . . ."

"Not many but vital." He ticked off his points. "One, you must build and fence. Chester's done the building, I hear. Don't know about the fencing." He put up his forefinger. "Two, you got to cultivate. Most folks go for flax at first; easier to plant. As I said, one-eighth of the claim." His middle finger stood at attention next to the first. "And three"—his ring finger joined the others—"it's all gotta happen in three years. Chester staked his claim in November 1915, so that gives you—" He glanced at the Citizens National Bank of Wolf Point calendar behind his desk. "Ten months to finish proving up. And don't forget the final fees."

I managed a wobbly smile. "I know. Thirty-seven seventy-five. For free land."

Mr. Ebgard stopped shuffling papers and looked up at me. He laughed. "Quick learner." He scribbled something in his ledger book. "Miss Hattie Inez Brooks, I sure hope to see you here in this office in November."

"Me too, sir." I stood up.

He stood too and offered his hand. "Take good care of yourself, young lady. You need to lay in some supplies?"

"That was my next task," I said.

"Head over to Hanson's Cash Grocery. Mr. Hanson will give you a fair deal." Mr. Ebgard's door opened again, and he turned his attention to the man coming in. I tried not to stare, but the newcomer was most eccentric. A thick, shoe-polish-black beard hung to his waist. Wire-brush eyebrows, dusted with snow, rested atop a pair of eyes that looked thirty years younger than the face in which they were set. An improbably long patchwork scarf was wrapped around his neck, and a fur hat perched askew on his large head.

He wore no fewer than three coats, all of them of fabrics and colors I'd certainly never seen in Arlington.

"Miss Hattie Inez Brooks, allow me to introduce another of your neighbors. This here's Mr. Jim Fowler."

"Ebgard, don't you go confusing the girl." Mr. Fowler peeled off a glove and stuck out a paw. "Ever'body calls me Rooster Jim. Shouldn't be no different for you."

"How do you do?" I took Mr. Fowler's—Rooster Jim's—hand and shook. Mr. Ebgard's office was suddenly quite potent. It seemed Rooster Jim may have come by his nickname for his barnyard aroma.

"I hope you play chess." Rooster Jim let my hand drop. "I got mighty accustomed to whuppin' Chester at the game."

"I'm sorry." I fished a handkerchief from my pocketbook and held it to my nose. "I don't play."

"It won't be no trouble to teach ya." Rooster Jim chuckled. "Won't mind a bit."

26

"Th-thank you. But I think I'll be awfully busy." I edged toward the door.

"Busy trying to stay warm!" Rooster Jim crowed at his own joke. "That's the prime entertainment in these parts. That and staying cool come summer."

"Now, Jim, don't scare the poor girl away." Mr. Ebgard smiled at me. "She's only been here a few hours."

"Well, neighbor, I'll let you be about your business. See you over to the homestead!" Rooster Jim removed two of his overcoats, and another odiferous wave crashed over the room.

"Yes, fine. Thank you." I nodded good-byes to both men and hurried outside. Now the cold air felt heavenly—exactly what I needed to clear my thoughts. A chess-playing, pungent neighbor was the least of my worries. What had Mr. Ebgard said? Forty acres of crops. Four hundred eighty rods of fence. I took a deep breath of the wintry air and pulled my shawl closer around me. No sense borrowing trouble; that's what Uncle Holt always said. Besides, in her first letter, Perilee said she and Karl would help me. I'd talk to them tonight. Surely they'd be able to answer many of my questions. I would take it one step at a time. If others could prove up on their homestead claims, there was no reason why I couldn't as well.

Hanson's Cash Grocery and Bakery was directly across the street—no doubt a short trip on a balmy spring day. Now, however, the snowdrifts tugged at my wool skirt as I wobbled my way along a packed and icy trail. I felt like a tightrope walker, balancing the urge to hurry out of the cutting wind and the need to step carefully so as not to fall on my hind regions. I slipped and slid, teeth chattering all the while, until I found sure footing on the swept wooden steps. Warmed by the effort of this short walk, I pulled open the door and stepped inside. The smell—dill pickles mixed with tobacco and peppermint—took me right back to Uncle Holt's store.

The clerk was helping another customer when I entered. He nodded to me but kept his attention on the plump woman at the counter.

"I'm not certain, Mr. Hanson, whether this yellow silk flatters my features," she fussed. "Perhaps the dove gray is better."

"You'll be a ray of sunshine in the yellow," he assured her.

I fought back a smile. Ray of sunshine! More like a lightning bolt.

I browsed the shelves while Mr. Hanson worked with the older woman. When she finished, she and her length of yellow silk swept out of the store without so much as a how-do-you-do to me.

"Good afternoon." I stood up taller. "Mr. Ebgard said you could help me put together some supplies."

"Let me see—you wouldn't be Chester's niece, would you?"

"Why, y-yes, I am."

"Welcome, neighbor." Mr. Hanson shook my hand. "Perilee sent word to tell me to take good care of you." He smiled. "She'd mother-hen the whole country if she could." He stepped out from behind the glass counter. "My stocks are low right now and we've got those darn flour and sugar limits, but I believe we can put you together a kit."

He began to assemble items at an alarming rate. He must have caught my panicked expression. "Young lady, when it's sixty-five below and your front door's froze shut, you'll be glad for this twenty pounds of beans."

Soon I had my stores: a quarter barrel of wheat flour, fifteen pounds of cornmeal, twenty pounds of coffee, kerosene, raisins and other dried fruits, a tin of loose tea, some tinned meats, canned goods, and an assortment of spices.

"Most I can sell you is twenty-five pounds of sugar," apologized Mr. Hanson. "The war."

"That should be fine," I said. I couldn't imagine using that much sugar.

Mr. Hanson added the sugar sack to the pile on the counter, then clicked his tongue in satisfaction. "This should hold you."

"Me and fifty others!" I laughed. If only Charlie could see me now—one medium-sized girl with enough supplies for his whole regiment.

The door swung open and Perilee bustled inside, bringing a blast of cold air with her. "Thought I'd find you here." She inspected my stores and gave approval. "That Silver Leaf Lard's the best for baking," she said, patting the number-five tin. "You'll also need some feed for Violet and Plug, though." Mr. Hanson tallied another set of figures. I counted out fourteen of my precious five-dollar bills. Perilee turned to Mr. Hanson, tugging the lid off the covered basket she'd been carrying. A heavenly fragrance filled the room. "I'm running low on coffee." She reached into her basket. "Can I trade you for two strudels?"

Mr. Hanson began to rub at an invisible spot on the glass counter. "I don't know, Perilee. Folks don't want much to do with anything German. The war . . ." Mr. Hanson shook his head. "I have to call my sauerkraut 'liberty cabbage' in order to sell it."

"But I won a blue ribbon at the county fair for this strudel!"

The shopkeeper lowered his voice. "Maybe you'd better stop making it for a while," he said. "And tell Karl to—"

The shop door creaked open. An icy gust announced another customer. Mr. Hanson didn't finish his sentence. "I can let you have some coffee," he said quietly to Perilee. "On credit."

Perilee closed up her basket. "No, thank you. Karl—" Her voice grew louder with this word and nearly cracked. "My husband is a good provider. We don't need credit."

"Perilee—" Mr. Hanson reached out a hand to her.

"He will be in soon to load Hattie's supplies in the wagon." She turned and left the store.

I followed her but hesitated outside the door. She was down the street before I could think of anything to do or say. I recalled the one letter I'd gotten from Charlie so far, written before he went overseas. He'd been full of spit and vinegar about the bayonet the army had given him. *I'm ready to take on the Kaiser himself,* he'd written. The war—and our enemies— were far away, like Charlie now in France. Surely Mr. Hanson understood that. Besides, couldn't he smell the cinnamon and apple perfume wafting out from Perilee's basket? I think even President Wilson would've been tempted.

Since it was noon, I stopped for dinner at the O.K. Café. After my ham sandwich, pie, and coffee, I put fifty-five cents on the table and stepped back outside. Despite the cold, I was determined to spend a bit of the afternoon exploring Wolf Point. At thirty miles from my claim, it wasn't likely I'd be back often. The imposing brick Sherman Hotel reigned from the far end of town. It fronted a town park, complete with bandstand. Where the walks were swept clean of snow and ice, I could see they were concrete, not wooden. Modern life had come to Wolf Point in other ways, too. The Wolf Point Motor Company advertised Buick, Chevrolet, and Dodge motor cars. I scurried past the Farmers Telephone Company to pop into the Citizens National Bank to open an account. Next door was Huxsol Drugs, where I bought a jar of Pond's Cold Cream. These few errands left me chilled to the bone, so cold that not even the window displays at the clothing store called The Fad could draw me in. Though I hadn't seen the entire town, my numb feet announced that my tour was completed. I hurried back to Erickson's Hotel, asked for a cup of tea to take to my room, and wrote letters until supper at six.

I treated everyone to a roast beef supper at the hotel. It didn't help my finances any, but it seemed only right. "The least I can do for all you've done for me," I said when Perilee protested. I wanted to start fresh in Montana, not owe anyone anything. That way, they couldn't remind me of it, like Aunt Ivy and all the other relatives that I'd lived with.

Supper proved to be the best part of the long day. The children were good as gold, and Perilee talked up such a storm that all Karl and I had to do was sit back and get warmed by the breeze. She didn't say a word to Karl about what had happened in the store. Leastwise, not that I heard.

After supper, we said our good-nights as they headed to their room and me to mine. Mr. Whiskers snored softly at the foot of the bed, and I wore my old flannel gown and said my prayers, just like always. But as I lay my head down to sleep, I knew that nothing would be "just like always" again. I'd boarded that train Hattie Here-and-There, but stepped off in Wolf Point Hattie Homesteader. Someone with a place to belong. Someone whose wish might come true.

With that sweet thought curling around my head like Uncle Holt's pipe smoke, I fell right to sleep.

❧ CHAPTER 4 ❧

January 4, 1918
My New Home
Three miles north and west of Vida, Montana

Dear Charlie,

I'm not officially at my home yet. In fact, we haven't even left Wolf Point. There's much to be done to get three children ready for a wagon ride. I am lingering over a second cup of coffee while Perilee and Karl shepherd their flock. If my penmanship doesn't meet Miss Simpson's standards, it's because my hands are shaking with excitement.

Soon they will be shaking with cold. Even packed together in the wagon, with woolen blankets to our noses, we are certain to be icier than the inside of Logan's icehouse!

Oh, I'm being summoned. This will be finished later . . .
from my new home! I hope you don't get tired of reading
those words, for I feel I shall never tire of writing them.

It was hustle and bustle getting everyone washed and dressed and breakfasted. Finally, gear, children, and cat were loaded into the wagon. With a small thrill in my stomach, I crunched through the snow and swung myself up next to Peri-lee. I was on my way to my new home.

Karl clucked at the horses, and they started off. I was grateful for the ride out to Uncle Chester's homestead. But what with Mr. Whiskers, Perilee, the three little ones, Karl, me, and my kit, there was hardly room to breathe in that wagon. Not that you could do much breathing in the stinging January air. Perilee, the children, and I snuggled deep under blankets. Karl's face was a chapped red mask as he drove, steady on, through the flat, treeless country.

"He's shy about speaking English in front of folks he doesn't know well," Perilee told me to explain his silence. "He hates making mistakes. I always tell him the only bad one he's ever made was marrying me and taking on my kids." She laughed, and Karl shook his head.

Perilee patted her middle. "Come summer, he'll have his own child."

"Mama, look there!" Chase pointed off to the left. The wagon road had twisted down into a shallow coulee. We were tucked between two banks of a long-ago river. On the near side of the left bank, a wolf posed against the bitter blue sky.

"Are—" I cleared my throat. "Are wolves a problem here?"

"I'm not afraid of wolves," said Chase. "I'd shoot one if it came too close."

"Have you ever had to? Shoot one?" I asked. Nowhere in that vast array of purchases from Mr. Hanson was a gun. Maybe Uncle Chester had one lying around. Not that I'd know how to use it.

"They won't bother you," Perilee said. "They get hungry, like that one there, and they go after calves or sheep. Not sweet young Iowa schoolgirls." She poked me in the ribs and laughed heartily at her own joke.

I wrapped my shawl more snugly around my face, as if that piece of wool could protect me from wolves and whatever other dangers lay ahead. All that peeked out were my eyes, watering from the cold. I'd figured out the trick of breathing in through the woolen scarf to warm the sharp air before it stabbed my lungs. My feet felt like clumps of ice at my ankles; two pairs of woolen socks provided a meager shield against this Montana cold. Shifting on the wooden seat sent a tiny surge of warmth through my veins and gave me a better angle to study the landscape through the narrow slit between scarf and hat.

How would I describe this scene to Charlie? So far, there had not been one tree to enliven the view. To say the land was flat was not quite true, though that would be the quick and easy assessment. No, it more resembled a giant's quilt—white, of course, because of the several feet of snow—spread out over an enormous bed. Here and there were the bumps made by the giant's toes or knees. In the distance, his covered head raised up a larger bump in the bedding. As I studied longer, I could see the creases where the quilt fell away from between his arms and sides. No, not flat in the tabletop sense of the word. *Remember that sheet cake I baked for your birthday last year?* I would write Charlie. *Montana is a bit smoother of surface, but not much.* I turned to find Perilee studying me.

"Chester's eyes were that same hazel color," she said. "Course, he didn't have no hair, but I suspect it was chestnut, like yours, when he was younger." She seemed lost in herself for a moment.

"What was he like?" I asked.

Perilee pursed her lips. "Quiet. But if he ever said something, folks would listen. And Lord, did he read—that man was a regular library." She smiled at some memory. "But there was a sadness in him. Never knew what the trouble was, but no matter how big his smile or loud his laugh, you could hear the hurt underneath."

"Was he alone?" I tried to envision this uncle I never knew, with my eyes and no hair. "When he died, I mean."

A tender smile flickered on Perilee's face. "A man like Chester? No, he was not alone. Me and Karl were there. Leafie Purvis and Rooster Jim, too." She patted my arm. "He talked about you, Lord almighty, right up till the very end. He'd be so pleased to know you had come."

We rode in snow-tipped silence for several minutes. "I wish I'd known him," I said aloud.

"You would've been fast friends," Perilee pronounced. That thought comforted me. At least it comforted my soul.

Comforting my body, however, was a completely different cup of tea. The glamour of my mode of transportation had dimmed considerably since leaving Wolf Point. This icy, jostling wagon ride had shaken the last bit of humor right out of my bones. The same bones through which, at least according to Uncle Chester, coursed some of my mother's starch. But that starch was frozen solid by the time we reached my new home.

"There it is!" Chase called, excitement and cold shrilling his voice. "Mr. Wright's house."

I looked in disbelief. *House* was a Charlie term—kind and generous. Aunt Ivy's chickens had better accommodations. The structure wasn't much bigger than Uncle Holt's tool shed and was put together with about as much care. Gaps in the siding revealed black tar paper, like decay between haphazard teeth. Two wood-block steps led up to a rough-hewn door. A small window—the only window, I was to find out—left of the door stared dully at me. My own gaze in return was no doubt equally as dull.

Karl slowed the wagon.

"Home sweet home!" Perilee chirped. "We'll help you get your things inside, sugar. But we can't stay. It's getting dark. We need to get on home."

"Home sweet home," I croaked. This cockeyed, slapped-together nine-foot by twelve-foot claim shack . . . my *home*.

"Ach, Schnee," Karl muttered as he swung open the door. "Snow."

"Oh, dear." Perilee stamped snow off her shoes. "No one plugged the keyhole."

Even in the gloom, I could see an icy slash of white that the wind had forced through the keyhole and across the cabin floor. It was as if Nature herself had drawn a line to keep me out. I fought back the urge to throw myself on Perilee's mercy and beg to go home with them.

Mattie slipped her tiny hand in mine. "You can sweep that up, boil it, and make coffee," she said.

Perilee smiled proudly. "Out of the mouths of babes."

"I sure can." I cleared the tears out of my throat. "Thank goodness I packed a broom."

"That's the spirit." Perilee patted my arm. "I know it don't look like much. Claim shacks never do. After you get proved up, you can work on a proper house."

"Do you . . ." Would it be bad manners to ask Perilee if she lived in such a shack? "I mean, have you? Proved up?"

"Sugar, I'm an old-timer!" Perilee laughed. "I have a cozy house now. But everyone started out like this. Or worse." She shifted Fern to her other hip. "My folks had a soddy—you know, a house built from bricks of sod. It was warm in the winter and cool in the summer, but oh, the bugs! And dirt. Dirt everywhere." She took a handkerchief from her pocket and wiped at Fern's drippy nose. "Trust me, this is a castle compared to a sod house."

Chase burst in through the door, a blast of cold air on his heels. "Here, Miz Brooks. I fetched you some water. For washing and such tonight." He set the bucket on the stove.

"Why, thank you, Chase." I was surprised by his kind act.

"Your well's right out there." He pointed. "You'll need to fetch more in the morning."

"*Das ist das* last." Karl brought in the last of my boxes.

"Right," said Perilee. She turned to me. "We've got to go, hon."

Mr. Whiskers complained from his carrying case. He didn't seem any too pleased with our accommodations, either.

"I'd leave him inside for a few days," advised Perilee.

"He's a pretty tough old puss," I said. "He can handle the cold."

"No, dear." Perilee patted my arm. "Because of the mice."

I shuddered. "In the house?"

"Chester was none too neat. And the house has been vacant awhile, and——"

I held up my hand. "No more ands."

Perilee hooted with laughter. "Sugar, you are a stitch." She handed me a lamp and my small box of books. Karl passed over a covered dish, wrapped in a towel, and one of the strudels.

"Get the fire lit," said Perilee. "And you can heat this up for your supper."

"You've done too much!" I protested, but Perilee covered her ears. "At least, let me repay you." I reached for one of the bags of coffee beans. "Please. In trade."

Her hands hovered in the air for a moment. Then she took the coffee. "I'd say the family resemblance goes beyond looks." She reached out to wrap me in another hug. This time I didn't back away.

With a jingle of the harness, they were off. I watched until they were a speck on the horizon.

"Yee-oww." Mr. Whiskers sounded pretty insulted at this step down in his living arrangements. The shack—oh, it was a shack, no poetry of home and hearth allowed—was a flimsy cage, keeping me in and very little else out. The essentials appeared to be present: stove, coffeepot, bread pans, skillet, and such, plus a few rough and splintery shelves for storage.

I collapsed in a nerve-worn heap on the floor. I imagined my first letter home. *I told you,* Aunt Ivy would say as she snapped it under Uncle Holt's nose. *Nothing good would come of this Montana mania. She's living worse than our hogs.*

I wanted nothing better than to lose myself in a good long cry. But the floor, in addition to being dirty, was cold. "Dear God," I cried out. "What should I do?" I leaned my forehead on my upraised knees. A tear trickled onto my woolen traveling skirt. Then something happened. I heard an answer to my prayer.

Pick yourself up, Hattie Inez Brooks, said a voice in my head. *And get a fire lit before you freeze what's left of your brains.*

The message stunned me into action. I brushed myself off, lit a lamp, and began to make some sense of my new home. The broom got put to good use as I tried not to think about what the little hard pellets in the growing dust pile meant. A low growl rolled up from the back of Mr. Whiskers' throat. He crouched in front of the stove, tail twitching wickedly. Suddenly the tail stopped and his right paw flew out. There was a tiny squeak, almost fairy-like, and then Mr. Whiskers ran into the far corner. I could hear him crunching away.

I drew a shaky breath. "All right, then." I fumbled for matches to light the fire. "You've got your supper, Mr. Whiskers. I'd best get mine."

A chipped enamelware pail by the stove held a fat collection of juniper kindling. I loaded the stove with twigs. Soon the juniper crackled fragrantly.

On the ride out, Perilee had explained that homestead fires were fed with dried buffalo chips. "The buffalo are gone," she'd said, "but thank goodness for their calling cards." I slipped on the work gloves that had been a gift from Charlie's mother and reached into an old lard bucket filled with dark objects. I swallowed my pride and tossed them quickly in the stove. Soon the little shack was tolerable; that is to say, as long as I kept moving, my innards would not freeze solid.

I'd followed Mattie's advice and scooped the top layer of intruding snow into the coffeepot, now heating on the stove. To the back of the range, I set the dish of Perilee's stew to warm. Since Aunt Ivy had been reluctant to trade in her wood cookstove, I was well versed in how to use one, at least for cooking; baking was beyond me. I rounded up some cutlery and found the table, which had been buried under a stack of dime novels and Shakespeare's plays. Uncle Chester and I shared one Wright trait: we loved our books.

Now that I was thawed out a bit and the little shack lit up by my trusty kerosene lamp, I could see that every shelf and surface was covered with books, newspapers, and old magazines. What Uncle Chester had lacked in niceties—Aunt Ivy would be horrified to find not one doily in the entire room—he'd made up for in reading materials. Under a goodly pile of the *Dakota Farmer, Popular Magazine,* and *Saturday Evening Post* magazines, I found a serviceable empty wooden crate that was recruited as a bookcase.

An old rag, lukewarm water, and elbow grease soon brought a sheen to the table. I set out an enamelware plate and a tin fork and spoon. "Just like the Vanderbilts!" I told

Mr. Whiskers. He'd bellied up to the stove to warm himself after his first course. There was no proper chair, but an upturned empty lard bucket suited me fine. I wondered if this had been Uncle Chester's favorite perch as well.

By the time my supper was hot, Uncle Chester's house—my house—was on its way to being cozy. I poured myself a mug of coffee and Mr. Whiskers a saucer of tinned milk. "Here's to our new home," I toasted.

Thinking of the Almighty's earlier guidance, I bowed my head. "Thank you, Lord, for Uncle Chester. May he rest peacefully in your care. Thank you for Perilee, who provided this good supper, and for keeping me safe thus far. Mr. Whiskers thanks you for the mouse. Amen."

I dug in, spoon clinking against the plate. The stew tasted of sage and carrots and hope. The flavor lingered on my tongue long after the plate was empty. I let Mr. Whiskers lick it clean while I sliced Perilee's strudel. It was even more delicious than it smelled. I shook my head thinking of Perilee's trouble trying to trade in town. People were gosh-darned thickheaded sometimes.

A rhythmic rasping told me Mr. Whiskers was sound asleep. It'd been a long day. I dipped a few ladles of warm water from the stove's reservoir into the largest enamel bowl, then dropped in a bar of soap and rolled it into a lather. I quickly washed up my few dishes, then ladled clean water over each item to rinse off the suds. The dishes rested briefly on a clean flour-sack towel while I dug another out of my things. Never let it be said I let my dishes air dry! When everything was set to rights, I turned to making ready my bed.

Because of the tight quarters—the whole house would have fit in Aunt Ivy's parlor—the bed had been hinged to the wall. I pulled the bed down. Uncle Chester's bed linens were fit for rags and barely that. I briskly made it up using the one set of sheets I'd brought. Within minutes of my banking the fire, the inside temperature took a huge step down the ladder. "Hope we don't turn into icicles," I said to Mr. Whiskers. He jumped up on the bed.

I pulled off my skirt and blouse and yanked on a flannel nightgown, singing at the top of my lungs to keep warm. "Onward Christian soldiers, marching off to war!" Bellowing and marching in place, I blew out the lamp and hopped into bed. After a few minutes, I hopped right back out. I added several layers of clothes, a hat, and two pairs of socks. Finally, with Mr. Whiskers curled at my feet, I warmed up enough to fall asleep.

I woke, bleary-eyed and hungry. And cold.

I started out of bed, then snagged the quilt to wrap around my shoulders. "Brrr!" I bounded across the cold floor to the stove. "I could chisel out the air in here and use it for ice in my lemonade next summer!"

"Meow." Mr. Whiskers scrabbled his way under my blankets and made a nest for himself in my bed.

"Don't get any ideas." I blew on last night's embers in the stove. "I've got to fold that up so there's room to move." I jumping-jacked to the chip barrel and tossed a handful onto the embers. "Let's get something warm inside us. Quick!" I grabbed the coffeepot. Then I remembered: the water was outside, the very cold outside. I began to bundle up. "Lesson number one: bring in a bucket of water each night for coffee in the morning."

Mr. Whiskers purred his agreement.

Any cowboy passing by at that moment might have fallen off his horse had he seen me step out the front door. Dressed in every stitch of clothing I could find, I suspect I looked like Mattie's rag doll, shuffling my way down the icy steps and across the snowy yard to the well.

The inside of my nose stung as I breathed in the icicled air. My eyes watered so much I could barely see the pump handle. To stay warm, I jiggled from one foot to the other. It was too cold to think. All the jiggling was reminding me of something else rather important.

I'd run out to the necessary the night before, right before bed. It had seemed a long way then, and it was even longer now—and certainly no warmer. I'd gotten awfully spoiled at Aunt Ivy and Uncle Holt's with their indoor plumbing. One more thing to get used to in Montana. I quickly used the facility, slipped off my mittens to grab a piece of the Monkey Ward catalog to dry off, and hiked up my underthings.

I hurried back to the well and began to pump. It took a significant amount of muscle—how had Chase with his little eight-year-old arms managed?—but soon I had a bucketful. That hot cup of coffee was one step closer!

I tried to let go of the pump handle . . . and couldn't. My naked hands, damp with the morning air, were firmly connected to the metal.

"Ouch!" My gyrations made my freezing hands raw and sore. And I was still stuck. Now my feet were tingling and

itching with the cold, too. I imagined them puffed up and black inside my boots. My teeth chattered hard enough in my head to loosen each and every one.

I was probably going to be the first homesteader ever to die from extreme stupidity. An image of my skeleton being discovered come spring spurred me into action. I began to tug and twist with renewed fervor.

"Hey there, Miz Hattie," a young voice called out. "Whatcha doing?" Into view rode Chase. He was astride one of the horses from Karl's wagon team and leading a large, boxy horse and a brown cow with white spots.

"Oh, hello, Chase." If I hadn't been stuck to the pump handle, I would've thrown myself down the well rather than bear this humiliation. "I seem to be in a pickle."

He slipped off his horse and tethered him to the well bracing. "Mama keeps an old mitten tied to the handle," he said. "In the winter."

"Yes, well, that's a wonderful idea, but . . ." The sentence hardly needed finishing.

Chase ran inside and fetched the small bit of water left in the stove reservoir. He poured it slowly over my hands.

"Oh!" The sudden warmth sent shooting pains into every knuckle and joint. My hands slipped free, and I tucked them under my arms. "That hurts."

Chase picked up the bucket and took my arm. "Come on inside, Miz Hattie. You better get warmed up."

I fell against my lard can chair, a frozen, useless lump, while this eight-year-old boy bustled around my shack. He stoked the fire, put coffee on, fed Mr. Whiskers a saucer of tinned milk, and fetched me another pail of water to fill the reservoir.

"Have you had breakfast?" I asked him, a mug of coffee finally cradled in my hands.

"Yes, ma'am."

"Well, I haven't. Can you eat a second?" Not bothering to wait for an answer, I flipped open the pamphlet Mr. Hanson had tucked in with my purchases. Put out by the Royal Baking Powder Company, "Best War Time Recipes" was packed with ways to cook to save flour, eggs, and such, what with the war on. I measured two coffee mugs of buckwheat flour into a bowl, stirred in four spoonfuls of Royal Baking Powder— the only kind Aunt Ivy ever used—and half a spoonful of salt. "Could you please reach two tins of milk from that shelf there?" Chase handed them to me, and I added the milk slowly to the flour mix, as the recipe said.

I licked my fingers and touched them to the greased frying pan heating up on the stove. *Sssss.* "It's sizzling all right!" I stuck my stinging fingers in my mouth. One thing I could make was flapjacks. Soon a stack rose on each of our plates, and we ate.

Warm, full, and humbled, I pushed back my plate. "So your mama ties a mitten to the pump handle," I said. "Anything else I should know before I do some other foolish thing?" Somehow, I didn't feel such a failure talking with Chase this way. I prayed he didn't tell Karl and Perilee what a featherbrain their new neighbor was.

Chase relished his role as teacher and, for the next hour, showed me this trick and that of homestead life. "Use the juniper sparingly," he said after peeking in my kindling barrel. "It's hard to come by." When we'd finished my hearth and home lesson, he took me out to the barn and helped me get Violet and Plug settled.

"Do you know how to milk a cow?" he asked.

"That's one thing I do know how to do," I said. One of my stays had been with a second cousin dairy farmer.

"Violet's kind of cranky." Chase patted the cow's broad flank. "Watch out for her tail."

"Will do."

"Chester gave us her calf. I named her Fawn 'cause she looks like a baby deer I saw once, over to Glendive."

"That's a wonderful name." I gave Violet a pat, though more tentative than Chase's.

Chase gave me a few more instructions about Plug. "He's a good old range horse and can practically take care of himself," he said. "I better head on back, Miz Hattie, or Mama will fret."

I walked him back out to the yard, where'd he left his horse.

"How can I thank you?" I was so touched by how easily he and his family had taken me under their wing.

"You can give me a boost up." He lifted up his foot.

I cupped my hands, he stepped into them, and up he went. "Tell your mama hello from me."

"I will." Chase wheeled his horse around. "Thanks for breakfast, Miz Hattie!"

And with that, my eight-year-old knight in shining armor rode off.

I went straight into the house, rummaged through my things, found an old mitten, and went back out and tied it to the pump handle.

That night my prayers were full of thanks. "For Chase and Perilee and for lessons learned," I said. "But Lord, if you could help me not learn every lesson the hard way, I'd sure appreciate it. Amen."

Mr. Whiskers meowed his amen to that, too.

CHAPTER 5

February 5, 1918
Three miles north and west of Vida, Montana

Dear Uncle Holt,

You asked me to tell you more about my everyday doings. Such a life of glamour, you cannot imagine! Water must be fetched first thing each morning, and my breakfast is just a hope until I have fed and watered Plug and Violet. This is not such an easy task when the snowdrifts are piled high as a Chicago skyscraper! Now it is not so bad: Mr. Whiskers and I have beat a path to the barn. But the first day—it was over an hour before I had paddled my way through the snow. Sometimes I feel as if this Montana winter is Goliath and I am David. I only hope my ending is as victorious as his!

*After I milk Violet, I must also clean out the barn
each day. You would think the cold weather might put a
damper on the smells. Not so. Plug is self-sufficient; after
a handful of oats, he is turned out to find his own grub.
Thank goodness for such a smart range horse.*

*I am eternally grateful for your old work boots. I
know you worried that they would be too big, but they
are a perfect fit after I've wrapped my stockinged feet in
newspapers. If I didn't do this, I don't think I'd have any
toes left come spring.*

Your niece,
Hattie Inez Brooks

After I finished my letter to Uncle Holt, I added a post-script to Charlie's:

I read this in the Wolf Point Herald. *I do not know
the author, but it may give you and your comrades a
laugh: "My Tuesdays are meatless, my Wednesdays are
wheatless, I'm getting more eatless each day; my house it is
heatless, my bed it is sheetless—they've gone to the
Y.M.C.A. The barroom is treatless, my coffee is sweetless,
each day I grow poorer and wiser. My stockings are
feetless, my trousers are seatless, Jeroosh, how I hate the
d——n Kaiser." Though our sacrifices at home are small
compared to yours, we make them with a sense of humor!*

Your wheatless, et cetera school chum, Hattie

Sealing both envelopes, I hurried to my morning chores. I
dressed in every stitch of clothing I could find, all the time

knowing I'd be an ice block the minute I stepped out that door. Back in Iowa, my smooth hands and face had been my one vanity. No more. No amount of fancy Pond's Cold Cream would soothe the chapped cheeks and nose that were now my badge of homestead honor.

Mr. Whiskers and I waded through the snow to the barn. More than once I cursed Uncle Chester for placing it so far from the house. As we struggled along, I heard sleigh bells jingling like Christmas. A painted sledge skimmed the snow, drawn by a pair of ashy horses.

"How do, neighbor!" Rooster Jim called out a greeting.

Even though I was in the middle of chores, I'd learned enough about Montana ways to know I must invite him in. "The coffee's on," I said.

Rooster Jim spoke some quiet words to his horses. Steam rose from their backs, and they shook their heads and stamped their hooves. "I'm on my way to Vida. Better not this time."

"Your team is beautiful," I said. "Such an unusual color."

"That they are." He grinned. "It gets Traft Martin's goat that I won't sell them. He prides himself on saddling up the best-looking horses in these parts."

I could tell by Rooster Jim's tone that he was pretty pleased about vexing Traft Martin. I hadn't met him yet. I'd heard from Perilee that he and his mother—the yellow silk lady at Hanson's—ran the largest ranch around. The Tipped M butted up against the northeast boundary of my claim.

"How are you handling this weather?" he asked.

"Well, I will be glad when winter's over," I said. "I'll bet spring is lovely here."

He hooted with laughter. "Yep, spring's lovely all right. If you like mud. And summer's even lovelier, long as you don't mind the fires of Hades."

My face must've given evidence of my dismay. Rooster Jim grinned and sniffed the air. "That Chinook that blew through yesterday will warm things up some." He must've seen the question on my face. "That's a warm wind that comes through sometimes in winter."

"Chinook." I'd have to remember that term and tell Uncle Holt about it. And about Rooster Jim.

"You know, Hattie, Chester and me had a deal."

"Oh?" My heart sank a bit. What kind of deal? And would I be expected to honor it? My reserves were slim after traveling here and getting set up.

Rooster Jim pulled an enormous blue bandanna from his pocket and blew his nose with astonishing energy. When he pulled the bandanna away I was amazed to see that his nose was still attached to his face.

"Yep. He let me win at chess, and I took his mail to the Vida post office for him."

"But as I told you at Mr. Ebgard's, I don't know how to play," I started.

"Perfect. Then it'll be easy for me to teach you how to lose." He laughed heartily at his joke, reminding me of a ragged version of Clement Moore's Saint Nick from the old poem "The Night Before Christmas."

"Well, I do have letters ready to mail. . . ."

"Get 'em, then. I'll wait."

I turned and hurried back to the house, dashing inside

without even stopping to take off my boots. On the way back out, I nearly tripped over the coil of rope Uncle Chester had left behind. I kicked it back into the corner.

I handed Rooster Jim the letters to Charlie and Uncle Holt.

"Aha." He nodded wisely. "Two sweethearts. That's the way to do it. Keep 'em guessing."

I was glad my cheeks were already red from the cold, so Rooster Jim couldn't know I was blushing. "Oh, they aren't sweethearts," I said.

He laughed his belly laugh again. "That's what they all say!" He flicked the reins over the horses' backs. "I'll stop by soon to give you that chess lesson." The horses started off with a merry jingle.

"Well, he'll be an interesting neighbor, don't you think?" I asked Mr. Whiskers. He answered with a small meow, and then he and I hurried back to the barn to take care of Plug and Violet. The barn was a small structure, with room enough for the two animals, some bales of hay, spare parts, and a pitchfork. I'd never had much to do with livestock before. Plug, sturdy, loyal range horse that he was, forgave my every mistake. I suspected he could run things better than I could, but he never let on. He contentedly munched the small portion of feed I gave him each day before turning him out to forage.

Violet was a cow of a completely different color. She felt it her bovine duty to make up for each and every one of Plug's kindnesses. It only took me a day to learn never to turn my back on her. That tail scratched like barbed wire as it flicked across my winter-frozen face. Nothing suited her better than to wait until the milk bucket was nearly full, then kick it over with a back hoof.

"It's a lucky thing for you you're too tough for stew," I threatened that morning after she'd pulled her favorite trick once again. I smacked her hind end in frustration and righted the now-empty milk bucket. If it weren't for the fact that she was my only source of fresh milk, I would have driven her off that very first day. And gladly.

"Ouch!" Her tail scraped my face. It was almost as if she could read my mind and was punishing me for my thoughts. I smacked her again and practiced a curse word I'd heard on the train. There was no Aunt Ivy to recoil in horror at my language and, truth be told, there is nothing like the occasional outburst of profanity to calm jangled nerves.

Barn chores finished, I turned Plug and Violet out. As Rooster Jim had noted, a Chinook had blown through a few days before, warming the prairie. Tiny patches of green poked optimistically out of the cold earth. It wasn't much, but both horse and cow seemed content with the change of fare.

I turned back to the house. It was Monday, laundry day. Last night I'd set the clothes soaking in two tubs. Before breakfast I'd put the wash boiler atop the stove and lugged in kettle after kettle of water from the well to fill it. It had been heating all morning and was nearly aboil. Perilee had planted the notion that there were two or three bachelor neighbors who might pay me to do their laundry. Rooster Jim was no doubt one of them, but I wasn't sure I'd want to tackle his wash.

The whites would boil away on the stove awhile. I poured

off some hot water into the bread pan, leaned the washboard inside, cut off a hunk of soap, and began to rub. Rub, rinse, wring. Rub, rinse, wring. By the time I got through all the clothes and the last of the whites were rinsed and wrung, my hands were raw and my back was grumbling something fierce. But I still had to hang the clothes. For this, I put on my woolen mittens. They made pegging the clothes to the line clumsy work but kept my fingers from freezing solid.

To keep myself company, I'd taken to conducting chore-time conversations with God. My self-imposed rule was that each conversation must start on a thankful note. Sometimes that kept the discussion from really getting going. I lifted my petticoat out of the wash basket.

"Lord, I do thank you for that warm wind and the promise of spring." I bent for another clothespin to secure the petticoat. "And I am very thankful that my wash load is small." Here I thought of Perilee, washing for her family of five. "I count it a true blessing that there are no diapers in my wash." I shuddered to think of that. "Now, you know I've been working on keeping a sunny lookout on life, but I must speak to you about Violet, who is more devil than cow."

Mr. Whiskers pranced around my feet in the snow, batting at a clothespin that had tumbled out of the laundry basket. When we'd first arrived, he'd shoot into the house every time he got the chance. Now, fattened up on mice and wearing a thicker coat of fur, he was content to play outdoors most days.

"Hey there, Mr. Whiskers." I reached out to scratch behind his ears.

"Ye-owww!" He pulled away from me and arched his back.

"What's wrong?" I asked him. He crouched low, growling an eerie warning, ears flattened tight against his solid head.

I looked around the yard, unable to see what might be spooking him. "Now, now, Mr. Whiskers. Everything's all right."

The growling grew louder.

"You stop that now." I'd never seen him act like this. "You're giving me the heebie-jeebies." A trickle of sweat wriggled down my spine. I kept talking, as if my voice might calm us both. "It's all right now. It's all right." I moved toward him, but he sprang into the air, hissed, and flew under the shack.

"What on earth?" Then I saw it: a wolf, silently, stealthily making its way up the coulee to the very spot where Violet had found a patch of needle grass for dessert. Fear clamped its fist around my throat. I croaked out a warning. Violet couldn't hear me from where she was, and even if she could, she was ornery enough not to budge.

I stamped my foot against the frozen ground. "Ha!" I yelled, my voice finally loosened from fear's fingers. "Hya, hya!"

The wolf did not even flinch.

"Run, Violet! Run, you crazy cow!" I screamed the words at the top of my lungs. Fear must have frizzled out the thinking part of my brain, because next thing I knew, I was dashing toward that wolf. I would have scared the bejeebies out of myself had *I* seen me coming—dressed like a scarecrow, screeching like a banshee.

The wolf had one thought: dinner. Without even a glance my way, he hunkered into a lopsided crouch, rear haunches raised, head down.

Violet was drunk on the allure of fresh needle grass, blissfully unaware of mortal danger. She took a step toward another patch of green.

Even in Uncle Holt's old work boots in the settled snow, I made pretty good time up the coulee bank. Now my antics caught the wolf's attention.

"Git!" I shouted.

Violet bellowed, her long tongue sticking out. "Rrroo!"

Without a sound, the wolf propelled himself forward, leaping at my cow.

Violet snorted in surprise. She flicked her head to see that wolf firmly attached to her tail. She started to run, as fast as a stupid old cow can run in snow.

"Let her be!" I took off my cap and slapped it against my thigh.

Startled, the wolf let go of Violet's tail.

"Run, Violet!" I waved my arms like a butter churn gone mad. "Run!"

The wolf recovered from its shock and snatched Violet's tail once again in its jaws. I searched frantically for something to throw. The Chinook had uncovered a patch of rocky ground near the crest of the bank. I picked up the biggest stones I could find and began to pitch them at that wolf.

One thing the wolf could not know is that I learned to throw from the best pitcher in Fayette County, Iowa: Charlie. One rock clipped the wolf on the hindquarters, another on the back of the neck. Still, that wolf hung on. He must've been starving. He yanked and jerked at Violet's tail.

I reached for the last rock. This one had to count. I let it fly.

"Yip!" The wolf yelped, turned, and hightailed it, a good chunk of Violet's tail dangling from between his jaws.

I was frozen by the time I chased Violet down. She was bawling like a lost calf as I grabbed her thick leather collar. A little stub twitched at the end of her rump. That was all that remained of that whip of a tail.

"Bless it all, Violet!" Fear turned to tears and relieved laughter. "Aunt Ivy's right again. The Lord surely does work in mysterious ways." Seems that the wolf and I both made out okay in this affair: He got a little snack, and I got an eternal reprieve from Violet's vicious tail. It was a fair enough trade.

I picked up my muddied hat and led Violet back to the barn, quieting her with an extra portion of hay. I examined the raw stump of a tail, oozing blood. It needed doctoring, and I had not one clue about what to do. A clean rag tied tightly seemed to stanch the bleeding. My good humor turned to fear as I thought about losing my cow.

I was going to have to get help. I whistled for Plug and mounted up. We plodded through the drifted snow to Perilee's. I hadn't been to visit yet but knew to follow the path to Vida, a path Rooster Jim had freshly marked with his sledge. The way must have been familiar to Plug, who picked up the pace as we drew close.

"Come in, come in." Perilee waved me inside her warm house—a real house, with two doors, a bedroom, and a parlor. Perilee fetched two thick white mugs. "I'll bet your blood's about frozen." She motioned for me to sit. "A cup of coffee will fix anything."

"How about a cow's tail?" I took the mug from her,

warming my aching hands, then relayed to her the morning's misadventure.

Perilee laughed out loud. "Hon, what I wouldn't have given to see that." Her laughter softened to a chuckle. "Wouldn't Chester love to know that Violet finally got her comeuppance?"

"I do worry about caring for the wound," I said.

"Karl would know, but he's not here." Perilee set her coffee mug down. "My pa always swore by a poultice of brown sugar and cobwebs—though where you'd find cobwebs in this bitter cold, I have no idea. Flour paste and brown paper should work fine, too."

"What's Karl doing working in this weather?" I shivered. "My wash is going to be frozen on the line by the time I take it down."

Fern let out a little squeal from her apple crate bed. Perilee stepped over and patted her on the back till she quieted.

She pulled a newspaper from the shelf and brought it over to me. "He's not working."

"Alien Enemies Must Register," blared the headline. I began to read.

The following instructions and suggestions are sent out from the United States Department of Justice through the office of the United States Marshal for Montana to all male German alien enemies of the age of 14 years or more. February 4 to 9, 1918, inclusive, between the hours of 6 a.m. and 8 p.m. have been designated as the dates and time when registrations must be made. Excepting in nine of the larger cities of the state all postmasters are registrars for their respective districts.

I put down the paper. "I don't understand."

Perilee picked up her coffee mug but didn't drink. She rolled the mug back and forth in her hands. "Karl's at the post office in Vida right now, registering."

"Karl? An alien *enemy?*"

"He was born in Germany."

I looked at the paper again. "There must be a good reason for this, Perilee."

She held my gaze. "What good reason is there to treat neighbors—someone like Karl—like this?"

I thought of all the articles Uncle Holt had read aloud. Awful stories about starving Belgians and cruelties of war. Unbelievable stories. But it was the Huns who were responsible. The Germans over there. Not here. Not people we knew. "I don't know. But it wouldn't be required if there wasn't one." I held out my hands, helpless. "Would it?"

Thwack. Perilee set her coffee cup down hard. "I guess we're supposed to be grateful there's no fee to register." She rubbed at her eyes. "But there'll be a price to pay. Traft Martin and his County Council of Defense will make sure of that."

Fern started fussing again. "Now, see what I've done." Perilee placed her hand on mine. "I'm sorry, sugar. I get so darned angry sometimes. It's not your fault."

I slipped my hand on top of hers. "It would take more

60

than that to scare me off," I said. "You've got nothing on Aunt Ivy."

That drew a smile from Perilee. "You'd better get back to that cow of yours," she said, picking the baby up.

"I'd better." I drained my coffee cup.

"Do you have enough flour for a paste?" Perilee jiggled Fern. "I can spare some if you don't."

I'd started to tie my shawl around me and stopped mid-knot. "I've got plenty." Perilee would do anything for me. For anyone. Same with Karl. Where did you go to register for that?

"Nothing bad will happen." I hoped she knew I was talking about Karl, not Violet.

"I wish." Perilee patted Fern's back, then shook her head. "Mix some sugar with that flour, put it on her tail, and wrap it in brown paper. Tie it on and leave it for a week."

"Thank you." I patted her back as she patted Fern's, then snugged my shawl tighter around me and left.

An uneasiness settled on me as I jostled and jolted on Plug's back. First the strudel and now this registration. The war was in Europe, not here. Why all this fuss about where someone was born? Wasn't it where he lived—rather, how he lived—that counted? I worried these questions the way Mr. Whiskers worried the mice he caught; worried so, in fact, that I barely felt the piercing wind the whole ride home.

❧ CHAPTER 6 ❧

February 14, 1918
Three miles north and west of Vida, Montana

Dear Charlie,

*I expect I might not do too badly in that army of
yours. I am now quite adept at keeping warm no matter
how low the mercury falls. Perilee says their thermometer
hit sixty-five below last week.*

*One of my neighbors, Mr. Durfey, is cutting ice out of
Wolf Creek eighteen inches thick. But the snow is banked
in beautiful mounds around my claim (oh, how I love to
write these words). Sometimes I think I am in a true
fairyland.*

*Perilee and the children were here a few days back
and Chase and Mattie nearly wore through my wash*

bucket. One drift is even with the roof of the barn and they climbed up there and slid down in that bucket over and over again. Their little toes were purple when we finally made them come in. Mattie's stung and itched so. "Do you think I have the froch bite?" she asked me in her sweet worried voice. I bathed her feet in warm water and thus staved off the "froch" bite. Perilee calls her their little magpie, and the nickname fits like a glove. We popped corn and I read aloud a chapter from Treasure Island. You should have seen Chase's eyes light up.

Violet and I are eternally grateful that you taught me to pitch. I wish you'd seen it. There was a hungry old wolf after Violet but thanks to her orneriness and my dead aim, I still have fresh milk every morning. I also have the funniest-looking no-tail cow in eastern Montana. Perhaps I will be able to introduce the two of you someday.

There is much to do here and only nine months now in which to do it. But I can't hurry spring, which is when the real work begins. For now, I drool over seed catalogs and study up on how to build a fence. And how to play chess. Though it hasn't done me much good yet with Rooster Jim. Odd duck that he is, he is very kind. Twice now he's given me a sleigh ride into Vida, the nearest town. (Pin dot is more like it!) The three miles from here to Vida will make a pleasant walk come spring. I devour each scrap of newspaper that falls in my grasp. Perilee and Jim keep me well stocked. There is much news of the war, of course, and those wicked Huns. But Charlie, I

felt so odd when Perilee told me that Karl had to register
as an alien enemy. Yes, he was born in Germany, but he
is Karl—no Hun who bayonets babies. If you were here,
you could explain this to me as well as you used to
explain how to diagram sentences.

I wish I could send you one of Perilee's strudels. She'd
even beat Mildred Powell in a baking contest!

Your old friend,
Hattie Inez Brooks

The wind, rumbling like an approaching train, diverted my attention from my letter to Charlie. I shivered in my bed. "I'm not eager to go out there, are you?" Mr. Whiskers answered by burrowing deeper under the quilt. No matter the weather, there were still chores to be done. I hopped out of bed and glanced at the Vida National Bank calendar by the stove as I put the coffee on.

"Happy Valentine's Day to us!" I put the coffee on to boil while I milked. "I wonder if Charlie got the valentine I sent him." I was certain Mildred would send one loaded with mush, so I'd found the funniest penny postcard I could at Bub Nefzger's little sod-house post office and store in Vida. I figured Charlie could use a laugh more than anything else, so far from home.

I peeked out my one window to be greeted by a sky like a gray flannel crazy quilt. Snow fell so thickly I could barely see the barn. There was nothing for it but to carry on with my chores, pulling my overcoat even tighter about me as I slogged to the barn. I hesitated to turn Plug loose. But I'd seen how clever he was at pawing through the snow to the tender grass below. And I didn't have enough feed to keep him and Violet going all winter. I eased my conscience by giving him an extra-large portion of oats before opening the stable door for him. I fed, watered, and milked my cranky cow.

"Easy there." I patted Violet's twitching flanks. She shifted back and forth, back and forth, lowing in a most mournful manner. "What is it, girl?" I made up my mind to rummage through Uncle Chester's books for one on animal husbandry. I hadn't saved this varmint from a wolf to lose her to some cow disease.

"Moo-oo," she moaned again, her brown eyes rolling in her head. Her tail had healed nicely, her nose felt fine, and she gave milk pretty good. Perhaps she wasn't ill after all. But something was certainly unsettling her.

I discovered it for myself when I hefted the milk pail and stepped outside. The wind, brisk before, had worked itself up into a temper. It whirled around my head, threatening to suck the very life out of my lungs. I couldn't catch my breath.

"Plug!" I screamed against the wind. Or tried to. Nature forced my words right back down my throat. Another gust nearly knocked me over. Surely Plug would know enough to get out of this storm. I had to get back to the house.

Icy snow slashed at my head and shoulders. For weeks I'd tripped over that length of rope Uncle Chester had curled up inside the door. I'd let it be, not having another place to stash it. Now I guessed its use: I must fasten one end to the house and one to the barn. If this blizzard lasted more than a day, I'd need a way to get to the barn to take care of Violet.

I set the milk pail inside and grabbed up the rope. Uncle Chester had already fastened a great metal eye to the front of the shack. In dreamier moments, I'd thought I might use it to stake up some hollyhocks come spring. Tying off a secure knot, I let out the rope and fought my way back to the barn. The angry wind snatched away every breath I tried to take. My chest tightened in panic, but I forced myself forward. Icicles formed on my eyelashes. I could not close my eyes. They felt frozen open. And yet I could barely see. The icy wind whipped and scratched worse than Violet's tail ever had. I placed one foot in front of the other in the snow.

One minuscule step at a time, I battled toward the barn, praying for help: "Lord, I can't do this alone." But no help came. It was up to me. I drew in an icy, ragged breath. I couldn't fail. Couldn't lose my way. Or lose my cow. That thought propelled me forward the last few steps. Finally, finally, I reached the barn, gasping and sobbing for air. My face was raw. I tasted the salt of blood trickling down my cheeks. I worked my shawl over my face. It was a frail barricade, but it did help.

My hands, clumsy in mittens, could not tie the knot at this end. I pried off my mittens and felt as if I'd plunged my hands into a glacier-fed stream. The ache in my joints rocked me back on my heels.

"Come on, come on." My fingers no longer belonged to my body. They were lifeless wooden sticks at the ends of my hands. "Over, under. Pull it snug." I nearly had the knot secured when a shrieking gust knocked me to my knees. Again and again, I fought to stand. It seemed hours passed before I finally finished tying the knot. My legs were rags; I leaned heavily on the rope. Left hand, then right hand, then left again. I dragged myself back to the house.

A small dark object perched at the top of the steps. Mr. Whiskers! We both nearly fell into the cabin, I panting, he mewling. The flimsy wood and tar-paper walls were no match for this wind. It bullied its way through every crack. My eyes warmed and grew runny. Another handful of chips in the stove barely took the edge off. I nailed a precious spare blanket over the door and kept feeding the fire.

Uncle Chester's cabin rattled and creaked and moaned and shifted as the wind battered it again and again. It surely could not hold. I pulled on another sweater. I would not leave this cabin. Would not be driven out.

At one point, I heard—what? A noise. A strange noise riding on top of the wild wind. The noise sounded almost human. And it sounded like my name.

I shook my head and listened again. Nothing but the screeching of the storm. But there—listen! It *was* a human voice. A child's voice! I pulled back the blanket, opened the door, and peered out.

At first, I could see nothing but the wildly swirling snow. "Hello?" I called, my voice instantly sucked up by the wind. I tried again. *"Hello!"* This, screeched at the top of my lungs.

I heard the voice again. "Hattie. Miz Hattie!" What I saw next brought me to my knees more suddenly than any slap of wind. A large figure fought its way toward the house. Plug. Dear Plug. And hanging to his tail for dear life—literally for dear life—were Chase and Mattie.

I ran out without a thought for overcoat, hanging on to the rope I'd just strung. "Here, Plug. Here, children," I screamed, my voice raw. After an eternity, Plug staggered into range. I swept Mattie into my arms and motioned for Chase to take hold of the rope. Head down, he scuffled with snow and wind until he reached it. We made our way, hand over hand, to the cabin. Plug settled himself in the lee of the house, out of the wind.

Mattie's hands felt deathly cold as I brought her inside and began to take off her frozen things.

"What happened?" I could not disguise the tremble of alarm in my voice.

Chase rubbed his own purple hands together and stepped closer to the fire. "We were at school and saw the storm coming. Mr. Nelson told us to get on home. I thought we could make it but . . ." Chase's voice cracked.

"You're safe now," I assured him. *Thank you, Lord, for that good horse, who led these children out of the storm.* "And what a hero you are—to find Plug and let him lead you here."

Chase crumpled to the floor. His shoulders shook with sobs. I turned to distract Mattie, to spare him the further pain of having witnesses to his tears.

"Now, little miss." I rubbed her feet briskly. "What do I have that will fit you?" By the time I got her dressed in dry things, she looked more scarecrow than six-year-old. But she was content chatting to her doll as her clothes dried by the stove.

"We've got to get Chase warmed up, too." I surveyed my remaining wardrobe. Not much was appropriate for an eight-year-old boy. I held up my flannel nightgown.

"I'd rather freeze to death," he said.

"Don't blame you." In a far corner, I'd made a neat stack of Uncle Chester's clothes. Much too large for me to wear, I'd thought to use the shirts for a quilt and pants for a rag rug but was now very glad I hadn't. The pride—and survival—of an eight-year-old boy depended on a flannel shirt and pair of man's wool pants.

The clothes were a bit sniffy, but then, from my meager experience with Chase, it seemed that eight-year-old boys could be a bit sniffy themselves. "Perfect fit," I proclaimed.

With both children in dry clothes, my thoughts turned to feeding them. "Have you ever had milk coffee?" I asked.

"Mama don't 'low us to drink coffee," said Mattie. "Do you think she's worried about us?"

"She knows how clever you are," I said. "That you'd find a safe place to weather this storm." That seemed to comfort her.

"She let me drink coffee last harvest," Chase bragged.

I nodded. "Well, milk coffee's what my mama used to make me when I was little." I poured some milk out of the pail and into a small kettle and set it on the stove to warm. "Even littler than you, Mattie. So I suspect it will be okay with your mama." I took three mugs off the shelf. "Now, what do you think about something to go with this coffee?"

"We don't need anything," answered Chase.

"Yes, please," answered his more truthful sister. "And Mulie's hungry, too."

I sliced up some bread. "This isn't too bad with lots of jelly," I said, setting plates before the kids. Bread making was not one of my more highly developed skills. They both ate bravely, without comment. Perilee had raised them right.

"Say, have either of you ever played Five Hundred?"

Mattie shook her head. "I don't think so," said Chase.

I got out my one deck of cards and explained the rules. "Mattie and I will be partners," I said. "So watch out, Chase!"

The game went on fast and furious. I was amazed at how quickly Chase picked it up. The boy had a knack for numbers. And his memory! He tracked nearly every card played.

"You must be the star pupil of your class," I said in amazement.

He shrugged. "I do all right."

I took the cards and shuffled them. We had played Five Hundred all afternoon. "Do you want to play a different game?"

"Let's play I Wish," said Mattie. "I'll start." She chewed on her lip. "I wish I had a doll made of china, like Sarah Martin." She patted Mulie's bedraggled yarn hair. "So Mulie would have a friend."

"I wish for cinnamon rolls every day," Chase said. He laughed.

I leaned back on my lard bucket chair. "Well, I guess I wish it was spring and I could start planting wheat."

Chase perked up. "First you plant flax, then the wheat. Karl says maybe end of April."

"That's not a wish," scolded Mattie. "That's work."

"You've got me there." I could imagine what a disappointing wish that would be for a six-year-old, but I had to plant crops. It was part of proving up. Part of my dream of having a place of my own. November was mere months away; the clock was ticking. Here it was the middle of February and I hadn't set one fence post or plowed one foot of dirt. I'd had to content myself with reading about it in that book Miss Simpson gave me.

"You can wish for anything," Chase said. "There are no rules. Mama said."

"Your mama sure is smart." I added a precious scoop of coal to the stove.

The children got quiet—so quiet I could hear the coal hissing.

Mattie clapped her hands. "I wish for *two* dolls!"

"That's the spirit. Now, Chase, how about you?"

He looked over his shoulder at my library. He stood up and walked over, tracing his fingers down the spines of several volumes. "I wish I could live somewhere where there were books all around. In a real town, with a real library. And I could read about pirates or explorers or anything." He gazed off into space for a moment, and I knew he was seeing himself in just such a wonderful place.

"I hope your wish comes true," I said to him. "Yours, too, Mattie."

"What's your real, true wish?" Chase asked. He came back to sit at the table, searching my face with an eight-year-old's earnestness.

I flipped my hands up. "Oh, I don't know." How to explain to these two children the longing in my heart for what they had? To be part of a family. To have a place to call home. Better leave it all unsaid. I glanced over at my books. "So, Chase, shall you pick one out for a story time? That storm doesn't look like it's settling down any. I think you're here for the night."

"We've never stayed away from home before," said Mattie.

Her elfin face clouded over. She drew her legs underneath her and rocked on the wooden crate. Silent tears dribbled down her cheeks. She cuddled her rag doll close.

"Now, now. There'll be none of that." I cringed to hear Aunt Ivy's sharp tone accompanying my words. I softened my voice. "Or I'll feed you another slice of my bread." That won a smile from both children. I reached over, took Mattie's hand in mine, and squeezed it, *one-two-three*. "That's a secret message," I told her. "My mama taught it to me, and now you can teach it to your mama."

"What's it mean?" Mattie rubbed the tears from her cheeks.

I blushed, embarrassed to say the words aloud. I leaned to whisper in her ear: "It means 'I love you.' "

Mattie regarded me for a moment with her big brown eyes. Then she reached out and squeezed my hand, *one-two-three*. I blinked back a tear of my own.

Chase had made his selection. "Mr. Nelson's going to read us *Treasure Island* by Robert Louis Stevenson at school, so I pick this one." He held out *A Child's Garden of Verses* and scooted his apple crate chair closer to the stove.

Mattie stood at my knee. I opened the book. She inched closer.

"Mama lets me sit on her lap when she reads," she said.

"Oh." I felt myself get all flustered. "Then I guess you'd better sit here." I patted my legs. Mattie scootched up and snuggled her wiry body close. She smelled of coffee and jelly and damp wool. As I began to read, her body relaxed into mine, until it was difficult to tell where she left off and I began.

After two poems, she was sound asleep. After two more,

Chase was snoring. I slipped them both into my bed and pulled the covers up tight. Then I got myself ready and joined them. Once Mattie cried out, "Mama!" but she didn't waken. I settled the covers over her again, then watched them both, amazed. With a sigh, I curled up on the edge of the bed and slept the soundest sleep of my entire sixteen years.

I woke to the jingle of sleigh bells. Two warm children were flung every which way across my bed. For a moment, my head was fuzzy. Children?

"Hallo!" A voice rose above the jingling bells. "Hallo, Miz Hattie!" There was an edge to that familiar deep voice. Not even Karl's thick accent could cover up fear.

I snatched up my overcoat and flung open the door. "They're safe," I called out. "Plug led them here."

Karl tethered his team and slid down off the sled. He caught himself—it was almost as if his legs weren't strong enough to hold him. I waved him inside.

"You're frozen!" I hurried to warm up some coffee.

"Karl!" Mattie leaped off my bed and into his arms.

I caught the glitter of a tear in his eye. "I'll warn you, Karl," I chattered, "I've turned these two into card sharks. Corrupted them with coffee, too."

Karl sat down heavily, Mattie still clinging to him.

"This cold air makes my nose run worse than Niagara Falls," I said lightly.

He fished out a huge red handkerchief and blew his nose. *Kalt, ja,* he said.

I set the coffee in front of him. "I've got some bread and jam."

73

"Danke." He nodded and reached an arm out for Chase.

"You might want to dunk it in your coffee," said Chase. "Soften it up a bit."

I laughed. "Insult my baking, will you?" I pretended to box Chase's ears. "Ungrateful child." He wiggled away and grinned from safety behind Karl.

I don't know that Karl understood all of our silliness, but I could tell by his face he knew Mattie and Chase had been safe with me. *"Danke,"* he repeated.

"See, he does like my bread," I said, cutting several more slices. I set some bacon to frying, too. "Let me get some warm food in you before you go on your way. Your ma's probably worn through the window glass watching for you to come home."

Karl reached a cracked and bleeding hand for another piece of bread. Bits of white flesh dotted his cheeks. Frostbite. "Off with those boots," I ordered. He obeyed. I swallowed hard when I saw his chalk-white toes. From the looks of him, he'd been out all night looking for Perilee's children. I blinked back my own tears.

"Hand me that tub there," I ordered Chase. "A warm bath is the ticket for cold toes." I kept my voice light and the children busy so they wouldn't get a look at Karl's feet.

Karl grimaced as I poured warm water over his feet into the tub. I soaked a rag in warm water and had him press against the bad spots on his cheeks. Some folks said rubbing snow on frostbite was the best cure, but it seemed to me that getting the flesh unfrozen made more sense.

As his toes and face turned purple, I questioned my

wisdom. His feet swelled and sprouted blisters. I wasn't sure how he was going to get his boots back on, even after daubing the worst of the blisters with a paste made of baking soda.

I wasn't done doctoring, but Karl was done being a patient. *"Perilee macht . . ."* He left the sentence hanging, but there was no need to finish. He wanted to get the children home. We gathered up their now dry clothes from around the house. I helped them dress while Karl downed a second cup of coffee.

"I wish there'd been time to dry out your socks." I rummaged through Chester's things. "Here, you must take these." It wouldn't do his feet much good to be back in those cold, wet socks and boots.

He put on the dry socks, then his boots and mittens. He patted my hands. He opened his mouth as if to say something, then simply cleared his throat.

Mattie jumped into his arms again, and he tilted her toward me. "Mwah!" She gave me a juicy six-year-old's kiss. But I did not wipe the dampness from my cheek.

"Oh, wait!" I took two steps to the bookshelf. I pulled off the book we'd started and handed it to Chase. "On loan." I squeezed his shoulder.

Chase tucked the book carefully inside his coat. "I'll take very good care of it, I promise."

"Safe trip home, you three!"

They rushed out into the cold and into the sled. My one small window was placed so that I could not watch them leave, but I could hear them go. I strained to capture every jingle.

❧ CHAPTER 7 ❧

March 5, 1918
Three miles north and west of Vida, Montana

Dear Charlie,

*The beautiful snow is melting, turning everything
into pig heaven, what with all the mud puddles. I
walked right out of my boots this morning on my way
to milk Violet, the mud was that thick. I was ready to
start planting last week, but Karl and Rooster Jim
both laughed at me. "The seeds will drown," said Jim.
So today I will perfect my fence-building skills
instead.*

*Your letter—the first one received at my Montana
home—arrived so full of holes I thought the moths had
got into it. The censors take their work seriously! It makes*

your letters a great puzzle to read. When the censor slices out the offending phrases on one side of the page, it creates a challenge on the opposite side as well. I was able to discern that you are now sleeping in barracks at your new camp instead of tents. Though they don't sound much better than tents if you must sleep with your raincoat to keep the rain off at night.

Over our last chess game (I lost), Jim was full of war news. He says the Allied forces pushed the Germans back in Paris, but my heart broke to learn of the Tuscania being torpedoed. All those sailors lost. I am thankful you are on dry land at least. When I am not worrying over our valiant doughboys, I worry over what's happening here at home. Every day there are notices of folks being charged with sedition; it seems anything can be interpreted as treasonous. I read that that funny little dachshund dog is now to be called a "liberty dog." Can you beat that? There is even talk here of outlawing speaking any German at all. Jim says it will be pure hardship for Reverend Schatz and his parishioners over at the Lutheran church. "The padre might as well speak in Greek," he said. "They won't be able to follow him at all." Because Jim's vocabulary is particularly lively, I can't write everything he said. But I do wonder, as he does, what harm it is for our neighbors to worship God in their native language.

Sometimes I do not know what to think.

Your bewildered friend,
Hattie Inez Brooks

Since I couldn't plant, I turned to another big chore: fencing. It was the other part of the requirement for proving up on my claim. No way around it. Uncle Chester had made a stab at it, but a halfhearted stab. I could pace off the length of fence he built in ten strides. He'd laid in plenty of materials, enough for the 480 rods of fence that had to be built. One cold and lonely night I'd done the math to calculate how many feet that was. Sixteen and a half feet times 480 rods. Seven thousand nine hundred and twenty feet. I nearly cried. No wonder farmers talked of rods; it was an easier number to face. No matter how I calculated it, you can be sure I said a prayer of thanks that it was all paid for. There it was, stacked up behind the barn, waiting for willing hands. Which turned out to be mine.

"Lord, I am thankful for the gloves Charlie's mother gave me," I said, starting my daily upward conversation. Wouldn't Aunt Ivy get a wrench in her whalebone corset to see me dolled up? Uncle Holt's old work boots on my feet, a pair of Karl's patched overalls, rolled up, those heavy canvas gloves on my hands, topped off with my straw hat. I chuckled as I picked up a roll of barbed wire, a hammer, and a sack of fence staples and prepared to slog my way to the far side of the coulee to pick up where I'd left off yesterday. I was fencing a line at the southeast edge of my claim, right where it butted up against Karl and Perilee's.

A person can take something commonplace like a fence completely for granted until that same person has to try to build a foot or two of it. Seems like it should be a simple thing. It's not. First you break your back trying to dig a hole in the ground. Then you wrestle a post into the hole. Then you bury the base in dirt so it's nice and sturdy. Then you go on to the next hole. And the next one. I spent a week with a pickaxe and shovel digging postholes. The first night, my hands were so blistered and sore, I couldn't even spoon up my supper. The second night, I applied a liberal dose of white liniment—Uncle Holt's own concoction of hartshorn, arnica, witch hazel, camphor gum, eggs, and cider vinegar. Thankfully, it was as soothing as it was strong-smelling. By the third night, I was too hungry and tired to even feel my hands anymore.

I'd rigged up a stone boat for Plug to pull. I'd felt a bit like Noah as I studied the countless boulders scattered across my claim. Noah looked to build a boat to float on the rising waters; I was looking for a stone boat to "float" on the rolling prairie land. Finally, I found a stone flat enough and solid but not too heavy for Plug. Karl put me wise to this trick when I saw him using a stone boat to bring his supplies out to our common boundary. It would've taken me till I was ninety to get the diamond willow posts and wire out to the field if I hadn't.

Now I lashed a load to the stone boat, clucked to Plug, and we were off. The day before, I'd stopped work near an enormous chokecherry. Today I planned to string wire to that spot and, with luck, plant a few more fence posts.

Plug and I battled through the gumbo mud to the fence line.

"What on earth?" I reached the chokecherry and dropped my tools. I looked back and took my bearings. This was the right bush, all right. But my fence didn't stop here. It now stretched out for another good ways, maybe forty rods or so. I moved in for a closer inspection. It wasn't hard to identify my handiwork of the prior workday: my staples were crooked, catching the wire in a haphazard but adequate way to hold it to the posts.

But from the chokecherry on, the nails were square in and true as true. I remembered a story my mother read to me long, long ago. It was about a shoemaker who used the last of his shoe leather to outfit a trio of fairies. After that day, each morning he'd find a handsome new pair of shoes on his workbench. The fairies repaid his brand of kindness with their own.

The one I suspected at this moment was not of the fairy world but firmly in this one. I picked up where my fairy fence builder had left off. As I stretched each strand of wire, tapped it into place with a staple, stretched and tapped, stretched and tapped, I thought again of that conversation in Wolf Point between Mr. Hanson and Perilee. About folks who called sauerkraut "liberty cabbage" in order to swallow it down with their supper. And of Charlie doing his duty, eager to finish off a German or two. I thought about all the fences that get built in this world—the ones that divide folks and tear them up, like the actions of the Kaiser and his henchmen, and the ones that bring folks closer together, like this stretch of fence Karl Mueller had built for me.

"Plug." I patted the old horse. "It's like I wrote to Charlie. This world is surely a puzzle. I wonder how old I'll be before I get it all figured out."

His only answer was to step sideways to a greener patch of grass.

I finished up what I could and headed back for dinner at noon. Mr. Whiskers perched himself on the still-empty chicken coop—I hoped to order some chicks soon from Sears and Roebuck—earnestly licking the mud from his white paws.

I started for the house—and stopped. There were noises coming from the barn. Decidedly un-cow-like noises. A chill crept over me. I couldn't imagine what—or more likely who—was in there. I swung up my hammer and eased over to the barn. Before I could make a plan, the door slapped open and a tall, bony woman stepped out. She took me in with a glance.

"You planning to knock me a good one?" She took a step toward me. That's when I noticed the shotgun leaned up against the wall.

"Who are—"

"Leafie Purvis." The woman stuck out a large, four-fingered hand. "Came to pay a call."

"Most folks come to the house, not the barn." She may have told me her name, but I didn't know this woman or what to make of her.

That drew a huge laugh. "If that isn't a Chester remark."

"I'm his niece." I lowered my weapon. "Hattie Brooks."

"I know." She reached behind a stack of bundled hay. "Give me a hand, will you?" Pushed up against the back wall was a wooden chest fastened shut with three heavy leather straps. The initials *CHB* were etched into the leather strap in the center.

"This is Uncle Chester's?" I ran my fingers over the worn leather, stopping at the buckle. Did this chest hold anything of my past? Anything of my mother?

"He was the private sort," said Leafie. "Asked me to move it out here when he got so sick. Wanted to make sure nobody went through it before you." A wistful expression flickered across her lined face. "He so hoped to show you himself." Leafie patted the trunk with her hand.

"You were here when he died." I recalled Perilee's words. "Thank you."

"He'd have done the same for any one of us." She reached into the pocket of the man's shirt she wore and pulled out a pouch of tobacco. Aunt Ivy would've fainted dead away, but I watched with fascination as Leafie deftly rolled a cigarette.

I fought my curiosity about the trunk and managed to remember my manners. "Would you like to come inside for some dinner? Do we need to water your horse?"

Leafie's laugh rolled out with the cigarette smoke and turned to a cough. "I'm traveling by shank's mare."

"I don't understand."

She lifted her skirts to show sturdy boots. "I'm walking. Trouble with this gumbo is that walking means one step forward and two steps back." She laughed again. "Only way I can get anywhere is to walk in the opposite direction."

I laughed, too. It was hard to resist Leafie's enthusiasm. "And Rooster Jim says summer's worse than spring!" I exclaimed.

"He's right there." Leafie wiped her brow. "I'd rather slip

and slide than sizzle any day." She pointed to herself. "So though I've no horse, I could stand to water this old beast."

"I can heat up some coffee real quick," I said. "And if you don't mind beans—" The ground rumbled and rolled as I stepped out of the barn. "What on earth?" I glanced around and saw the cause of the reverberations.

Several riders, maybe as many as six, pounded across the prairie. Ahead of them, at breakneck speed, they drove a cow. She zigged and zagged, frightened by the men and horses. Then she turned and bolted down the coulee. Right toward my cabin.

"No!" I screamed. "Watch out!"

The riders didn't slow. Now I could see there were four of them. Four horses and a cow bearing down on my home. "Stop! Stop!" I ran toward them.

Ropes of saliva swung from the frantic cow's mouth. Her eyes rolled up in her head. All I could see were whites. I don't think she could even see me.

"*Stop!*" I screamed at the top of my lungs. I thought I heard a rider laugh. Still they thundered toward my home. They were going to drive that cow right through it!

Ka-boom! An explosion went off behind me. I whirled to see Leafie there, cocking the shotgun to fire again. *Ka-boom!*

The lead rider pulled up short. He raised his arm in the air, signaling the others. They swung around, almost as one rider, and rode off, the cow forgotten. Its frantic pace slowed and it trotted to a halt beyond the house, sides heaving.

I realized I'd been holding my breath and let it go. "Who

were they?" I wiped sweating palms on my overalls. "Do you think they'll come back?"

Leafie squinted. "If they get a burr in their britches about something, they will. But I don't expect you've got anything to worry about. Stay out of their way. That'd be my advice." She handed me her gun.

"We better water that poor thing." Leafie strode over, fearlessly grabbed the cow's heavy leather collar, and led it to the barn. "You've got a guest, Violet."

I followed, carrying the gun in shaking arms. "What was that all about?" I sank down against Uncle Chester's chest.

She shook her head. "The last thing this county needed was Traft Martin on that so-called Dawson County Council of Defense."

"But isn't that a patriotic organization?" I'd read about the councils in the paper. They'd been organized by the governor. "To encourage people to follow the food rules and buy Liberty Bonds and such?"

"Far as I'm concerned, it's nothing more than an excuse for grown men to behave like schoolboys." She snorted. "Tell me this—what's patriotic about driving a good man's cow to death?" She slapped the cow's flank for emphasis. It startled but resumed eating. "This war's making folks forget what it means to be neighbors."

"Whose cow is it?"

"Let's just say I'll be leading it back to Perilee's on my way to check on Ellie Watson over at the sheep camp."

My stomach rocked at Perilee's name. "I don't understand. Why would they do something like this? Karl and Perilee are

84

good people." There was a section of strong fence out there to prove it.

"This war gives them all the reason they need." She rubbed the cow down with an old horse blanket. "All this fuss about where people are from. Seems like how they live now that they're here should be what matters." Leafie tossed the blanket aside and stepped toward me. "Oh, don't pay me no never mind. I fuss and peck like a cranky old hen." She gave me a sound pat on the arm. "I best be on my way."

I got her a rope, and she fastened it around the cow's collar.

She brought her gaze back to me. "You got a gun here?"

"No." I thought about the wolf. "I've never even fired one."

"Don't always have to use a gun in order for it to make an impression," she said. Before I could say anything in reply, she was across the yard, she and the cow squelching their way through the gumbo toward the sheep camp. By way of the Muellers' place.

When Leafie was out of sight, I realized she'd never got her water, or the coffee and beans. I hoped someone would feed her at the Watsons'. I went back into the barn. On knees still shaking from the cow episode, I knelt by the trunk and ran my finger over the leather straps. What had Uncle Chester wanted to show me? Would I find any answers about his mysterious life? I undid the left strap and then the right. Slowly I lifted the curved lid. It was solid, heavy. Strong enough to keep nearly any secret safe.

The chest was as neat and tidy as the cabin had been

cluttered and dirty. Careful piles rose from the bottom. Tucked in between old woolen socks and pants were mementoes: circus bills, a dance card, penny postcards, a few photos. I stared at each face in each photo but saw no one I recognized. I dug a little deeper, pushing aside a cache of books. A packet wrapped in brown paper and tied with a bit of calico proved to hold girlish bits of fabric. It looked like the start of someone's quilt. But whose? The fabric was bright, some even new and unwashed. Was this part of Chester's sadness? A quilt started by a young love and never finished for some tragic reason? I rocked back on my heels.

I couldn't see one thing inside this chest that would warrant Chester asking Leafie to hide it from others. No clue to his "scoundrel" past. No—I couldn't help but voice the hope— photos of my mother or father. I replaced the chest's contents, lowered the lid, and refastened the straps.

This day had been as full of mystery as Uncle Chester's life. It reminded me of a pitch Charlie had tried and tried to teach me. He called it the "snake ball." There was no way a batter could predict which way that ball was going to break. Sometimes there was no way for the pitcher to, either.

This had certainly been a snake ball day. From Karl's work on my fence to meeting Leafie and learning about the trunk to the Council of Defense and their wild cowpunching, there was no way to predict which way this day was going to break.

I pushed myself to my feet. My nerves had calmed and my stomach was complaining. The mysteries of life would have to wait; now I needed some dinner.

· · ·

The day after Leafie's visit, I was about a third of the way through my wheat field, picking rocks. When I'd asked about all the rock fences weaving drunkenly along others' fields, Perilee had provided an answer straight from the Bible. "Don't you remember the parable of the sower?" she teased me. "And how the seed died when it was planted on rocky ground?" She had scooped up a handful of loose soil. "You have to clear out the rocks before you can plant, sugar. Or nothing will grow."

So here I was ruining back and hands, picking rocks and building my own wobbly rock fences while Mr. Whiskers chased after the garter snakes I scared up. One tiny snake twisted itself up and launched at Mr. Whiskers. The old cat jumped four feet off the ground. I laughed out loud. "If there was a market for rocks and snakes," I told Mr. Whiskers, "I could buy up the whole of Dawson County." Mr. Whiskers' response was to chase off after a worm-hungry killdeer.

I stood up straight to retie my bonnet and caught sight of a single rider drawing near.

"Howdy, ma'am." The rider sat straight in his saddle. "Here we are neighbors and haven't even met yet." At this, he dismounted and extended his right hand.

I stepped across the cleared patch and took it. "Hattie Brooks."

"Traft Martin."

I started. Surely anyone this good-looking could not be all bad, no matter what Leafie said about him and the Council of Defense.

"Seems a shame we haven't met until now." He smiled. It was a nice smile in an even nicer-looking face. He couldn't have been much more than twenty.

"I thought Sunday was come-calling day." I pushed my bonnet back on my head.

He smiled again, this time with his eyes as well. "Well, I was out this way to speak to Rooster Jim about a horse."

I remembered Jim talking about Traft Martin wanting his horses. "No sale?" I guessed.

Something behind his eyes shifted. "Not yet."

A chill snuck over me. *Handsome is as handsome does,* Aunt Ivy used to preach. Right now those words seemed created with Traft Martin in mind. I bent back to my work. "If you'll forgive me, Mr. Martin, I've got ground to cover before sundown." I waved my hand over the rocky patch.

"I admire you." He pulled a pouch from his pocket and began to roll a cigarette. "This is hard work. And lonely, too."

I had leaned over to pick up another rock, then stopped. Something in his words caught me. It was the tone of someone who knew what it was like to be lonely. Alone. "I'm getting used to the hard work part," I said. *Clunk clunk clunk.* Three more rocks.

Without saying anything, he strode over to where I was clearing and began picking rocks, too. *Clunk clunk clunk.* "You don't have to do this," I said.

He talked around the cigarette in his teeth. "Just being neighborly." *Clunk clunk clunk.*

I felt very confused. According to what I'd heard, the devil himself was a saint compared to Traft Martin. What kind of devil helps someone pick rocks? Didn't figure. We worked together for an hour or more. The sun slipped to the horizon. Traft rubbed his forehead with the back of his wrist. "I best git going."

I brushed dirt off my hands. "This was so kind of you."

"Neighbors should help one another," he said. "Don't you agree?"

"Do unto others," I said.

He nodded at me, then mounted his horse.

"Let's go, Trouble." He and the horse wheeled around. "It was nice meeting you, Miz Brooks." He rode off. Mr. Whiskers padded up behind me, rubbing against my legs.

"Trouble," I mused, bending down to scratch Mr. Whiskers behind the ears. "I have a feeling that could be Traft Martin's middle name."

That night, the four walls of that shack squeezed so snug that I did my reading on the front steps. After a few pages into my book, I set it aside. Traft's help in the field had brought up a memory of me and Charlie painting half the fences in Arlington that one summer. With the two of us, it seemed more like a taffy pull than work.

I leaned back against the rough siding of Uncle Chester's house and studied that Montana sky. I know the same sky hangs over Iowa—over Charlie in France, for that matter—but I don't think it looks like this anywhere else in the world. There weren't many trees or mountains to catch at that sky and keep it low. No, it stretched out high and smooth and far, like a heavenly quilt on an unseen frame. Back in Iowa, I'd spent my fair share of time studying the clouds and the stars. Sometimes, lying out on Aunt Ivy and Uncle Holt's back lawn, it'd felt as if I could stretch out my arms and my fingertips and rake them across the underside of the heavens and end up with a fistful of stars.

Not even the biggest giant I could imagine could brush this Montana sky with his fingertips. It made me feel like one of the prickly pear cactuses I crunched under my feet: small and unimportant on the prairie near Vida. Was I feeling lonely? How could I be? Mattie and Chase stopped by after school most days, and Rooster Jim had deepened the path from his shack to mine. Was there a word in Uncle Chester's big dictionary to describe what I was feeling? Solitary? Desolate? Forlorn? "It's like when you play Old Maid," I said to Mr. Whiskers. "That's what I feel like. Leftover." He wiggled into my lap, purring away. I stroked his dark head. "Not that you're not good company," I told him. "But there is something to that two-by-two business."

Mr. Whiskers flipped over for a belly rub. All he cared about was a warm place to sleep, something to eat, and someone to give him a pat now and then. Maybe I should learn from his example, quit moping, and think about November, when I'd march into Mr. Ebgard's office. I closed my eyes and pictured the flax field come fall. Perilee had said it would look like the ocean, all bloomed out in blue. And the wheat, golden and whiskery. I saw the fence—every inch of it— marking off the lines of my claim.

"It's going to be mighty fine to be land barons, isn't it?" Mr. Whiskers batted at my hand. He was done with petting.

And I was done with moping. Here, under this big sky, some-one like me—Hattie Here-and-There—could work hard and get a place of her own. A place to belong. Wasn't that my deepest wish?

A warmth wrapped over me, like I was being covered with a quilt. I whispered a prayer of thanks, then went back inside, turned out the lights, and crawled into bed.

❧ CHAPTER 8 ❧

The Ides of March
Three miles north and west of Vida, Montana

Dear Charlie,

Mr. Whiskers sends his greetings. You might not recognize him, he's gotten so full of mice and who knows what all else. He's still not warmed up to Chase but lets Mattie fuss and pet at him to no end. One day she even dressed him in one of Mulie's bonnets! That little girl could sweet-talk anyone into doing anything.

And now you are an engine fitter. How exciting to work with aeroplanes. Mind the propellers!

Have you heard about the Daylight Saving Time plan? It seems so odd to begin it on Easter Sunday. President Wilson says it will save millions of tons of coal

*and thus help the war effort. When I think of you
bunking in leaky barracks, and all of the other sacrifices
you and the other doughboys are making, such a change
seems a small thing.*

*I have puzzled out what the stars mean that you put
in the margins of each letter. Each one is a sad
accounting. I weep to think of each mother who stitches a
gold star on her service flag to signify her son's ultimate
sacrifice.*

*I pray every night for an end to this war. And that
every single soldier, including the best pitcher in Fayette
County, comes home safe and sound.*

*Your fretful friend,
Hattie*

A stitched sampler hung on Aunt Ivy's kitchen wall: "Monday, Wash Day; Tuesday, Ironing; Wednesday, Mending; Thursday, Market; Friday, Cleaning; Saturday, Baking; Sunday, Day of Rest." It was Tuesday, so both sad irons were heating on the stove and I'd covered the kitchen table with a clean blanket. The sheets were the hardest to iron, so that's where I started. When one iron cooled off, I'd set it back on the stove and pick up the hot one, running it over a piece of old flour sacking to clean off any ash. I had my camisoles and underthings laid out to iron next when I heard a horse in the yard.

"Hello there!" a male voice called out. "Miz Brooks?"

I peeked out the open door. Traft! For a fleeting moment I wished I'd put on my skirt that morning instead of the more practical pair of Chester's old overalls.

"Good morning, ma'am." The range horse was slick with sweat. "Wonder if I might water Trouble?"

I nodded. "Out for a long ride?"

"You might say so." He slid to the ground with a jingle of spurs.

"Would you like a cup of coffee?" I motioned him toward the house. "And some bread? It won't compete with Perilee's, but it won't kill you."

Traft laughed. "Sounds about like my own cooking." He watered and tethered his horse, then stepped inside.

"Won't you sit—" I stopped. There for all the world—and Traft Martin—to see were my underthings. I snatched them up and deposited them in a nearby empty lard bucket.

"You've made it very homey around here," he said. A crinkle at his eyes betrayed him. He'd seen. Oh, Lord, what would Aunt Ivy think?

I pointed to the apple crate. "This chair is especially comfortable." I quickly tipped over the lard bucket so he couldn't see its contents, then set out some refreshments.

Traft devoured several slices of bread with Uncle Chester's buffalo berry jam and two cups of coffee. Then he pushed his plate and cup away. "Thank you," he said. "That did hit the spot." He shook his booted left foot. "Right down there."

"I'm working on getting it lighter," I said.

He grinned. "It's hard to get light bread in damp weather. Maybe next time set your sponge over the water reservoir in the stove. That's what my mother does."

"Why, Mr. Martin, you are better than a subscription to the *Ladies' Home Journal*." I finished my coffee.

94

"Speaking of my mother, she wanted me to invite you to church on Easter. There'll be supper after and a sewing circle. For the Red Cross." He stood up. I couldn't tell if his cheeks were badly chapped or if he was blushing. "I'd be pleased to come take you."

"Oh, thank you. But I don't know—I mean, if I'm not planting, perhaps I'll go. But I'll bring myself." I wasn't sure what it meant out here to ride to church with a man, but back home, that was reserved for courting couples.

"Suit yourself, then." He picked up his hat and set it on his head, holding my gaze as he situated it just so. The look he gave me nearly undid my resolve to decline his offer. "Oh, I nearly forgot. I stopped at Bub Nefzger's store this morning, and he had some mail for you. I said I'd bring it out." He reached inside his shirtfront and brought out a small bundle.

"That's so kind of you."

"No trouble at all." He shrugged back into his jacket. "I like the scenery out this way."

It was my turn to blush.

With a nod, he slipped out the door. I watched him mount his horse and ride away. I fanned myself with the packet he'd brought; funny how the cabin had warmed up so quickly. I shook myself and untied the packet holding two letters and the *Wolf Point Herald*. The first letter was from Uncle Holt, with a small postscript that pleased me to no end: *I surely enjoyed your last letter.*

The second letter was from Charlie. It was dated several months before and sent on from Arlington; the envelope was stained and creased. The words "Opened by Censor" were stamped heavily on the back.

February 10, 1918

Dear Hattie,

You know I'm not one to complain, but I've been in France for three months without one letter from you. Could it be that you don't think of your old pal Charlie anymore? I sure hope not.

Well, I haven't won the war yet. Give me a few more days! So far, it's mostly drills and drills and trying not to get sick. My bunkmate's in the hospital now from the dysentery. We hope we don't all end up in the wards before we see some action.

You would swoon if you saw how handsome your old pal looks in his uniform. A Red Cross nurse took my photo yesterday. If it turns out, I'll send it to you.

I can't tell you much about where I am—the censors turn most letters into Swiss cheese as it is—but I hope I can come back someday. The buildings here have been standing for centuries. And the food even beats Ma's cooking. Don't tell her but I've sampled some of that French wine. It slips down pretty fine.

Today was hand grenade practice. No trouble at all for the best pitcher in Fayette County. Couldn't help thinking of the day I taught you to throw. Remember when you beaned old Jack the rooster? You straightened out your throw considerable after that but I'm not sure poor Jack ever fully recovered.

Guess what? They asked for volunteers to learn to be aeroplane mechanics, and you can bet I stepped right up. Suits me fine, and my sergeant says I'm picking it up real quick.

Don't forget about your old pal. Write me a line now and again.

Charlie

The post was so frustrating. I'd sent Charlie five letters since my arrival in Montana. It took forever for mail to get to him, and our letters were clearly crossing each other. Still, no matter when he got it, he'd get a chuckle out of my wolf story letter. Odd, both of us using our baseball skills for survival. I reread his letter, then poured myself another cup of coffee and savored every word of the paper. The ironing could wait. According to the front page of the *Herald,* the British had staged daylight raids on Stuttgart, and another hospital ship had been torpedoed, but not sunk this time. Nothing about what was happening in France. Aunt Ivy would say no news is good news, but still my stomach tightened as I scanned the front page. Nothing much more but the earthshaking report that Henry Hahn's gray mare had wandered off again. And the Glacier Theater was showing *In the Balance,* starring Earle Williams. I hadn't been to a show since I saw Kitty Gordon in *The Purple Lily,* right before Charlie signed up.

The old Hattie would've lingered over the movie ad, but not the new one. I turned straight to the market report and learned that flax was going for $3.66 a bushel. Chicago markets were paying $2.20 per bushel for wheat. I scribbled some figures in the margins of the newspaper. Uncle Chester had planted twenty acres in flax and harvested eighty bushels. Surely I could do as well, too. Eight times six and carry the four—that'd be $292.80. It was tight but no red ink yet, as Uncle Holt would say. So if I put twenty acres into flax and twenty into wheat, that would be the needed forty acres. I wondered how much wheat I could count on. Another question for Karl. I rubbed my eyes. No wonder farmers looked grim all the time.

I slapped the paper closed. The back page advertised "opportunities." The Shamrock Café wanted "experienced Chinese cooks." I didn't exactly qualify. The Smith Rooming House was getting ready to open: "experienced chambermaids wanted." I sighed. I'd left Iowa rather than work for Iantha Wells, but to save my claim, I might have to hire out to the Smith Rooming House. Folks did it all the time—worked a job as well as their claim. How they had the time, I had no idea. Mr. Gorley's sister, Clarice, taught at the Powder Creek school, Wayne Robbins from church helped out at Nefzger's store, and Leafie had told me about a young man from England who rode from town to town taking photographs of folks. His claim was down by Brockaway.

I couldn't teach school, and Bub Nefzger had plenty of help at the store. And I sure didn't own a camera. My prospects looked puny.

"Lord, now would be a good time to move in your mysterious ways," I said aloud. Mr. Whiskers jerked awake. Assuming the crop came on strong, I couldn't harvest forty acres on my own. Rooster Jim told me most folks hired Wayne Robbins or Mr. Gorley; they had binders and threshing machines.

I hadn't asked him what that would cost. I'd have to ask him next time I saw him. Dollar signs flitted before my eyes.

I drained the last of my coffee and stood to finish my ironing. Enough money or not, I would make it—prove up Uncle Chester's claim. I *had* to.

Little routines crept into my life. Chase and Mattie had worn a path next to my house, which was on their way home from school. Sometimes they didn't do more than wave, and sometimes they stopped and we discussed all manner of things. Chase was going places, that's for sure. He had ideas that most men never had, let alone eight-year-old boys. He trained his calf, Fawn, to come when he whistled like a killdeer. Last week he'd made an elaborate trap to catch a prairie dog. "Then I'm going to harness it to this wheel-and-pulley gizmo," he'd said, showing me a remarkable contraption. "This goes in the chips bucket and"—he rolled his hands around—"yee-haw! The chips flip right in the stove. No more mess." While he had successfully trapped the prairie dog, the rest of his invention wasn't quite the success Chase imagined. But he kept after it.

And read! He seemed purely starving for stories.

Where Chase preferred words on a page, Mattie favored the spoken word. She could talk rings around anyone, and from her and Mulie I learned much about the doings in Vida. Even if I'd had a telephone, like some of the folks closer to town did, I wouldn't have needed to listen in on the party line. Mattie would keep me up to snuff on goings-on. Those that mattered to a six-year-old, at any rate.

It was a cool day, damp from a recent rain. Another good day to pick rocks from what would be my wheat field. This land was shy on trees but flush with rocks. I could've built a wall to rival that one I heard about in China. Some days I was certain I'd be picking rocks even in heaven.

The angle of the sun clued me in that I should be seeing two small figures anytime now. I'd made some of what Perilee called "sore finger biscuits"—when your fingers were too sore to knead the dough, you'd pinch off balls and bake them. I'd sprinkled them with some cinnamon sugar, thinking they might shorten the walk home for two certain schoolkids.

While I chunked rocks into a pile and waited for Chase and Mattie to pass by, I mentally composed my next letter to Uncle Holt. I wanted so badly to describe the prairie smell to him, the sweet promise of spring after a Chinook, the warm, edgy rub of sage, the rib-eye steak smell of my fields. *I feel as if I need to make up a new alphabet to be able to create the words that would summon up the stew of smells out here. I've learned not to take too deep a whiff when mucking out the barn, but most of the smells are good, wonderful, and hopeful, if smells can be such a thing.*

I got to turning words over in my mind so, I nearly forgot about my little trespassers.

"Unhh." I straightened up, aching from toe to hip with the strain of bending over, hour after hour. I scanned the horizon. Oh, there they were. I waved and hollered. "Fresh biscuits," I called gaily.

But they didn't come toward me. In fact, they were running—stumbling—away. Two figures, the larger one tugging the smaller along, kept to the top of the cutbank.

"Mattie! Chase!" I called again. They probably hadn't seen me, hunkered over in the field. Then I saw three other figures behind them. It didn't look like a happy situation.

"Children!" I hollered. I hitched up my skirts and cut a diagonal to meet up with them. It took some effort on my part; their legs were short but determined.

Panting, I crested the cutbank. I found myself smack between Chase and Mattie and the three rough-and-tumble boys chasing them. "Ow!" I hollered as a stone clipped my shoulder. "What is going on here?"

The trio stopped in their tracks, arms cocked back, hands loaded with rocks. No one answered me.

I rubbed my shoulder where I'd been hit. My presence evened up the sides; I could tell they were thinking that over.

"Young man." I addressed myself to the tallest of the three. He seemed to be the ringleader. "I asked what's going on here."

He just glowered at me. And held his ground.

I slowly bent down and picked up the rock that had struck me. The other two boys lowered their arms.

"We're just having a game," the leader said.

"Throwing rocks at people isn't a game." I took a step closer to Chase and Mattie. "It's cowardly." I'd hit a bull's-eye with that remark. The taller boy took a step forward. I squared my shoulders.

"Where do you boys live?" I rolled the stone in my hand like a die in a game of chance.

No answer.

There was something familiar in the taller boy's face. "You wouldn't be a Martin, would you?"

"Don't have to answer to you."

"No. But I'm sure your mama will want to know I've had the pleasure of your acquaintance," I said. "When I see her at church on Sunday."

"Why do you care?" he asked, though in a somewhat deflated tone. "You a Hun-lover, too?"

It was painful to hear childish voices using such names and labels. "I am a friend to these children." I tossed the rock up and down in my hand. It was clear my conversation was not making much of an impression on him. Time to change tactics.

I looked for something to aim at. A wild plum tree yonder made a fine target. I let loose. The stone hit the tree trunk with a satisfying smack.

"I gotta get home." One of the smaller boys took a shuffling step backward. "Pa'll skin me if I'm late for milking." He and his buddy emptied their hands. "C'mon, Lon," they urged.

Lon gave me one last defiant look. "Hun-lover," he spat.

I held his gaze. "So you say." I bent to pick up another stone. All three boys made elaborately casual turns, then loped back down the cutbank and out of sight.

"What was that all about?" I asked.

Chase shook his head. He began to march away.

"They took Karl's book," Mattie said. Her soft gray eyes wore an expression so sad, it cut me.

"Chase!" I ran a few steps, snagged his wiry arm, and turned him toward me. "Oh!" A smear of dried blood traced his cheekbone, and a small moist trickle leaked out of his nose. His face wore raw red marks, and a shiner threatened his right eye. "Here." I dabbed at him with an apron corner held in trembling hands. He stood it for a moment, then jerked away.

"I'm never going back there," he said through clenched teeth. "Mama can't make me." He swiped at his nose again, forcing another streak of red across his face.

"At least come to the house and clean up." I hated for Perilee to see him like this.

He hesitated. "All right."

I dragged the story out of him on the walk down the bank. Mattie, with help from Mulie, filled in details Chase overlooked.

"It belonged to Karl's mother," said Chase as we climbed the steps to my front door. "Old fairy tales."

"And Lon threw it—" Mattie held her own nose and covered her doll's. "In the necessary."

I ladled warm water from the reservoir on the stove into an enamelware bowl, soaked a rag, wrung it out, and handed it to Chase. He gently dabbed at his face.

"Why?" I asked.

"They said it's against the law to have German books." Chase's answer was so quiet I nearly didn't hear.

I took the rag from him and rinsed it out again; the water was sunset pink. "What did your teacher say?"

Chase shook his head.

Mattie shook Mulie at me. "Mulie's mad at Chase for not telling."

"You didn't tell Mr. Nelson?"

Chase winced as I daubed ointment on his raw cheek. "I can handle Lon."

I stopped doctoring and studied his face. "I can see that."

"It's not funny." He jerked away.

My hands dropped to my lap. "You are right. I was trying to make light, and this is not something to make light of."

"Mulie says those biscuits smell good," said Mattie. At this hint, I served them up, wrapping a few in a napkin for them to take home.

"It'll be all right." I patted Chase's shoulder as they took their leave. "They won't bother you anymore. And if they do, you tell Mr. Nelson."

"Won't need to." Chase grabbed Mattie's hand and tugged her forward. " 'Cause I'm not going anymore."

I watched them climb the cutbank hill and trudge toward home. The words I'd intended to write to Uncle Holt came back to me. I inhaled deeply, but the air didn't seem as sweet or hopeful. Some new odor was wafting on the breeze. One that caused my throat to catch and heart to ache. Was this what mistrust and fear smelled like?

I bent to pick up my work gloves. Whatever the ways of the world, there were still rocks to pick in my field. I got back to it.

❧ CHAPTER 9 ❧

March 30, 1918
Three miles north and west of Vida, Montana

Dear Uncle Holt,

Aunt Ivy can cease in her praying for my soul. I am going to attend my first church services here in Vida tomorrow, Easter Sunday. And it should please her all the more that I am staying after for the Ladies' Knitting Circle. As for actually knitting—my spirit is willing, but my fingers don't seem to cooperate. I can wind balls of yarn, at least.

Traft Martin, a neighbor, asked to take me to church, but I declined. He runs his family ranch, one of the largest around. He's nice-looking and has twice stopped to help me pick rocks in my field. That's enough to commend even the biggest sinner. But my heart is already promised—to this 320 acres of mine. Perhaps after November, after I prove up, I can think about beaus.

I finished Campbell's 1907 Soil Culture Manual and am now reading some of Rooster Jim's poultry journals so I can be ready for my chickens when I get them. Quite a change of reading from my usual fare. It's only been three months and I already look the part of farmer in overalls and clodhoppers. Soon I'll be fluent in farmer as well.

The Saturday before Easter, I cleaned. First, I did up my breakfast things, then scrubbed the plank floor. I used the floor water to wash down the front steps and threw the last of it on the seeds I'd planted in coffee tins by the door. I smiled to think of the sunflowers bursting forth from those cans come August. After a long day of inside work and a supper of lima beans and ham, I lugged the washtub from the barn and slowly filled it, kettle by kettle, from the warm water reservoir on the stove. After my Saturday night bath, I set my hair on rag rollers. This was the first time I'd gone to such bother since leaving Iowa. But I'd decided that Easter was a good time for such primping.

Plug was quite the gentleman as we picked our way around patches of mucky gumbo the next morning. I carried a basket filled with two Mason jars of Uncle Chester's canned wild plums to share at the after-service dinner. The ride to town was pleasant and quiet. It would've been pleasanter with a friend, but when I'd asked Perilee to attend with me, she shook her head. "It's been so long," she'd said.

"No time like the present to start up again." It would've been a comfort to have company. "And there's Sunday school for the children."

But she was resolute and most mysterious about her reasons for turning me down. So I plodded to town alone.

Now, as I drew closer, the faint strains of organ music caught my ears. A wave of longing swept over me; I hadn't heard that hymn since Charlie's last Sunday at church.

"Hello, hello!" A young woman greeted me and introduced herself as Grace Robbins. "So glad to finally meet you." She linked her arm in mine and led me inside. We sat together in the pew. "We're going to knit a bit after supper," she whispered as the organist cranked up the volume. "For the soldiers."

Mrs. Martin, resplendent in her yellow silk, silenced Grace's whispers with a dour look. Grace pouted but shushed all the same.

After the service, and shaking hands with Reverend Tweed, and eating a fine dinner with the congregation, the women broke into two groups. One group tidied up from the meal, and the other—the one Grace dragged me into—stayed seated at the sawhorse tables and took out handwork.

"I have an extra set of needles," said Grace. She rummaged in a large basket. "Oh, and a ball of yarn." She handed it to me.

I stoically cast on the requisite number of stitches, recalling the pair of socks I'd finally finished and sent to Charlie. They had more holes than a wheel of Swiss cheese. I glanced around the room. Other sets of needles clicked and flew; mine stumbled and rubbed.

Grace gave me a sympathetic glance. "What do you think about this Daylight Saving Time plan?" she asked, tugging on the yarn ball to free up more yarn.

"They say it will save on coal," I said. "Twelve countries are going to do it." Would Charlie be getting up an hour earlier, too, in France?

"Doesn't seem right that they start such a thing on Easter Sunday," grumbled a plump woman I'd not yet met.

"What do you expect of President Wilson? That human icicle," complained Mrs. Schillinger. "And him the son of a Presbyterian minister, too."

Grace frowned at her work. "I think I dropped a stitch."

"It's our patriotic duty to support this and any other law that helps the war effort," Mrs. Martin pronounced.

"Did I tell you my brother joined up last week?" Grace smiled proudly. "He's on his way to Camp Lewis."

Mrs. Martin's mouth twitched. It appeared that Grace had hit a sore spot.

"One need not be in uniform to serve our country," bristled Mrs. Martin. Her comment made me wonder why it was that Traft had not yet gone. To be fair, I knew many men who had registered, as required, but their numbers had not yet been called. Of course, Charlie hadn't waited to be drafted. He had to up and enlist.

Mrs. Martin continued, her voice edged with anger. "My son serves on the Council of Defense, for example. And Mr. Nefzger on the draft board, and—" Each word she spoke got higher and more shrill. Grace had clearly struck a nerve.

"Leona," soothed Mrs. Schillinger, "I hear you've some news for us."

Mrs. Martin rustled importantly in her yellow silk, then turned toward Mrs. Schillinger. "I suppose it's fine that you ladies are the first to know." She sat back as if waiting for us to beg her to tell us what she knew. No one begged. She went on. "Reverend Tweed and I are in agreement that it is time for a choir for the Vida church. He has asked me to direct."

Grace looked my way and rolled her eyes.

"A choir's a wonderful idea!" I said, trying not to laugh at Grace's outrageous expression. This little congregation was fairly ragtag in the singing-in-unison department. A choir would brighten up services considerably. And it was the perfect excuse to invite Perilee again. "And I've got just the person to join."

"Do you sing, Miss Brooks?" Mrs. Martin peered at me over her spectacles.

"Heavens, no. Not me!" I laughed. "The person I'm thinking of is a far better singer than I."

"Hattie." Grace patted my arm. "My cow sings better than you do."

I joined the laughter. "At Aunt Ivy's church, I was asked to leave the children's choir because of my caterwauling."

"So if we are not to be graced with your presence," said Mrs. Martin, "whom are you suggesting?"

"Someone with the voice of an angel." I set down my needles. "Perilee Mueller."

The room grew quiet. Grace glanced at me, but I couldn't read the meaning in her look.

109

"You should hear her sing," I continued, trying to fill up the silence. "And she knows nearly every hymn."

Mrs. Martin dabbed her thin lips with a handkerchief. "I do not like to speak ill of others," she began. It was a wonder she wasn't struck down as she spoke. "But Perilee, uh, Mueller, does not attend services."

"Not yet," I said.

"I don't think that'd be a good idea," said Mrs. Martin.

"Why not?" My blood began to simmer like sage hen stew.

"Oh, you've got a tangle there, Hattie," said Grace. "Let me help." She reached for my knitting.

Mrs. Martin cleared her throat. "I would say she has more than a tangle in her yarn," she said, her voice one shade oilier than normal. "In a calmer moment, Miss Brooks, I am sure you would agree that Perilee Mueller would not be an appropriate addition to our choir." She stuck her needles in the ball of green wool in her lap. "Of course, you are young." She fixed a cold eye on me. "How old are you?"

Surprised by the question, I blurted out the answer. "Sixteen. Seventeen in October."

"And you are proving up on a claim. On your own." Mrs. Martin put her knitting in her carry bag, stood, and gathered her coat. "Quite interesting." Her tone twisted the bland words like a knife in my heart. "The County Council of Defense will find it interesting as well."

My stomach knotted. "What do you mean?" I moved toward Mrs. Martin.

Grace put her hand on my arm and whispered one word to me: "Don't."

I swallowed the bitterness back down and pushed myself out of the chair. "Excuse me. I must get home to do my evening chores."

It was a three-mile ride home from Vida, and yet I did not recall one step of it. I sat on Plug as if I were a sack of flour. I had read an article in the *Herald* about soldiers suffering from something called shell-shock. That was exactly how I felt: shell-shocked.

I settled Plug in the barn, rubbing him down. I held up a handful of oats for him. His velvety lips brushed my palm in a comforting manner. Maybe Mrs. Martin didn't know what she was talking about. Why would the Council of Defense bother me about my claim? What did my age have to do with anything? Uncle Chester had left the place to me. To *me.*

With a lighter heart, I patted Plug and even had a kind word for Violet.

The lightness quickly fell like my last batch of bread dough when I reached my house. The door was ajar. I edged toward it and tapped it open.

"Leafie?" Maybe she'd dropped in again. It was her habit to stop on her way to and fro. "Are you there?"

No answer.

"Mr. Whiskers?" I stepped through.

Again, silence.

I moved inside. There was no one there. But someone had been there. . . . And had left something on the kitchen table. I picked it up.

It was a broadside of sorts. *Join the Montana Loyalty League,* it read. *It hunts home huns, checks class conflicts,*

*promotes pure patriotism. Membership free to all Loyal Montana
men, women, and children.*

I whipped around my house, checking on my meager
possessions. It did not appear that anything had been
disturbed—aside from my peace of mind.

CHAPTER 10

April 2, 1918
Three miles north and west of Vida, Montana

Dear Charlie,

I hope to send you a packet soon—don't worry! It's not another pair of socks. I'm glad the pair I made brought you and your chums such amusement. What I lack in knitting prowess I am making up for with a quilting needle. Perilee is pleased by my progress. To be honest, so am I. I'm sure you have guessed that I am making you a quilt. I call it Charlie's Propeller. It's my version of a windmill pattern. It's in honor of your promotion to mechanic. It's not waterproof, but it should help keep you warm.

Speaking of warm, my chess-playing skills are heating

up. Rooster Jim was by last week for another chess game and I held my own, though he beat me. He heard some troublesome news from his cousin over to Lewiston. A mob marched on the high school there, pulled out all the German textbooks, and had a bonfire. It was a miracle the school didn't burn. One of the teachers was so upset, she quit and left town.

I try to keep focused on my goal, which is to prove up. Karl showed me how to test the earth to see if it is ready to plant. His method is much preferred to Rooster Jim's, which is to taste it. Karl grabs a handful and squeezes it in his hand. Mine is still too clumpy; the seeds would rot. Bub Nefzger says not to worry, that I may plant as late as the middle of next month, but I hope I don't have to wait that long.

Do you laugh at my little farm reports? It seems humorous to me sometimes that I fret over soil and weather and such. My worries are not all selfish. Being a farmer is now very patriotic. We are encouraged to grow as much as we can. Think! My wheat may be some soldier's supper.

I hope not yours, however. I hope you are home well before my crop is harvested come August.

Your friend,
Hattie Inez Brooks

I took a hard look at my pocketbook. Any moths in there would soon starve. I thought of Moses leading the Israelites through the desert and God answering their hunger by raining down manna from heaven. I studied the never-ending Montana sky. No sign of manna or anything else falling from it anytime soon. With no small amount of concern, I spelled out my situation in daily prayer. "Lord, I need a bit of income to see me through to harvest," I explained. "I'm not particular but would appreciate Your help." I was eager to once again experience the Lord's mysterious ways.

With no ideas—and no lightning-bolt suggestions from the heavens—I finished my barn chores. Spring was firmly nudging winter on its way. The prairie was speckled with purple prairie crocus, yellow bells, and furry kittentails I couldn't resist petting as I passed. I thought about gathering up a bouquet and taking them to Perilee. As tempting as that thought was, there were fence posts calling my name. I gathered up the fencing supplies and went out to work.

A familiar horse meandered its way toward me with a familiar rider. Traft Martin had taken it upon himself to pick up my mail from Bub Nefzger's in Vida and bring it out when he was headed my way. It saved me the walk to town, but I wished he wouldn't do it.

"You're making great progress." He slipped off Trouble, landing lightly on well-worn boots.

"Will it ever end?" I pounded in another staple.

Traft took off his hat and hung it on the pommel. A cowlick at the back of his head stood up like a question mark. I could smell the warm pine scent of hair tonic. "Want me to pound for a while?"

My arms begged me to say yes. But my stubborn heart answered, "No. No, thanks."

"I brought your mail." Traft patted his coat pocket. "And some newspapers. I know how much you love to read them."

"Thank you." I wriggled my hand out of my work glove.

He hesitated, as if he was going to say something else. Then he handed me the packet. "Another letter from France," he said.

"My school chum, Charlie," I answered the question in his voice, then tucked the letters in my lunch basket.

"A good friend?" His words made my stomach turn a somersault for some reason.

"We've known each other a long time. He gave me my cat."

Traft nodded briskly, as if shaking that bit of information into his mind's proper file.

"I'd better get back at it," I said.

He moved toward his horse. "Good afternoon, Hattie."

"Afternoon." I started hammering before he'd even stepped into the stirrup.

"Oh, there was something else." He stopped. "A dance. At the Vida Community Hall. Wondered if you'd be going?"

"I don't dance." I could imagine Aunt Ivy's shrieks of disapproval: *Next thing, you'll be drinking and carrying on!*

"What if I said it was your patriotic duty?" he asked. "It's to raise money for the Liberty Bond drive."

I stiffened at the word *patriotic,* still on edge from that message left on my table. "Like joining the Loyalty League?"

He started. "What?"

I told him about finding the note. "I'm not sure what it means."

116

He toyed with Trouble's reins. He acted like he had something to say, so I waited. "Have you . . ." He stroked his horse's neck. "Have you said anything about the war? Given anyone the impression that you might be against it?"

"I've never had call to discuss it much with anyone," I said. Except Rooster Jim, but that was none of Traft's affair.

"Well, then, maybe . . ." he paused again. "You know, Hattie, folks are looking at one another hard these days."

I waggled the hammer in my hand. "If anyone's looking at me, all they see is unpatriotic activity like picking rocks and setting fence posts." I forced a laugh.

"Don't take such things lightly." His tone had cooled more quickly than a doused fire.

"Name one thing I've done that might cause someone to suspect me of being unpatriotic." The current running under this conversation had changed. I felt as if I might be caught in a whirlpool at any moment. No matter how charming he was, Traft was still head of the County Council of Defense. Still his mother's son.

"I know this is not going to sit well with you, but I'm going to say it flat out. There's talk about Karl Mueller."

"What?" I nearly dropped my hammer. "What kind of talk?"

"You heard about the Verne Hamilton case over in Roundup? Been charged with making seditious comments, saying he wouldn't go to war, that they'd have to take him feet first if he was conscripted?"

I nodded. I'd read about it in the paper.

"Over to Bub's one day, Karl said the man had the right to say such things. Said it was free speech and all that."

"And isn't it?"

"It's war, Hattie." He looked me in the eye. "And Karl's an alien enemy."

"He's no enemy," I said. "He's the finest man you'd ever want to meet."

Traft smiled at me, but it was an Aunt Ivy smile, the kind she wore when she would tell me the switching I was about to receive was for my own good. "Last thing I'd want to do is upset you. I told you because I thought you'd want to know." He shrugged. "Maybe some kids were playing a prank on you. With that notice, I mean."

If he was trying to shift the topic, it didn't work. "Traft, he's my friend."

"I know." He nodded. "And he's lucky for that."

He swung his hat off the saddle and snugged it on his head. "About the dance—I didn't mean to set you off. It *is* for a good cause. And I hope, if you come, you save one dance for me." Now he flashed a smile so warm and genuine it made me think perhaps I'd taken offense where none was meant.

I smiled back. "Your toes will be sorry. I'm not much of a dancer."

"I'm a good teacher," he said.

"I best get back to work." I turned toward the fence to hide my red cheeks.

"See you at the dance, Hattie." In one movement he was up on Trouble. They wheeled around and pounded away.

My heart pounded to the rhythm of Trouble's hooves. I felt behind me, found the stone boat, and sat against it. Being with that man was like walking the circus tightrope. I breathed deeply a few times to slow my heart. Of course he was right about the pamphlet. No doubt a prank. And, really, he was doing me a favor, telling me about Karl. I could speak to him, let him know to be more careful about what he said in town. Maybe Traft and I were more alike than I realized. Him, stubborn about things that mattered to him, like his ranch and this country. Me, I had my own stubborn streak, still going strong no matter how many times Aunt Ivy had tried to switch it out of me.

I pictured myself at the dance, trying hard not to step on Traft's feet. One dance and he'd find another partner, you could bet on that. Wouldn't Mildred Powell be fit to be tied to see me dancing with such a charmer? I thought back to the eighth-grade graduation ball. "Oh, Hattie," she'd said to me, "how clever of you to dress so plainly for the event." Her friends had laughed, too. I would've left right then, but good old Charlie had stepped up and asked me to waltz. I'm sure his feet regretted the invitation, but Charlie never said a word about my clumsiness. "You look pretty in blue," he'd said.

I sighed to remember his kindness. Then I looked down the row of fence posts waiting for wire. And sighed once more.

I hefted the hammer and began again, keeping at it until I couldn't lift the hammer one more time. Then I tucked into the lunch I'd packed, sipping cool well water from a glass jar. With a little imagination, I could envision I was sipping a strawberry soda from Chapman's Drug back in Arlington. Or an icy bottle of sarsaparilla from Uncle Holt's store. Imagining

119

even turned the cold pancakes, mushy apple, and handful of dried fruit into a tasty meal. Brushing off my hands, I reached for my mail. The papers would be dessert after supper and the evening chores.

Charlie's letter was terse. He mentioned finally receiving a letter from me, and working twenty-four-hour shifts at the airfield. He concluded:

> *Men are falling here, but more from various ailments than the war. Our unit's managed to avoid it thus far, but the Spanish influenza is taking its toll. It's as bad an enemy as the Huns. Yesterday we passed a line of men blinded by mustard gas—they stumbled along like a string of elephants, one man's hand on the next man's shoulder.*

The next section of Charlie's letter was sliced out by the censor's knife. I read on:

> *I met three fellows from Montana—Great Falls, I think. They are mad to get a baseball game up soon. I may join in and show them what Iowa can do!*
>   *Your (lonesome) chum, Charlie*

I closed the letter with a shiver. The spring sun seemed to have cooled several degrees. Charlie had been so excited when he signed up. He'd been going to save the world! And how excited *I'd* been to get Uncle Chester's letter and leave Aunt Ivy behind. I guessed Charlie and I were in the same boat. We'd both signed on for something we'd envisioned as heroic and glamorous. The heroism and glamour might be there somewhere, but you had to dig and scrape and scrabble through the dirt, pain, and misery to find it. Assuming you *could* find it.

I shook such thoughts out of my head and reached for the letter from Uncle Holt. It was a thick one. It wasn't like him to send such a long letter. Perhaps he'd tucked in another magazine article, as he had a few letters back.

I tore open the envelope and a slip of paper fluttered to the ground. *Pay to the order of Miss Hattie Inez Brooks: $15.* A check? I looked again. It was from the *Arlington News*. I shuffled through Uncle Holt's packet for an explanation.

> *Dear Hattie,*
>
> *Your letters have provided me such entertainment and enlightenment that I have shared them with Mr. George Miltenberger, editor of the* Arlington News. *He concurred that such lively observations about homestead life would be of general interest to his readership. As you will see from his letter (enclosed), he hopes to publish more of your stories. I hope you can accommodate him.*
>
> > *With affection,*
> > *Uncle Holt*

I snatched up the letter from Mr. Miltenberger. He offered $15 an installment, "preferably monthly," until my claim was proved up and I was no longer a homesteader.

"Hallelujah, Plug!" I startled the old horse with my outburst. Manna did fall from the Montana sky—at least from writing about living beneath it. "Cold hard cash!" I ticked off the months on my fingers. "April, May, June, July, August, September, October, November—Plug, that's eight months. Eight times fifteen is . . ." I did a quick calculation. "One hundred and twenty dollars!" I reached my arms to that vast blue sky. "Thank you, Lord, for your mysterious ways!"

Carefully I tucked the letters and the check back in the lunch basket. With each nail I pounded the rest of the afternoon, I hammered out my next installment for Mr. Miltenberger. Fifteen dollars a month! Until I proved up! I'd set aside the $37.75 I needed for final fees. Of course, there'd be some other costs, but my savings should cover them. Maybe now I could buy some new boots, ones that really fit my feet, not Uncle Holt's old ones. And I could get my own subscription to the *Wolf Point Herald.* That and boots would take only $7 out of my stash. I couldn't contain my excitement. "Plug, I think we're going to make it." The hammer felt like a feather as I finished the next section of fence.

When I'd pounded in the last nail and gathered up my tools, I fairly floated across the blooming prairie. "What do you think all the other millionaires are doing today, Plug?" I asked. An image flashed behind my eyes of Perilee pointing out the $3 oak rockers in the Monkey Ward catalog. "Wouldn't that be fine for rocking the baby?" she had asked. They were saving for a new tractor, so I knew she wouldn't even think of spending that money on herself.

Violet was crankier than ever as I milked her that night. Almost as if she knew what selfish hands were on her teats.

"All right," I said, slapping her ornery hide. Devil cow that she was, I felt she was giving me a message from heaven this time. "I'll make do with these old boots. Then I can get Perilee that rocker."

Violet looked at me with her big brown eyes . . . and stepped hard on my right foot. So much for signs from God!

CHAPTER 11

April 5, 1918
Three miles north and west of Vida, Montana

Dear Uncle Holt,

How can I ever thank you? My monthly checks will grow like the wheat I hope to plant soon. Just think—Miss Simpson may read my first article to my old classmates. I'm sure she'll find a way to point out my dangling participles and awkward syntax. I am so pleased, I don't even mind being a bad example!

Karl shakes his head at me when I try to tell him about the scientific studies Mr. Campbell set forth in his Soil Culture Manual. *If I take Mr. Campbell's advice, I should order seven bushels of seed, all told, for my forty acres. Karl says I should order twenty! That is a difference*

of thirteen bushels. I would be floundering without Karl's
guidance, but Mr. Campbell is a scientist. And with
wheat seed going for $2.50 a bushel, his plan means
nearly $33 more in Hattie's coffers. I would appreciate
any advice you might have for me.

There are big doings at the schoolhouse this weekend:
a dance to raise money for the Liberty Bonds. This will be
my first social outing, aside from church (yes, Aunt Ivy, I
have been attending). Perilee is baking one of her cakes,
but I thought it safer if I brought sandwiches. My bread
is not nearly as heavy and dry as it was at first.

Your niece,
Hattie Inez Brooks

"What do you think, Mr. Whiskers?" I laid out my clothing choices on the table the night before the dance. "The yellow gingham dress or the navy wool skirt and bodice?"

Mr. Whiskers sniffed at both outfits. He sneezed at the
navy wool.

"My thoughts exactly." I picked up the dress. "Time for a
little color around here!" It was foolishness, certainly, but I
even took some care with that bird's nest on top of my head.
First I washed it and rinsed it with sugar water. Then I set it
in rags all over my head. I left the rags in place till it was
nearly time to go on Saturday. With some fussing and coaxing, my hair looked presentable. I held it back at each side
with Mama's tortoiseshell combs. Mr. Whiskers meowed his
approval.

I'd finished making a stack of sandwiches when I heard

125

Rooster Jim's team trot into the yard. I set the sandwiches on my least chipped enamelware plate, covered them with a clean towel, and grabbed my overcoat and shawl.

"You look awful nice, Hattie." Jim even clambered out of the wagon to help me up.

"You aren't so hard to look at yourself," I teased. Since becoming my chess partner, Rooster Jim had improved in the olfactory department. Or maybe I was getting used to his smell.

"Hope you wore comfy shoes." Rooster Jim hopped back onto the seat and clucked to the horses. "You're going to be dancing all night."

I blushed but managed to get the topic off me and onto news of the war. The Germans had launched new attacks in France, between the Somme and Arve rivers and were now claiming to have taken ninety thousand prisoners. I couldn't help but think of Charlie.

"You ever figure out where your chum is?" Jim asked.

"No. Once he wrote down the name of some town, but the censor cut it out." I sat quietly for a moment, thinking. "I like to think they keep the airfields back of the worst of the fighting, to keep the planes safe," I said.

"That's what you'd hope," said Jim.

"Hope *and* pray," I said, pushing away a sense of dread. Last week we'd had our first local casualty, Mr. Kirkpatrick from Terrace. Though I hadn't known him, his death brought the war all that much closer to home. We were both quiet, Jim and I, the rest of the ride.

"Come on in!" Leafie waved to us from the doorway. "It's nice and warm in here."

Soon we were inside, coats off, helping to set up tables of

126

sandwiches, cake, beans, and cottage cheese. I helped make coffee. Perilee brought over a cake.

"This smells like heaven!" exclaimed Leafie. "How on earth did you bake a cake like this with all the shortages?"

"I've been hankering sweets something awful. My gran used to whip up cakes out of nothing. I figured I could do the same." Perilee smiled shyly. "You cook up the raisins first. That's what makes it sweet and moist."

Mattie came over and threw her arms around my legs. "We have kittens!" She let me go to smooth out what was left of Mulie's hair. "We each get to name one—me, and Chase, and Mulie." She leaned closer. "Mulie had a hard time choosing, so I helped her."

Before I could ask about the kittens' names, Mattie was off, playing tag with a little girl I didn't know.

It wasn't long before the room was filled. I waved at Grace Robbins, stepping inside with her husband, Wayne, and her two children. Her daughter, Olive, skipped over to Mattie and her other friend. The Schillinger brothers warmed up their violins as older children chased each other around the school room. I saw Chase in the far corner, snugged behind a desk, reading. Folks were laughing and chattering. I didn't see Traft.

"You think the Martins will come?" I asked Leafie.

She made a face. "And miss the chance to make a show of buying Liberty Bonds? Not likely."

"It's for a good cause," I said.

Leafie crooked an eyebrow at me. "Hattie, don't you know that man is trouble?"

"Thought that was his horse," I said, trying to make light.

"You." She laughed, then patted my hand. "I'll tell you what my mama told me: handsome is as—"

"Handsome does," I finished. "Your mama and my aunt."

"Speak of the devil." Leafie tilted her head toward the door. In walked Traft Martin with a handful of cowboys.

A few men nodded at these late arrivals, but the music started up, turning the crowd's focus to the dance floor.

"Don't them Schillingers play some toe-tappers?" Leafie asked me, with an elbow to my ribs. We watched others dance for a while, clapping and shouting and having a grand time.

After a particularly lively two-step, I felt a pat on my shoulder. I turned and found myself facing Traft Martin.

"Nice to see you again, Miz Brooks," he said. His slicked-up hair smelled of Packer's Scalptone. It was the same stuff Charlie used to wear; he snitched it from his father.

"Evening." I smoothed a stray lock of my sugar-stiffened hair.

"Would you like to dance?" He held out his arm.

I glanced over at Leafie. She frowned and turned away. "I'm not sure I've got the hang of it yet," I told him.

Traft smiled. It was the same kind of smile he'd worn the day he helped me pick rocks. "And you won't, just standing there."

Though I could feel Leafie's eyes boring a hole in my back, I took his arm and we moved toward the dance floor.

The Schillingers launched into a lively tune.

"Don't say I didn't warn you!" I stepped into line with the other women.

It wasn't so hard after all. Pa Schillinger hollered out the steps.

"Ladies bow low and the gents bow under, couples up tight and swing like thunder!" His walrus mustache wiggled as he sang. "Leave that lady and home you go. Opposite the gent with a do-si-do. Jump right up and never come down. Now swing that calico round and round."

The floor was so crowded, there wasn't room to make a mistake. If you did, you laughed, grabbed your partner, and picked it up again.

The next dance was a waltz. "One more?" Traft asked. I nodded.

He slipped his right hand around my waist and took my right hand in his left. When our hands connected, I swear to Christmas I felt a current of electricity jolt through me. "Oh!" I jerked my hand away.

"Is my hand too rough?" He wiped it on his jeans. "Or too sweaty?"

"No. No." I couldn't in a million years tell him. "I—my hands are still chapped from putting up fence." I hoped I told the white lie smoothly enough for him to believe it.

"I know how that is," he said. "I'll be real careful." Then he took my hand again, as gently as if he was holding his own mother's very best china teacup.

We twirled this way and that around the room. I'd never danced with anyone like this before. True, Charlie had danced with me at the eighth-grade ball, but he was a worse dancer than me. We'd tromped all over each other's feet. Traft made me feel like a fairy-tale princess, dancing in a gingerbread castle. Too soon, the song was over.

"Time for supper!" Leafie called, banging on a pot. Traft

thanked me, then stepped away, and I was caught up with the crowd of folks lined up for sandwiches.

Grace slipped in line behind me. She poked me in the back. "Hattie's got a beau!" she teased. I could feel my cheeks were hot, and not because of the stuffy room.

"Oh, Lordy!" Leafie threw her hands up.

"No such thing," I mumbled.

"Friends and neighbors," Pa Schillinger called out, "get you something to eat and then let's talk about why we're gathered together tonight."

Folks filled their plates and coffee cups. Mr. Saboe began his pitch to sell Liberty Bonds. He wasn't as smooth as the Four Minute Man I'd heard back home at the Excelsior Theater, but his heart was sure in it.

"Now, you all know my own sons are over there right now," he began.

"Mine too, don't you forget," called out a woman—was that Mrs. Ervick?

Mr. Saboe nodded. "I've heard that there are more Montana boys fighting than from any other state in the Union."

That brought a loud cheer from the crowd.

Mr. Saboe waved his hands to get everyone's attention. "No one can accuse this state of not supporting the war effort." Another cheer. "There's one more way we can all help, and that's to buy Liberty Bonds. Montana's quota of the Third Liberty Loan is three million dollars."

Someone let out a shrill whistle.

"Sounds impossible, I know," said Mr. Saboe. "But it figures out to about thirty dollars for every man, woman, and child in this great state. That's a small price for Liberty. I know you'll all do what you can. I'll be in the back, so come on over and humble the Huns. Every dollar adds up to victory."

"You go buy those bonds," hollered Leafie, "then git on over here and have some of this cake."

"Build up your strength for the next bit of dancing," added Pa Schillinger.

I carried my limp and worn five-dollar bill to the back table. Mr. Saboe wrote my name down in his book. "That's your down payment. Four more payments of just ten dollars each and you'll have yourself a bonafidey United States guaranteed Liberty Bond," he said. "Next payment is October twenty-first." He handed me a pen. "Sign here."

I thought of Charlie as I wrote my signature. My little bit wasn't much, but if everybody all over the country helped a little bit, it would add up to something. Add up to victory, like Mr. Saboe said. I was so thankful for my newspaper money. I wouldn't have been able to buy even a penny's worth of war stamps otherwise, let alone a Liberty Bond.

"Here you go, Hattie." Mr. Saboe handed me a green button. "Wear this to show you're Uncle Sam's partner."

As I pinned it on, someone stepped up behind me. Traft.

"Let me take a look at those names there, Saboe," he said.

Mr. Saboe closed his receipt book. "This is none of your business."

"Well, I see that different," Traft replied. He surveyed the room like he was surveying the range. "As a member of the Dawson County Council of Defense, I'm sworn to identify slackers and encourage them to do their patriotic duty." His loud words stopped the children's game of tag. Perilee scurried across the room and grabbed Mattie; I couldn't see where Chase was.

"This county measured up in the first two Liberty Loan drives," answered Mr. Saboe. "No reason to doubt it won't happen again."

Traft stared down the table at Karl. "Seems like there's some that might like to see it not happen."

I held my breath. Karl's loaf-sized hands curled into two rock-hard fists. *No,* I willed him with my eyes. I knew all too well how easy it was to feed a bully's fire. I learned that the hard way, when I first moved in with Aunt Ivy. Frannie Thompson had been wicked cruel about my being an orphan, and one day I couldn't let it go. If Charlie hadn't stepped in, we'd probably still have been at it hammer and tongs today.

Karl took a step toward Traft. That step was matched by one of Traft's own.

Leafie broke the spell. "Let's have some music, Pa." She slapped her hands together so loud it sounded like a gunshot. She crossed the room and held her hand out to Mr. Saboe. "Ladies' choice, Mr. Saboe, and I choose you." Pa grabbed his violin and began to play.

"But is everyone pulling their fair share? That's the question I'm asking." Traft's cowboys came to stand behind him, apparently oblivious to the music that signaled a lively dance called the racket. I caught a glisten of perspiration on Mr. Saboe's upper lip. Leafie wedged herself between Traft and the table. My own palms were slick and sticky, my feet stuck to

132

the floor. I glanced over at Perilee, Mattie clutching at her skirt, and back at Karl, whose hands had pounded hundreds of staples in my fence. My fence. Because he was my neighbor. My friend. I took a deep breath, wiped my hands on my skirt, and stepped forward.

"M-Mr. M-Martin." I took a breath and started over. "Mr. Martin." I reached out my hand. "This is ladies' choice. Would you please dance with me?"

Traft Martin turned to me with a bemused expression. The look he gave me seemed to see right through me, right to my back collar button. "A most gracious invitation, Miss Brooks." He took my hand and led me to the dance floor, where we joined the other whirling couples. I swung by Wayne and Grace Robbins, and Leafie with Mr. Saboe. Leafie wouldn't meet my eyes.

"Thank you for the dance, Hattie," Traft said as the music whirled to a stop. He walked me off the floor. "Take my advice on something."

"What's that, Mr. Martin?" I brushed my now-sticky hair back off my face.

He tipped his hat. "Don't ever play poker." He nodded to his men, and they all left.

Pa didn't miss a beat. He began picking out the next tune.

I realized I'd been holding my breath. I walked across the room on rubbery legs and found Perilee.

"Go, swirl a time or two with Karl." I took Fern from her. "It'll be good for you."

"He does love to dance," she said.

"Then go." I found a chair and settled in. Fern was a

sweet, round-faced baby, content with even the most inexpert of baby-handlers. And I certainly fell in that category.

"She likes to be held up so she can see." Mattie appeared at my side. "Like this." She turned Fern around in my arms so that her back was against my chest and her face was toward the dance floor. I was amazed to discover what a great comfort it was to hold that warm baby body next to mine. She calmed nearly all my jangled nerves. Mattie leaned against my side. I couldn't help but smile—it was as if these two babies were propping *me* up.

"Mulie made Mama cry." Mattie tugged at the bow in her dolly's hair.

"She did?" I said. "For heaven's sake."

Mattie nodded sadly. "Mulie was singing me a song. One Karl's mama used to sing to him."

"A song made her cry?" Little Fern had grabbed my pointer finger and was working on it with her new bottom tooth. I glanced across the room. Two couples stepped off the floor just as it was time for them to square up with Karl and Perilee. Fueled by Traft's fuss, no doubt. I sat forward, holding my breath. In an instant, Grace and Wayne Robbins stepped across the empty space and snatched Karl and Perilee up in a new square. "God bless you," I murmured.

"But Chase said it was the fence falling down," Mattie continued. "He said that's what made her cry."

"Fence?" I turned to her.

She nodded. "Lots of it fell down. And there wasn't even a storm or stampede or anything." Mattie wiped Fern's baby drool off my hand with the corner of her dress. Then she turned her face up to me. "Hattie, is Karl a Hun?"

Hearing Mattie give voice to that word was worse than hearing the most vulgar profanity. I wrapped my free arm around her shoulders. "Don't you pay any mind to such talk."

Mattie fiddled with Mulie's ragged dress. "Karl's making a cradle for Mulie. Mama thinks it's for the new baby, but Karl and me know it's really for Mulie." She wiggled out from under my arm. "Miss Leafie baked snickerdoodles. You want me to bring you one?"

"A snickerdoodle sounds delicious." Fern leaned heavily against my arms. I gently eased her against my shoulder and patted her back. Soon she was sound asleep. I turned my face toward her downy head and breathed in the baby scent of her. Perilee and Karl spun by—he tall and solid, she round of belly and homely of face—and my heart filled up so full, it threatened to spill out my eyes. I took stock of my feelings then and there. Traft might cause my innards to flip-flop, but that wasn't what I was looking for. I was looking for something solid, as solid as 320 Montana acres. As solid as good folks like Karl and Perilee.

At midnight, the sandwiches and coffee were passed around again and folks danced some more. I danced several with Rooster Jim and Mr. Saboe and even once with Chase.

"Last dance," called Pa Schillinger. He launched into "Home Sweet Home Waltz."

Perilee yawned as we finished washing up the coffee cups and sandwich plates. We set them out on the tables so the women could pick out the ones they'd brought.

The sun was rising when we set off for home. Karl, Perilee, and I each carried a sleeping bundle of child and settled them in the Muellers' wagon. "Night, hon," called Perilee. She leaned her head against Karl's shoulder and looked to be asleep before they were even out of the schoolyard.

Rooster Jim and I rode along quietly as the night sky softened from navy blue to faded denim to pink.

"Sleep fast," Jim called as I slid down from the wagon bench in front of my cabin.

"I hope to." I covered a yawn. "Violet will want milking in another hour or so! Thanks for the ride." I gave a tired wave as he and his team jingled off.

I bumped open the front door with my right hip and swung the basket I was carrying through the door. Setting it down with a thump on the table, I yawned again. All that dancing had left my stomach hungry. I lifted the towel to grab one of the leftover sandwiches in the basket. My hands brushed against something. Mulie! Mattie would fuss like sixty when she figured out Mulie was missing. I took a bite of sandwich, then turned myself around. Who needed sleep anyway? Plug could get me over to Mueller's and back before milking time. I could catch a nap later.

I regretted my generosity before I'd even gone twenty paces. There is nothing like a predawn prairie to get the juices flowing. *Scritch, scritch, scritch.* Plug's hooves crunched against the stubby prairie grass, speckled with little cactus. *Crunch, crunch, crunch.* But what was that? No doubt some critter snacking on a late supper. My skin crawled, thinking of that hungry wolf from two months' back. He'd have long ago digested Violet's tail and be looking for something more substantial. Something a little over five feet tall and 130 pounds. I shivered, doubly glad to be up on Plug's back.

Folks don't appreciate how open a prairie is, how there is absolutely no place to hide. "Hey there, Plug." I kicked my heels into his sides to pick up the pace over the hardened sod. Lord knows how I could have thought that old horse would outrun anything, but there's not a lot of clear thinking when you're alone on the prairie at sunrise.

If I hadn't given myself the willies over the prairie's night-time noises, I might have noticed it sooner. At the bottom of a cutbank, about a mile along, I smelled it.

Smoke.

I urged Plug up the coulee. As we bumped over the top, the smell hit me hard, like a wildly thrown pitch. Smoke.

And it was coming from the direction of Perilee's.

CHAPTER 12

At the end of a sad day in April
Three miles north and west of Vida, Montana

Dear Charlie,

It's funny how you and I have been having similar experiences, despite the number of miles between us. I imagine that everyone benefited from your willingness to share the bars of soap your mother sent. I, too, have had a chance to share my bounty with my neighbors. And in doing so, I have lifted one chore from my ever-lengthening daily list.

Plug's hooves beat out a rhythm on the sod: *Let them be safe. Let them be safe. Let them be safe.* I urged Plug on even faster. "Dear God, please don't let it be the house."

Bouncing along on Plug's back, I scoured the horizon until my head ached. It's hard to imagine how far you can see on the prairie. It's as if a giant scroll of sod has been rolled out before you. The closer you get to the end, the more sod gets rolled out. Would we never get there?

One more dip down a coulee and back up again and I could see the house. The house. It was not on fire! The smoke was beyond it. I pushed Plug on.

We rode on for several more minutes, pounding against the prairie, until we pounded right into Perilee's yard.

Chase burst from the house with an empty bucket on each arm. Perilee stood at the pump, driving the handle for all she was worth. She took one look at me. "I'll pump—you carry."

I nodded. By the time I'd tethered Plug, Perilee had both of Chase's buckets full. He and I each took one and ran for the barn.

We handed the buckets to Karl, and he threw the water at the fire. Chase and I ran back to the pump. Back and forth, back and forth we went: Perilee hauling water up from the well, and the rest of us forming a bucket brigade.

We repeated this dozens of times. But the fire burned brighter. I staggered for another bucket of water. Karl grabbed my arm. *"Halt."* He took the bucket from Chase's hand and set it on the ground.

"Nothing more to do." He turned and signaled to Perilee to stop pumping.

"The barn!" Chase dropped to his knees. "The barn."

Perilee ran to Karl, her progress hampered by exhaustion and her round middle. He wrapped his arm around her shoulder and pulled her close. Tears streamed down Chase's face, and I dropped to my own knees to stroke his hair.

"There, there," I murmured. Real words could not comfort.

I was bewitched by the blaze. Blue flames gnawed the timbers like termites. The burning boards groaned and hissed. The barn, solidly built with Karl's own hands, put up a brave fight. But the fire was too hungry. With a final growl, it wolfishly snapped the barn boards like twigs. The last of the walls crumpled to the ground.

It was horrible and horrifying, yet I could not tear myself away.

Chase's sobbing quieted. "Me and Karl got the horses out," he said. "They're grazing the coulee over behind the house." He rubbed at his eyes. "But we couldn't get . . ." He choked.

I glanced over at the coulee and saw the horses. Only the horses. "Marte," I said. "And Fawn?"

Karl shook his head.

The cows were a huge loss. No milk. No butter. And sweet little Fawn. I glanced at Chase. His sooty cheeks bore muddy tear tracks.

"What happened?" I asked.

Karl stood with his face to the charred building, soot striping it like war paint.

"It was smoking when we got home," said Perilee, slowly stroking her burgeoning middle. "After Karl and Chase got the horses out, the hay caught, and before we could do anything—" She lifted her hands helplessly.

"I wonder how it started," I asked.

"*Schweine*," said Karl.

"I'm sorry, I don't understand." I looked over at Perilee.

"Pigs," she answered. She brushed at her eyes. "The two-legged kind."

She took Karl's hand and they walked away from us. Away from the remains of the barn. They walked to where the horses grazed and, wrapped in one another's arms, stood there.

I rested my hand on Chase's shoulder. "Let's get some breakfast for you and those sisters of yours."

He ran his sleeve under his nose. "I'm not hungry."

I patted his back. I could feel his backbone and his ribs, all tied together by stringy muscles. "Could you even eat one doughnut?"

"Maybe." Chase wiggled away from me. He trudged toward the house with the air of old man rather than eight-year-old about him. Watching him caused a dull ache under my breastbone.

I fed the children. Karl and Perilee didn't come in for a very long time. When they did, I gave Perilee a hug and patted Karl's hand.

"Karl will go for Myron Gorley. He'll help us clean up and rebuild." Perilee wiped her own sooty face with her grimy apron. "So will the folks from the Lutheran church."

"You'll have a new barn in no time," I said, wiping an already dry plate with a towel. "Do you want me to stay today?"

Perilee glanced at Karl. He sat at the kitchen table, oblivious to the mug of coffee at his elbow. "No. Thank you, but no."

I loosened the reins and let Plug amble his way home. I could barely see through the tears that kept filling up my eyes. Just when I thought I'd gathered myself together, Chase's face would flash in front of me and the faucet would turn on all over again.

That's why I couldn't trust what I saw as we rode up the cutbank closest to home. A solitary rider, astride an enormous horse, was riding away from my house. I knew of only one horse that big around here.

I clucked my tongue and once again nudged Plug to pick up his pace. By the time I reached my own yard, there was no rider—no sign of any rider—that I could see. I went inside. Nothing looked disturbed.

It'd been a long night and an even longer morning. As much as I wanted to lower my bed and crawl into it, I had a cow to milk. I changed into overalls and headed for the barn. An idea had planted itself during my teary ride home—an idea so ridiculous I couldn't believe I was entertaining it.

I stepped around to the back side of the barn. A charred bundle of hay, still smoldering, leaned at a drunken angle against a pile of rocks, spitting distance from the barn.

"Oh, Lord!" Snatching up the pitchfork, I smacked away at the glowing straw, all the while dragging the smoky bundle farther away from the barn. Then I ran for a bucket of water and doused the whole thing.

It was Traft. He had done this. Had to have. There was no mistaking his horse. Had he come here to leave this calling card—more to threaten than to harm—after setting fire to Karl's barn? Was he crazy? Was I?

The message sent was clear: my barn was no safer than Karl and Perilee's, not after tonight. I headed in to milk Violet, bumping against Uncle Chester's trunk. If he were here, what would he do?

Violet mooed her impatience. "Hush a minute. I'll be right there." I unlatched the straps, then flipped the lid open. He would tell me what to do. He'd cared enough about me to leave me this place; surely he was watching over me now. I closed my eyes and reached in. The first thing I touched would show me the way.

I opened my eyes and saw what my fingers were brushing. Tears pricked the underside of my eyelids. "You are a scoundrel," I said. "But you are right."

The next morning, I wrapped a rope around Violet's grumpy neck. I carried one end of the rope in one hand and the packet from Uncle Chester's trunk in the other. The closer I got, the more I could smell the sodden ashes and burnt dreams. *Crack crack crack!* The sound of hammering meant Karl was already busy with a lean-to for the horses. I smiled. And their new stable mate.

Chase was in the yard. "Ma!" he called when he saw me. "Company."

The door pushed open and there stood Perilee, wearing that winning smile of hers despite red-rimmed and tired eyes. She cocked her head when she saw Violet. "Hon, I've heard of walking your dog. But walking your cow?"

I handed the rope to Chase. "You already know how to handle her." He looked at his mother.

"Hattie, we can't—"

I held up my hand. "I can't keep her when you need the milk more," I said. "Besides, now I'll have to come over more often. To get some of that milk of hers." I shooed Chase. "Go get her settled." To Perilee I said, "Is there any coffee on?"

Perilee pressed her hand to her mouth. Then she took a deep breath. "And fresh biscuits. You get yourself in here."

After several biscuits, I brought out the slim packet wrapped in muslin and tied with a strip of calico. The calico slipped out of its knot; I pushed back the layers of muslin and uncovered a rainbow of patches—ticking and shirt cloth, gingham and calico, in faded blues and greens and yellows. I fingered the snippets, letting them drift through my hands like snowflakes.

"It's time to start a quilt." I pointed to the bulge under her apron. "For the baby."

She didn't say anything for a moment. "Are you sure about all this?"

Sure? I wasn't sure about anything. "I was thinking of an Ohio Star," I said. "You know, like 'Twinkle, Twinkle Little Star.'"

"Mattie's favorite song." She reached across the table and squeezed my hand. "Thank you."

We spent that afternoon cutting out the triangles, planning each patch. "What do you think of this piece next to that one?" I held up a blue calico and a green paisley.

She pursed her lips. "Too much friction," she said. "How about this?" She slipped another fabric over the green, a soft yellow stripe.

"You have an eye," I said.

144

"My mama always said piecing quilts is like making friends." She kept her eyes on the scissors as she cut up a piece of blue ticking. "Sometimes the more different fabrics—and people—are," she said, "the stronger the pattern."

I looked up at her. She smiled a sad, sweet smile at me. I felt as if she'd looked right into my heart and seen all my warts and flaws, and held her own heart out to me anyway. I swallowed hard at the lump that had gathered in my throat.

"I ever tell you about meeting Karl?" She layered blue ticking triangles in a stack. "It was after Lemuel left. Lord, what a sorry man. I told him to leave when he'd nearly drunk us broke. He grabbed the rest of our money and I tried to stop him." She patted her leg. "He got the money and I got this limp."

I sucked in my breath. "He hit you?"

Perilee didn't answer. She stroked her hand across the oilcloth on the table. "I was pregnant with Fern at the time. I thank God I didn't lose her. Leafie came to stay till I was up and around again."

I covered her hand with mine. "I am so sorry."

"Leafie knew Karl from back in Chicago. He'd recently arrived, and she told him I needed a hand. When he stepped across that doorway, it was as if he was supposed to have been here all along." She rubbed her lower back, all the while holding my gaze. "Really, Hattie. It might be easier if you didn't come here so much. For a while." She toyed with some triangles. "I'll send Chase with your milk."

Images flashed through my mind: the note on my table. Traft's face at the dance. The barn fire. The smoldering hay bundle. I drew in a ragged breath. Easier wasn't an option anymore.

"I think, as big as you are, we'd better get going on this quilt or we'll never finish it before the baby comes."

Perilee looked at me and shook her head. "Hattie, you are—" She paused, then patted her middle. "I am enormous, aren't I?"

We began to talk about babies and crops and tricks for keeping bedbugs out of our beds. We'd talked about such things before, but today it was different. It'd been something big for me to ship myself out here, to work on Uncle Chester's claim. But I was beginning to see there were bigger things in life than proving up on a claim. I was proving up on my life. My choices would no doubt horrify Aunt Ivy, but if they brought me friends like Perilee, it seemed like I was surely headed in the right direction.

CHAPTER 13

THE ARLINGTON NEWS

Honyocker's Homily ~ Sowing Seed

There are as many methods as there are farmers for determining the readiness of the earth for planting. I adopted the method preferred by my closest neighbor, Karl Mueller. The handful of dirt I squeezed did not clump together wetly or crumble drily. It held its shape. That means that planting can commence. Twenty acres of flax and twenty more of wheat. I thought this day would never come.

Once again, I am thankful for Plug. I hope he knows enough about plowing to make up for what I don't. But folks have been sowing seeds for centuries— surely even one such as I can manage.

"Oof." I tossed the harness over Plug's sturdy back and adjusted it and then the neck halter. "Good boy, good boy." I patted his withers. He stood patiently while I connected the chains from the bottom edge of the harness to the beam on the plow. I wrapped one rein around each hand and grabbed the plow handles. "Hi-yup!" Plug strolled out until the reins were taut. Then he stopped and turned his head back to look at me.

"Yes, we are going to plow this field. You and I. If it kills us." I flicked the reins against his back. "And it may."

Plug decided I was serious. He moved ahead. I put my weight onto the handles to keep the plowshare embedded in the sod. It sliced through the prairie grass, upturning a two-foot ribbon of chocolate-colored earth. "We're plowing, Plug!" I flicked the reins again, and we cut another six feet or so of sod ribbon. My gloves rubbed with each bump of the handles.

Another six feet, and blisters sprouted on each hand, even with the gloves. After one complete row, the blisters were bleeding. After the fifth row, my shoulders ached so that I couldn't feel my hands.

Several neighbors rode by and saw my "progress." "The general idea is to plow in a straight line," said Rooster Jim. "Not circles." He laughed till his face was red.

Leafie passed by after I'd fallen hard in the sod. "That's some kind of shiner," she said, and handed me a packet of herbs. "Mix this with some bacon grease. It should help. Can't stay. I want to check on Perilee." My eye did feel better after her treatment.

Later, Karl rode by. We stood side by side, staring at my field. I don't know what Karl was thinking, but I knew what I was thinking. I'd be ninety before I got forty acres plowed.

"Gar nicht gut." He shook his head. "You need a machine," he said, imitating turning a steering wheel. He had managed to get enough gasoline despite the shortages to run his tractor. Even with his rough English, he managed to make himself clear. He would plow for me, sixty acres, if twenty of it were his to harvest. I thought his offer over carefully . . . for about two seconds. We shook on the best deal I'd made in a long time.

A few days later, when Karl came to plow, I headed over to spend the day with Perilee. That was the other part of our deal; he didn't like leaving her alone. The baby was due in June, but Leafie and I wondered if she'd make it till then. "What are you carrying, girl, an elephant?" Leafie had asked her. Perilee laughed. "You remember how it was with Fern," she said. "You thought I was carrying twins." They went on to discuss Fern's arrival in great detail. Their conversation gave me pause. Of course, anything to do with babies and giving birth gave me pause. What I knew about those subjects would fit on the head of a pin. I was thankful Perilee wouldn't have to rely on me. Not with Leafie around.

It was Monday, wash day—again. While the whites boiled, I scrubbed a load of the kids' dungarees and overalls. Perilee's condition made bending over the washboard and washtub awkward and uncomfortable. When I finished wringing something, I handed it to Chase or Mattie and they carried it to their mama so she could pin it to the line.

"Now, Hattie, don't be surprised if our laundry attracts company." Perilee shook out Mattie's green gingham dress.

"Company?" I said. The last company I'd had was Rooster Jim. He'd stayed for supper and afterward beat me at chess. Again. His parting gift to me was to share his bedbugs. I used up nearly a quart of kerosene trying to kill them off.

Perilee stood up and rested her hands on the small of her back. "Last week a band of antelopes came up to inspect our skivvies flapping in the breeze!" She laughed—a sound I'd heard too few times lately—then a frown of pain flickered across her face.

"Chase, go on in and bring out that rocker for your mama." I was pleased that Perilee had accepted my gift of that chair, paid for with my newspaper story money. "For the baby" was how I'd offered it. And for the baby was how she had accepted it. Growing up, I hadn't been around children much. The relatives I'd been sent to all seemed to have raised their broods; I was an add-on. At first, after moving out here, Mattie's constant chatter and baby Fern's drooling had got on my nerves. But now I made a habit of carrying a handkerchief for Fern, and I'd come to enjoy Mattie's observations. I thought she had the makings of a good writer herself. Charlie would have laughed out loud to see me warming up to these little ones. And that Chase! He'd whittled himself a good-sized niche in my heart. So good to his mama. And loyal as a little Turk to Karl. Smart as a whip, too. He'd finished up *Treasure Island* and was now tackling *Riders of the Purple Sage.*

"Here's the chair." Chase brought it over. I set it up in the only sliver of shade around and pushed Perilee into it. There was cool buttermilk yet, thanks to Violet, and I poured some in a tin cup. I wished it could've been a nice tall drink in a real glass.

"A penny for your thoughts." Perilee settled herself in her chair.

I laughed. "I hate to admit it, but it was something Aunt Ivy used to say." I handed Perilee the buttermilk. "If wishes were horses, then beggars would ride."

"My mama used to say that, too." Perilee sipped at the buttermilk. "Course, sometimes wishes do come true." She patted her stomach and took another drink. "Oh, this tastes good." Fern wobbled toward her mother's lap. I grabbed Chase by the overall strap. "You and Mattie take your baby sister. Go pick me some wild greens. I'll throw them in the stew."

Chase stopped and looked at me. "You better at stew than you are at bread?" His brown eyes were as serious as Sunday.

"Chase Samuel Johnson!" scolded Perilee.

Chase laughed. Such a nice clean sound. Perilee joined in.

"See if I ever cook for you again," I said. But I laughed, too. My cooking had improved somewhat, but I'd never match Perilee in that department.

The children gathered up empty lard pails to collect the greens in and headed off to the coulee. Perilee finished her buttermilk. "I believe I'll close my eyes for a minute," she said. Her rocking slowed. Soon I heard soft snoring.

My arms and back complained like the dickens as I refilled the wash boiler, kept the water hot, rubbed grimy clothes on the washboard, wrung them out, and hung them to dry. Aunt Ivy used to say, "A man just works from sun to sun. A woman's work is never done." Let me testify to that!

I hung the last of Fern's diapers and stretched. Perilee slept noisily in her chair. I decided to go after the children. As I walked, I mentally composed the next section of my latest *Arlington News* installment.

> It would be dishonest of me to try to impress with my tracking skills, to hint that living out in this wild country had brought out the native in me, able to discern from this twisted leaf or that disturbed rock which way my prey had gone. The buffalo grass around Perilee's house was tall but thick as moss; I had no trouble picking up the tracks of three barefoot children. Plus, I had the advantage of knowing the exact location of the greenest patch of wild parsley.

In short order, I'd come upon the three urchins, more intent on skipping stones across the creek than filling their buckets.

I bent to pick up a dark smooth stone.

"That's no good for skipping," said Chase.

"It's a wishing rock," I said. "Better than a skipping stone."

"I want one, too," said Mattie. I showed her how to look for a dark rock with a circle of white around it. "When you're ready to make a wish, you close your eyes, then throw it over your shoulder," I explained.

She filled her pockets with stones. "I'm saving these for later," she said. "When I need a really good wish."

"I like that idea." I collected a dozen myself. One to wish for good planting. One for a good harvest. Two for Charlie's safe return. Another for Perilee's new baby. And a handful for proving up.

I looked up from my collecting. Fern had toddled off. "Fern must be part fairy, with the way she's so crazy about picking flowers," I commented to Chase. Her sturdy little legs carried her through the grass from one patch of wildflowers to another. In one pudgy hand she carried a slightly smashed prairie rose, in the other a bent wild iris.

"Let's gather a bouquet for Mama!" Mattie handed me her bucket and went to work. She and Chase scooped up a veritable rainbow of flowers. When they were done, Fern reluctantly contributed her two treasures to the nosegay.

"Won't your mama be pleased." I brushed the petals with my fingers. Would I ever be on the receiving end of such a bouquet from my own little ones? I'd never thought before that I might actually long for such a thing. I ruffled Chase's hair. "We'd better start on back if I'm going to tackle stew yet today."

Fern stuck a sap-sticky hand in mine. I picked up one bucket; Chase carried the two others. "I have to carry Mulie," explained Mattie.

We strolled along at an easy pace, careful of little legs. I breathed deeply of the sweetly scented air. It reminded me of the fragrance I'd caught when I first stepped off the train in Wolf Point. Someone practical like Perilee might tell me it was only the buffalo grass, warmed to sweetness by the spring sun. But it was more than that: it was the smell of home. Of a place to belong.

I'd marked off nearly five months on my calendar. Wouldn't Charlie be amazed at what I'd done in those five months? With my own two hands—and help from Karl—I'd set what felt like miles of fence. Soon my first crop would be planted. Come fall, I'd have flax and wheat to harvest. In November, the three years would be up on Uncle Chester's claim. On my claim. And I would have everything checked off, everything accomplished. I would step into 1919 a new person—not Hattie Here-and-There, reliant on relatives to give her a roof and board, but Hattie Inez Brooks. Hattie Big Sky, I added with a touch of romance. Hattie Home-of-Her-Own.

"Hattie." Mattie tugged on my skirt. "Is that thunder?"

I shook off my daydream. "I don't hear—" A deep rumble shook me from my toes up. "What *is* that?"

The ground rolled beneath us as a shudder of noise rolled over us.

"Horses!" Chase's face went white. "Wild horses!"

He'd no sooner said the words than I knew he was right. I pictured the wild, frothing herd headed right for us. "A stallion can bite through the neck of a grown horse," Rooster Jim had once warned me. I trembled to think what it could do to the children.

"Piggyback," I said to Fern, swinging her onto my shoulders. I snatched Mattie's hand. "We've got to run for it!"

Flowers, greens, and buckets forgotten, we ran across the prairie, joined at the hands and wobbling like an unwieldy snake. The earth roared and writhed as it must have during Creation.

I turned and saw them, a tidal wave of horseflesh, nearing the other side of the creek. They'd soon be upon us.

The stallion guided his herd this way and that, closing the space between us. The mares followed his every lead. I handed Fern over to Chase. "Head for home," I ordered.

"Hattie—" Chase started.

"Go!" I screamed. Off they flew. I thought of the stones in my pocket; they'd worked against wolves and boys, but they'd be worthless against wild horses. I had no idea what to do. But I would not let those horses cross the creek. Would not allow them to harm those children. My skirt flapped in the breeze as I turned. I remembered Perilee's comments about the clothes on the line attracting the antelope. Maybe they'd have the opposite effect on skittish horses.

I ripped off my skirt and petticoat and began flapping them like a demented bird in bloomers. The stallion froze at the creek's edge. His herd stopped, too, as one, whinnying and stamping as he paced back and forth.

"Hee-yaw!" I waved and yelled and danced around. The stallion twitched and snorted and took one high step into the creek. "Hee-yaw!" I screamed. I flailed my arms and wailed like a dime-novel dervish.

The stallion lowered his head, flesh quivering on his massive, gleaming neck. He stepped back. And back again.

My woolen wings fluttered and flapped at the ends of my arms. "Back! Back!" I stepped forward. The stallion hopped back again and stopped. He froze, wild eyes fixed on me. What kind of creature did he imagine me to be? I prayed a fearsome one. I inched forward one more step and gave a ferocious flap. He yanked his head back and wheeled around. He paced and pranced, there on the other side of the creek. Then, with a shake of his powerful head, he launched into a gallop and led his four-legged band in the opposite direction.

I collapsed, exhausted, to the ground. Something sharp bruised my tailbone. I shifted and fished around on the ground for the offending item. It was one of my wishing stones, no doubt flung from my pocket in my wild display. Was it the stone, my antics, or the Lord once again moving in mysterious ways that had turned the horses? Who could say? My ragged breaths turned to sobs as the full force of the close call hit me. If anything had happened to Perilee's children . . . I wiped my face with my petticoat. There was no time to wallow in what could have been. I shook myself off, clutching my limp and torn garments, and headed for Perilee's to bring in the dry laundry and start supper. When I got home that night and undressed, the wishing stone fell out of my pocket. I set it on the kitchen table—a reminder of wishes come true— lit the kerosene lamp and finished writing my *Honyocker's Homily.*

> As I close this installment, let me say this: for all the times my aunt admonished me that a lady never goes out without at least one petticoat under her skirt, I am most thankful. My trusty underthings saved the day for me and

for those three children. It seems that this season of sowing is not simply about planting flax and wheat. Along with the grain, it appears I have also sown strong seeds of friendship.

The next Sunday, I started off to church. I walked a bit out of my way, to pass close to Perilee's to see the progress on the new barn. Pastor Schatz from the Lutheran church had recently organized a barn raising. I'd even pounded a few nails myself that day. While it was wonderfully satisfying to see a sturdy structure arise from the ashes, literally, what had lifted my spirits most was seeing all the Vida folks come out. The County Council of Defense members were noticeably absent, but otherwise nearly everyone came by to lend a hand or a word of advice. Mrs. Nefzger had the grippe but sent three of her raisin pies. Perilee dabbed at teary eyes all day, and Karl kept shaking his head. "That'll hold till after harvest," said Rooster Jim, admiring the day's work. "Then we'll get the roof on."

I shook my own head, thinking about that day. Coming back to the present, I was startled to turn the bend and see Perilee, in her best dress, holding her girls by the hand and Chase right behind.

"Where are you going?" I asked.

"To church." Her look ordered no questions. "You stay right next to me, you promise?"

"Like a burr," I promised.

Perilee tucked her arm through mine snug, as we walked through a rainbow of wildflowers. We took turns carrying

Fern. Mattie and Chase followed behind like calves, distracted by this butterfly or that bug or newly bloomed lily.

Across the flat prairie, the church sailed into view, a small ship of salvation on the buffalo grass sea. Perilee's grip on my arm tightened as each step drew us closer. By the time we arrived at the front door, I thought my arm would fall clean off.

Mattie and Chase were pulled away by the Saboe kids, off to Sunday school. Holding Fern, I led Perilee to a pew near the back. It rocked as we settled in, smoothing wool skirts into place with callused hands.

"Let us pray." Reverend Tweed led the opening prayer.

I glanced at Perilee. Her eyes were squeezed so tight her eyelashes disappeared. A wrinkle weaved its way across her forehead. I reached over and squeezed her hand, *one-two-three.* Perilee's eyes opened, and I winked at her. She smiled, and the wrinkle dissolved.

"Open your hymnals to page ninety-seven." Reverend Tweed stood again. "We will sing 'Love Divine, All Loves Excelling.' "

Mrs. Martin crashed out a semblance of the tune on the careworn upright piano. The choir lurched and stumbled somewhere near the proper melody. The congregation tried to follow. It was painful, even for me.

Then, softly, surely, an angel's voice broke through the tumult, offering a place for that raggedy mix of voices to land. It pulled the hymn out of muddled confusion and lifted true praises to the Lord.

I stopped to listen. It was Perilee.

A few other folks had also stopped singing and were craning

their necks to find the source of the only real music in that little church. I nearly burst with pride.

"You have the voice of an angel," Reverend Tweed told her as he shook her hand after the service. "You'd be a wonderful addition to our choir."

Perilee's face lit up. Before she could reply, Mrs. Martin piped up. "We are already overloaded on altos," she said.

"Surely—" began Reverend Tweed.

"I do thank you for your offer, Reverend." Perilee tugged her shawl around her. "But with the baby coming, I don't see how I could manage." She started down the stairs, and I was close behind, shifting Fern to my other hip. I caught a glimpse of Mrs. Martin, moving in behind us, her face puckered up like a prune. Reverend Tweed was about to be on the receiving end of a sermon.

Perilee and I called to the children.

"She's awful," I said.

Perilee shrugged. "It was nice to sing," she said wistfully.

"Plenty of time to decide after the baby is born," I said. Then and there I determined to get Perilee in that choir. Maybe I could threaten to join if they didn't let her in.

Once again, she slipped her arm through mine. We girl-talked our whole way back to her house. The kids jump-frogged ahead of us, playing some kind of complicated game of tag. Perilee asked me to stay to dinner. "It's just make-do," she apologized.

"Your make-do is better than the Ritz," I said, helping myself to some more chicken and dumplings.

She smiled shyly. "It's the company, not the cooking, that

makes the meal." She pushed back from the table. "I'll bring out the coffee."

"Stay put." I poured coffee for the three adults and we sat and visited. I was beginning to understand almost all of Karl's conversation, with its mix of German and English. He got us all to laughing over Violet's new bad habit. Seems she'd turned goat, trying to take nips out of Karl's britches.

"Stop, stop!" My stomach hurt from laughing so hard. But it felt good. The good mood wrapped around me and kept me company on my walk home and through my evening chores.

CHAPTER 14

THE ARLINGTON NEWS

Honyocker's Homily ~ Chicken Farmer

I may not have finished high school, but my homestead life continues to provide essential education. I have learned that no price can be put on good neighbors. I don't mean to imply I merely treasure the folks around me for the way they help. Granted, I wouldn't be looking out at a quilt of sprouting grain as I survey my flax and wheat fields had my neighbors not intervened. Nor would I be blessed with several new additions to my homestead family.

Rather, the lessons this life has planted in my heart pertain more to caring than to crops, more to Golden Rule than gold, more to the proper choice than to the popular choice.

About two weeks after the stand-off with the wild horses at Wolf Creek, I hied myself to Vida. I had a check due from Mr. Miltenberger, and I hoped there were some letters. Since the fire, I had lost Traft's front-door delivery service. If I never saw that man again, it would be too soon.

To my very pleasant surprise, I was not the only pilgrim on the path that day.

"Leafie!" I called out to the figure striding purposefully ahead of me. She turned and waited for me to catch up.

"Doing any more of them burlesque dances out there on the prairie?" She grinned.

"Perilee told!"

"Honey, a story that good can't be kept under a barrel." Leafie shook her head. "Wouldn't you love to know what that stallion made of you?" She chuckled.

"What takes you into town?" I decided to shift the subject.

"Oh, a bit of this and a bit of that." She patted her knapsack. "And an errand for Karl."

"He's done planting." I sidestepped a patch of gumbo lilies. "What's keeping him so busy he can't get to town?"

She looked thoughtful. "Yes, well . . . He says he don't want to leave Perilee alone, but . . ." Her voice trailed off.

I picked up my pace a bit. "But what?" Leafie had about twenty years on me, but you'd never know it from her stride.

"It's this Council of Defense monkey business. Those Martins and their knucklehead friends have gotten the whole town worked up. Did you know they broke up services last week at the Lutheran church? Traft fined Pastor Schatz! Said next time he'd put him in jail!" Leafie shook her head. "You tell me the good Lord's in charge of this mess and I'll scream."

"Is that why Karl isn't going to town?" I shivered.

"Perilee asked him not to." Leafie flipped her tobacco pouch from the front pocket of the man's shirt she always wore. She expertly rolled a cigarette and lit it. "She also asked him not to go to services at the Lutheran church, but that he wouldn't do." She picked a shred of tobacco off her tongue. "That man. Never went before, but now that there's trouble, he's determined to attend."

We made the last turn on the path, and the Vida church popped into sight. I thought about Reverend Tweed's last sermon: "Winning the War at Home." "They wouldn't hurt anyone at a church, would they?"

"That wouldn't stop them." Leafie took an impatient puff. "Did you hear about Edward Foster? They nearly lynched the poor old man simply because he said too many of our boys are dying in the war. And him a distinguished veteran." Leafie stopped to loosen her bootlaces. "Rock," she grumbled, leaning on me to shake out her boot. Nothing came out. She peered inside and shook it again. "Like trying to find an honest man on that silly Council of Defense," she said. She laughed at her own joke and slipped her boot back on.

163

"You shouldn't joke like that." I looked around. "What if someone overheard you?"

She snorted. "Let them try to come after me." She patted my hand. "Listen, there are worse things than the wrath of the Martin brothers. And the worst thing of all is standing by when folks are doing something wrong." She seemed to turn her thoughts somewhere else. "As if there was something more admirable about Lemuel Johnson because he was 100 percent American—whatever that is." She turned to look me full in the face. "Now, you tell me—you think I should keep quiet when those peabrains turn their meanness on Karl because of where he was born?" She fixed her gaze at me.

I thought about all that had happened in the last month or so. "No, not keep quiet, but . . ." I stopped.

"Will you listen to me?" She shook herself like a hen unruffling its feathers. "All worked up over them toads. Sorry, Hattie. Let's stop in Charlie Mason's café and have us some pie and coffee."

I wondered how a person got like Leafie. Or even like Traft. So sure of what was right. Maybe when I was Leafie's age, such matters would be clear as glass to me, as they were to her. Right now it seemed to me that life was as clear as the cup of muddy coffee Charlie Mason served up.

"You want to walk back together?" asked Leafie, scooping up her last bite of buttermilk pie. "Meet back here in an hour or so?"

I agreed, paid for my pie and coffee, and left my nickel change for a tip. My errands would take me to Nefzger's store and the post office, all one and the same, and all connected to his sod house.

Mr. Nefzger greeted me as I stepped inside. "Got some mail for you."

"Thank you." I flipped through the envelopes. Thank God there was one from the *Arlington News*. That meant I could buy a few supplies. "I could use another bag of beans," I said. "And some kerosene."

He set my items on the counter. "How are things out your way?"

"Fine." I opened my pocketbook. "You should see my fields. They're green velvet quilts." I laughed at myself. "Never thought the sight of growing plants could be so thrilling."

"It's something I've never tired of," he said. "Wait till you see the flax in bloom. I've never been to the sea myself, but I imagine it couldn't be bluer than a field of flax."

"I'll look forward to that." I handed over what I owed him.

Mr. Nefzger cleared his throat. "I hate to mention this, Hattie. But Chester left a bill here."

"A bill?" My hand froze in midair over my pocketbook.

He nodded. "For the fencing." He fumbled under the counter and brought out a piece of paper. An IOU. I looked at it.

"Two hundred and twenty dollars?" I reached my hand out and steadied myself on the counter. "He didn't pay for any of it?"

"He took sick. I didn't want to push it." He cleared his throat.

I fumbled with my pocketbook. Two hundred and twenty dollars! "I'm sorry—it can't be all at once." I counted out every bill in my pocketbook and set the money on the counter.

He didn't reach for the bills. "I should have told you sooner." He looked as sick as I felt. "I know times are tough. I've got the bank pushing on me to collect on accounts."

"Thank you, Mr. Nefzger." I started numbly for the door. "I'll get this paid off as quickly as I can."

In a fog, I moved through the doorway. If I hadn't been in shock, I might have had the wherewithal to turn a cold shoulder to the person I next encountered: Traft Martin.

He made a fuss of tipping his hat to me. "Good day, Miss Brooks. How is the homesteader today?"

"Fine, thank you." I cradled my parcel to my chest and began walking. *Let's see, $220 from—how much did that leave me?*

"You heading to the café?" He fell into step beside me. "Allow me to escort you."

"Oh, there's no need." Oh, Lord. I envisioned my ledger in my mind. Would there be enough to pay for the binder? The thresher? The grain sacks? What kind of payments would Mr. Nefzger expect? Would I have to go to Wolf Point and take everything out of my bank account there?

"Think nothing of it." Traft smiled. "Are you all right?"

Would I need to take out a loan? Karl didn't believe in them, but—

"Hattie?"

"What?" I realized he was still walking next to me. I walked faster.

"I haven't seen you in a while," he said.

His words jarred me out of my shock. He hadn't seen me in a while, he says. Well, I'd seen him. And his handiwork.

"For a short woman, you cover a lot of ground, and

quickly." He put his hand on my arm to slow me down. "Is there some reason you want to avoid me?"

I couldn't believe his gall. "Some reason? *Some?*"

He spread his hands, palms up, as if inviting me to explain.

It may be true that discretion is the better part of valor. But Leafie's words as we walked to town were still rummaging around in my brain. And the nerve of this man. Was he stupid as well as mean?

"I saw you."

"Saw me?"

"After the fire. At my house."

Traft's body jerked back for an instant. It was as if he'd been struck. "You've got it all wrong."

"Don't tell me you weren't there." My hands curled into angry fists. "Don't add liar to your list of dubious accomplishments."

"I'm not lying." His voice lost all its bluster. "I *was* at your place. But to stop another fire. Not start one."

"Like the one you started at Karl's?" No matter how my voice trembled, I would finish this.

He held up his hand to stop me. His eyes looked sad. Genuinely sad. "That fire was none of my doing. It—" He stopped. "No sense in my explaining. I can tell by your face you wouldn't believe me."

The sorrow in his tone softened my anger. "No. Please. Explain. I have judged you guilty without—" My words were drowned out by a terrified male voice.

"Whoa! Whoa there!"

We turned to see what was happening. There, smack dab

down the center of the street, wobbled Rooster Jim on a brand-new bicycle.

"Watch out!" I warned. He appeared to be headed straight for the front of the café.

"Put on the brake!" Traft trotted after him. "Brake!" Other folks ran down the street, too, calling out one suggestion after another.

Rooster Jim didn't heed a thing anybody said. Bellowing louder than Violet that day with the wolf, he swerved this way and that. He narrowly missed a collision with Leafie, stepping out of Dye's store. "Jim, you fool, what are you doing?" she hollered.

"Trying to stop this darned thing." The street took a dip downward, and Jim began to pick up speed. Mrs. Schillinger jumped out of the way in the nick of time, pulling little Edward to safety.

"Yee-haw!" Rooster Jim crowed. His feet flew off the pedals as he barreled straight for Gust Trishalt's blacksmith shop. Traft ran all the faster to try to bring Rooster to a halt.

Gust stepped out of his door and quickly assessed the situation. "Head for the hay," he hollered, flapping his arms as if he could propel Rooster Jim toward the bundles at the back of the smithy.

Traft had given up the chase. He panted hard, leaning against a post in front of Gust. "He's going to roll clear to Circle," he said.

In one magnificent motion, Rooster Jim jerked the bicycle off course and careened—*thunk*—into the stacked bundles. He flew one way, the bicycle another.

Leafie and I grabbed our skirts and ran to his side. Straw stuck every which way out of his shaggy hair. There was even a stalk in his beard.

"Jim!" I reached him first. "Are you okay?"

Leafie cradled Jim's head. "Jim?" She patted his face. Finally he gave himself a shake.

"Last time I trade a pig for a bicycle," he mumbled. He pushed himself upright and picked up the wheeled terror. "Only thing this is good for is . . . is . . ." He spat straw and dirt out of his mouth. "Absolutely nothing." Despite the wild ride, he managed to leave town with a great degree of dignity, holding his head high and his back stiff as he pushed the bike along the path.

Gust picked up Rooster's forgotten hat. "I'll take it," I said. "We're due for a chess game soon." I took the hat gingerly between my thumb and forefinger. Good thing I'd bought kerosene; I could soak Jim's hat in it and evict all the bedbug roomers.

"Now, that was better than any movie show," said Leafie. She slipped her arm through mine. "Come on, girl. Let's walk on these slow but sure feet and git ourselves to home."

We were a ways down the road when I realized I'd never finished my conversation with Traft. Could it be that he'd really not been involved in the fire at Karl's? He'd seemed so sincere. I didn't know what to think.

Leafie chatted away the miles, so there wasn't much need for me to talk. My mind was a-whirl with what I'd learned in town. Here I'd been so thankful that Uncle Chester had laid in the fencing supplies. Only he'd forgotten one little detail— paying for them. It seemed small of me to be so unhappy when he'd done so much for me, but the IOU had been a bitter surprise. Would I ever stop fretting about money?

I don't even remember bidding Leafie good-bye. After we parted company, I walked on lost in thought. I was surprised when I found myself in my own yard, with Mr. Whiskers there on the steps, curled up next to the sunflower I'd planted in a coffee can. I couldn't stop thinking about Traft. Was he to be believed? Or had this war brewed up a sourness deep inside him, causing him to twist and turn like that sunflower as it tried to reach some sun? I reached down to scratch Mr. Whiskers behind the ears. "Cats are sure less complicated than people," I said. Mr. Whiskers purred in agreement.

A week passed after the bicycle mishap, but Rooster Jim didn't come by. In the meantime, I'd finished my fence. It was hard to even take that in. Finished! One of the major parts of proving up on the claim and I had done it. *I can't imagine how big one of those airfields of yours is,* I'd write Charlie, *but I suspect I've set enough fence to wrap around one many times over.* I shielded my eyes from the sun and admired my completed work of art. Four hundred and eighty rods of mighty fine fence, if I did say so myself. Four hundred and eighty rods of maybe the finest fence in Montana! All right then, perhaps not. But to my mind it was, since every inch of it—aside from a patch put up by my fairy godfather—had been set with my own two hands.

I needed to celebrate. I decided to do so by returning Jim's hat. After freshening up a bit, I was soon on my way.

His was a hard place to miss. For one thing, as you

approached, you'd find his prize pigs hobbled out on the prairie like most folks do horses or cows. It was a source of constant conversation for the cowboys I'd met, why old Jim would treat his pigs so. Past the pigs, you'd come upon the ghost tree, bleached white with wind and age. The poor thing served its purpose now as a landmark and a place for lovers to carve initials. From this spot, you could spy Jim's soddy—at least the roof, from which grew a cherry tree that Jim swore bore the best pie cherries in all of Montana. It would be hard to prove him wrong, as I didn't know of too many other pie cherry trees in these parts, least of all any that grew from anybody's roof. Maybe there'd be a cherry pie for the Fourth of July picnic on Wolf Creek.

As I drew near to the house, I had to laugh right out loud. There, planted in his garden, was that bicycle. Jim had found a use for it: as a trellis for his string beans.

"Hey there, neighbor!" Rooster Jim waved and, with a groan, straightened himself to a stand from the patch of garden he was weeding. "Out for a Sunday stroll?" He chuckled at this, seeing as it was Wednesday.

"I finished my fence," I said. There should be trumpets to herald the news. "Thought I'd celebrate with a walk. Being as it's getting so warm, I thought you'd be missing your hat." I handed it to him.

He took it from me and settled it just so on his head. "I wondered what happened to it after my run-in with that monster machine." He chuckled, then sniffed the air. "My, my. This spring breeze is so rich it smells like fresh-baked bread."

I held out the package I'd been carrying. "I think I'm

getting the hang of this," I said. "You can actually eat this loaf without soaking it in water first."

Rooster laughed. "Bread that delicious deserves a trade," he said.

"Oh, no need," I assured him.

"Seems to me I've been by the Hattie Brooks place a time or two and heard a most peculiar sound," he said.

"You have? What?"

"Most fearful sound." He shook his head. "The sound of a farm without any hens."

"Well, I plan on getting some after harvest."

"That's a long summer without fresh eggs." He motioned me to follow him. Over in his hen yard, he pointed out three scraggly hens. "Them's Martha, Rose, and June. They've got some setting left in them, and I need to thin out the flock. You interested in giving them a new home? Course, Albert"— here he pointed to a handsome white leghorn rooster—"is part of the package, too."

No more doling out eggs as if they were pearls! I could taste fried eggs for breakfast. Fried chicken for supper. Spice cake with an egg for richness. "Oh, yes."

Rooster Jim expertly rounded up the three ladies and their escort. He slipped all four of them, squawking and screeching, into a burlap sack. "Can you manage this?" he asked.

"I sure hope so." The bag twisted and jerked as if it was full of snakes.

"Them's good girls. They'll settle soon." He picked up his hat from where it had fallen during the chicken roundup.

I wobbled home with my prize. Mr. Whiskers meowed his approval when I set down the bag. "Don't you even think about it," I warned. He would be the least of my troubles. I needed to save my cluckers from coyotes and chicken hawks. Uncle Chester's efforts had included a chicken coop, but it wasn't fenced. I had to laugh. So much for thinking I was done fencing!

I turned my new family loose in the house and shut the door quick. I'd have to deal with their mess later. For now, I needed to keep them safe while I secured the chicken yard. A roll of chicken wire was the last item in Uncle Chester's stock of supplies stored in the barn. I said a prayer that it was paid for. My budget couldn't afford any more surprises.

Hours of practice had turned me into a proficient but slow fence builder. This was a little more challenging because I had to dig down to bury the bottom of the chicken wire to keep out hungry diggers like skunks and such. By working straight through supper and then by lamplight, I was able to enclose the whole yard. My fingers were raw and blistered, but I couldn't stop yet to tend them. I tidied up the chicken coop and got it ready for its new residents.

My stomach complained for its supper and my back cried out for its bed, but I finally had a suitable castle for my winged herd. With an indignant squawk, Rose led the way into their new domicile, tempted by a trail of grain. Martha, June, and Albert followed suit. I slipped in an old pan for their water trough and fastened the chicken coop door closed.

Too tired to fuss with supper, I ate a bowl of graveyard stew, breaking up chunks of bread and covering them with warm milk and molasses.

My first night as a chicken farmer passed far too quickly. Albert was persistent about announcing dawn's first—and very early—light. I rolled out of bed and began my daily round of chores even earlier than customary. A new chore included letting the chickens out into their yard. A run-in with Albert convinced Mr. Whiskers that he'd best forget about any chicken dinners.

Over the course of the next few days, I headed out to the chicken house full of anticipation. But every morning, I would find Martha, Rose, and June scratching in a pile of broken shells. These ladies seemed most disinterested in setting on their eggs. At this rate, I'd never be able to add to my flock.

As luck would have it, Rooster Jim passed by a few days later.

"Came to see how you and the girls were getting along," he said. "I could tell Albert took to you right off."

I couldn't say I had taken to Albert. The dark circles under my eyes spoke to the rooster's propensity for early morning announcements. Unfortunately, he was essential if I was going to increase my chicken family from four to many.

Rooster Jim inspected my fencing job. "Why, it's better than Andrew Carnegie could build with all his money!" He slapped me heartily on the back. "But, from the evidence, it seems the ladies aren't cooperating for you."

At least there were eggs this morning, and none broken. "I can't get them to set," I said. "I don't know what to do."

Rooster Jim nodded. "It takes a firm hand with chickens," he said. "Let me show you." Soon he had the hens hobbled inside their coop. A little string went from one chicken leg to a nail in the wall. The string was long enough to allow each member of the feathery trio to step off the nest and get a bite to eat and a drink of water.

"Now, tonight you set a bucket over each of them. That'll teach them to stay put." Rooster Jim finished his instructions as he stepped back to admire the chicken coop improvements.

"Won't that frighten them?" I asked.

"Naw." He smoothed his beard down over his broad chest. "And if that don't work, there's always the rain barrel."

"For the eggs?"

"No, for the ladies. If the bucket don't convince them to set, you dunk them in the rain barrel a time or two and turn 'em loose. Settles them right down."

I invited Rooster Jim in for dinner, and we ate in companionable silence. I didn't know if he'd been pulling my leg with his instructions. I would try the bucket trick tonight. But if that didn't work, I didn't know what I'd do. I couldn't see myself dunking any chickens.

By the next day, Martha and June were content on their nests. They bought right into the notion that they had a job to do. Rose was cut from the same animal cloth as Violet. She would not set. Another week passed.

I'd had a short night and was in a mood when Albert announced "rise-and-shine." When I saw the broken shells under Rose's nest, something snapped. Coyote quick, I snatched her by the feet and ran over to the rain barrel. I tipped her upside down and—*splash, splash, splash*—I baptized that bird but good.

She didn't move much when I pulled her up the third time. I set her down. She toppled right over.

175

"Oh, Lordy, I've killed her!" In my distress, I barely took note of Mr. Whiskers slinking along the ground. Perhaps he thought that a drowned chicken was fair game. I wiped my hands on my apron and cursed my stupidity. I shouldn't have listened to Rooster Jim. No doubt his surefire setting cure was a practical joke. Only now it had cost me one third of my flock. I leaned against the rain barrel and mourned my loss.

All the while, Mr. Whiskers slunk along. Since I wasn't screeching at him to get away, he must've thought he was free and clear to a fine, feathered dinner. At the sound of his deep-throated hunter's growl, however, I regained my senses and shrieked, "Mr. Whiskers! *No!*"

Too late. He pounced.

Unfortunately for Mr. Whiskers, he landed the moment Rose rejoined the living. She lashed out with her sharp little beak, right at the cat's soft underbelly.

"Yowl!" Mr. Whiskers launched himself straight up and ran off under the shack to lick his wounds.

Rose fluttered to a stand, twirled drunkenly around, and staggered to the chicken coop doorway. With Albert trumpeting her resurrection, she hopped inside the coop and settled herself down. She proved to be a good layer and an even better setter. But that was the last time I ever dunked a chicken.

Dear Hattie,

I have finally received another letter from you. I can't imagine what fills your days so that you don't have time to write to an old friend.

You, with your quiet farming ways, would be quite agog over all the activity here. We are tramping from hither to yon. My new purpose in life is to keep my boots, and thus my feet, dry. I must say I am losing some of my admiration for France. I did not intend to be her guest for so long! I miss my books and my folks and my friends. Let me tell you, soldiering is a lot more glamorous from the other side of the uniform! There are rumors of hot food and showers tonight.

I do not have it as hard as some. Do you remember Harvey Bloch? I have learned that he has been killed. That makes twelve gold stars hanging in Arlington's windows. I hope we get the job done here, and soon, without too many more.

> *Your muddy and tired chum,*
> *Charlie*

I took my pen in hand to write a reply.

Dear Charlie,

I am so sorry to hear about Harvey.

I set the pen down. *Harvey.* I thought back to how Miss Simpson had taken such pride in the wooden apple he had carved for her desk. How he had never hurried about anything. How he'd been so patient with his younger brother, who wasn't quite right. I remembered seeing his mother hang the service flag in their front window the very day Harvey left for camp. I could see it now—a blue star centered on a white field, surrounded by a red border. Now the blue star would be covered by a gold one. I ached for the Blochs. And for myself. I continued the letter to Charlie, writing about everything other than the war. Then I finished it with:

> *See that you keep those boots dry. And the boy who wears them safe.*
>
>

As ever,
Hattie

⚜ CHAPTER 15 ⚜

May 15, 1918
Three miles north and west of Vida, Montana

Dear Uncle Holt,

I wish you could see my fields. I never knew green could be so beautiful—but then I've never had a farm of my own before. Rooster Jim says all portents point to a good harvest. I certainly hope so; my meager budget can't stand much more of a diet.

You asked me about my far neighbor, Leafie Purvis. She is rough-and-tumble but doesn't think twice about lending anyone a hand. She came from Chicago but has lived in Vida as long as Perilee can remember. She runs some cows and trains horses. Rooster Jim says Leafie's the best around. Some fellow came clear from Havre one

*time to have her train his horse. She's good with
doctoring, too, which is handy since the nearest doctor is
thirty miles away in Wolf Point. I had a spring cold and
she made me some tea that had me on my feet quick as a
wink. I was her assistant a few days back when a young
neighbor boy fell and broke his arm.*

"I sure do appreciate the company." Leafie shifted the basket she carried from her left arm to her right.

"Let me take a turn carrying that," I said. She handed over the basket and rubbed her left shoulder.

"Weather's going to change. I can feel it in my bones." She turned her face up to the blue sky and studied it. "I expect rain anytime."

"The crops sure need it." I scanned the sky, too, but unclear about what signs I should be seeking.

Leafie reached in her shirt pocket for cigarette materials. I was used to her smoking now. The warm tobacco reminded me of Uncle Holt.

"You mind a little detour?" We were on our way to visit Perilee, who was recovering from a bad cough.

"Where to?"

She pointed to a small knoll about a mile away. "I'd like to stop in and see how Mabel Ren's getting along." Leafie shook her head. "She's got six little ones, four of them under six. And their oldest, Elmer junior, is a real pistol. Not afraid of anything, and one sandwich short of a picnic basket when it comes to common sense." She laughed. "Nearly broke his neck last summer when he decided to see if pigs might be able to fly. He and one of Elmer's weaner pigs took a nosedive off the barn."

I laughed, too. "That reminds me of Chase. Last time he was over, he helped me with the supper dishes. Nearly talked my ear off about how he was going to invent a washing machine for dishes someday." I brushed at a bluebottle buzzing at my head. "Of course, knowing Chase, he'll do it."

"That's one sharp mind that boy has." Leafie watched her feet as she picked her way down the coulee.

We were both quiet for a bit, no doubt thinking the same thing. You could line up all the boys in Dawson County and not find a brighter one than Chase. But since the incident with his fairy-tale book, he'd stopped going to school. No amount of pleading by Perilee could shift his mind. I'd tried reasoning with him, too. "I can learn more at home," he'd said. "On my own." And he was probably right about that. But it troubled me that a small boy would be forced out of school by a bunch of bullies.

"That's Elmer's place down there."

The Ren house was sturdier built than my cabin; from here, it appeared to have several rooms. As I got closer, I could see that three old homestead shacks had been fitted together to make the oddest-shaped house I'd ever seen. But it was fresh painted, and chintz curtains hung in the windows.

Mabel Ren was a sparrow of a woman, flitting here and there the minute we arrived. "Mabel, sit down and drink your coffee," Leafie scolded. "We didn't come to be waited on."

"I haven't had company in a long time," Mabel said. She showed us the quilt she was piecing for the county fair.

"Perilee and I are working on one together," I told her. "For the baby." I admired Mabel's tight stitches, feathered out in a very unusual pattern. "I've never seen this before."

"I made it up," she answered. "It reminded me of a curlew's feather."

"That it does," said Leafie. "This is blue-ribbon work." I nodded agreement.

Mabel smiled shyly. She reached for the coffeepot. "More coffee?"

Leafie held her hand over her cup. "No, thanks. We're on our way to see Perilee." Leafie patted her basket. "Made her some sagebrush tea and some tamarack syrup."

Mabel wrapped up some biscuits and a rasher of bacon. "Take this to her, please. She was so good to us when our Bernice took sick."

There was a commotion out of doors. Mabel turned to the window. "Elmer!" She dropped the package for Perilee and ran outside.

"That little dickens, what's he done now?" Leafie trundled after her. I followed the both of them, only to see that it wasn't Elmer junior who was the cause of the commotion this time. Elmer senior was with Deputy Patton in the yard, along with another man I didn't know.

"Blast it, Elmer," the deputy hollered. "You know you got to register for the draft."

"I got a family and a farm," Elmer senior hollered back.

"So do lots of other men," replied the deputy. "But the law's the law. Ages twenty-one to thirty-one. I gotta arrest anyone who hasn't signed up."

"I'm thirty-two," Elmer said.

"Says here you were twenty-nine when you registered to vote," said the other man. "Two years ago, in '16."

Deputy Patton let fly a stream of tobacco juice that landed next to Elmer's work boot. "I only went to sixth grade, but even I know twenty-nine plus two equals thirty-one."

"I've got a family. And my wife's still weak after the baby."

"Elmer," Mabel called from the porch.

Elmer turned to face her. "Go inside, Mabel." At that moment, both men slid off their horses and grabbed him.

"Let him go!" Elmer junior came running from the barn, brandishing a hoe. "Let my daddy go!"

"Now, son," said the deputy, "stand back there. We're just going to give your daddy a ride to town."

"Leave him be!" The boy rushed at the men, slashing at the air with his weapon.

"Junior!" both his parents called at the same time.

"Put that down now," ordered his father.

"Papa, don't leave us!" Junior dropped the hoe. "Please!" He reached his arms for his father, now tied, being lifted onto the deputy's horse.

Elmer sat ramrod straight. He didn't take his eyes off Mabel as the horse wheeled and they started off. Junior, hysterical now, ran after him. "Papa! Papa!"

The horses picked up the pace.

"Son!" Mabel called out to him frantically. "Come back. You hear?"

But the boy ran all the faster.

"Junior!" Mabel hurried off the porch and started after him. "Come here."

The distance between him and the horses grew longer and

longer. The men nudged their rides back up the coulee. Junior kept running, wiry arms pumping up and down like tractor pistons. The riders were now out of sight. But still he ran. As he crested the coulee, he stumbled. Must have been a prairie dog hole. He fell hard and rolled down the hill.

His mother caught up to him and cradled him in her arms. He yelped loud enough for us to hear.

"That don't sound good," said Leafie. She hurried toward them. I grabbed her satchel. When she reached Mabel, she knelt down to Junior's level.

"Let Leafie take a look." She spoke in the same tone Karl used when he needed to quiet his horses, Star and Joey. The boy's sobs softened to pitiful hiccups, then spiked again to shrieks as Leafie felt his arm.

"Broken," she said quietly. I gave her everything she asked for out of her satchel, and soon she had the arm splinted.

Mabel kept stroking her son's hair. "You are so brave," she said.

"But I didn't stop them." He sniffled. "They took Papa away."

"It will be all right." She bent to kiss his head. "Your father will be so proud of you."

Junior wiped his nose on his sleeve. "Mama, how long will he be gone?"

She and Leafie exchanged a look. Leafie squeezed Mabel's arm. "Why, you won't even have time to miss him, he'll be home that quick," Leafie said brightly. "How do you feel about taffy?" she asked. "Because I have a wonderful idea. Why don't you and I make a batch while Hattie here and your mother go see Reverend Schatz?"

I couldn't believe what I was hearing. I hardly knew Mabel. And I sure didn't want to get mixed up in this. If Elmer was supposed to register—

Mabel wiped her hands on her apron. "There's no need to trouble Miss Brooks."

Leafie looked at me. Hard.

I took in Mabel, how thin she was. Skin the color of wet muslin. "It'd be no trouble."

Junior held up his splinted arm. "How can I help with this?" he said.

"Why," said Leafie, "you can be the supervisor. Most important job of all."

The boy turned his head and stared off in the direction the deputy had taken his father. He sat that way for several moments. "Okay," he said, standing up. "Papa likes peppermint taffy. Let's make that kind."

"That's the ticket." Leafie brushed herself off, and I helped her to her feet.

Several hours later, Mabel and I returned. Reverend Schatz would see about raising money for Elmer's bond. "We should have him out of jail by tomorrow," he had promised.

We sat with Mabel over another pot of coffee, then Leafie and I gathered our things to make our way over to Perilee's. I wish I had thought to speak the words that Leafie did as we left. "No matter what," she said, picking up her satchel, "you got friends here. Friends help each other. You remember that."

Mabel nodded, then turned to go inside.

All I could think of on that walk to Perilee's were the

185

puffed-up words of my latest installment to Mr. Miltenberger's paper. I'd been inspired after reading a particularly gruesome report about Hun atrocities. *Every man must do his duty*, I'd written. *What is the small sacrifice of leaving one's family? Think of those Belgian babies and starving Frenchmen.* It seemed so easy to tell nameless, faceless men to march off to war. But to tell Elmer Ren, with a sick wife and too many children and his life tied up in 320 acres of Montana prairie, that he must leave all behind . . . that was a different story.

"It's no fun to beat you." Rooster Jim put my king in check. "You didn't even try."

"Sorry, Jim." Chess was the last thing on my mind these days. I'd heard little Elmer's arm was healing and his father's bail had been raised. That was small comfort in light of the daily reports of troubling news. Three railroad workers had been thrown in jail for mocking a Liberty Bond poster, and a woman had been fined for sending twenty dollars to her mother in Germany. It'd gotten so that Karl rarely left their farm. Seemed as if folks were seeing German spies and seditionists under every patch of buffalo grass. As if these worries were not enough, there hadn't been a drop of rain all month. I looked at my neighbor across the chessboard. "I guess this heat's wearing on me." I sipped at my iced tea. "The crops need some rain."

"Story of life out here," he said, tipping back in his chair. "There's always plenty of what you don't need. That's why folks call this next-year country. 'Cause next year, things will be better." He rocked forward, landing the chair on all four legs. "Wait until summer. *Hot* ain't the word for it. My pa used to say that hell would be a holiday for someone from eastern Montana."

Another week passed after Jim's visit and still not a drop of rain. There'd been several more reports around town of people being accused of sedition. I couldn't help but notice that most of the names of those being arrested or fined were German. And the paper was full of little notices like the one I'd just read: "Algot and Gudrun Solomonson were in the city on Monday to show their loyalty to their country by starting their son, Otto, off with a dollar's worth of Thrift Stamps. Follow their fine example and teach your own young ones two great lessons—that of self-denial and of patriotism." I had to wonder if there were Liberty Bonds and War Stamps enough for any Germans living here to prove their loyalty.

These thoughts dropped on top of the hillock of crop worries in my heart. I'd been walking through the fields kicking up dust all day. Each dusty puff added to the all-too-familiar gnawing pain in my stomach. Every farmer I knew was dosing liberally with bicarbonate of soda to ease the same pain in their own stomachs. If we didn't get some rain soon . . .

I bent to yank up another bunch of cheatgrass. I'd been at it all day. Bushels full of that sneaky weed stood as testament to my labors. The jug of water I'd brought out had been drained dry hours before. Common sense told me to walk back and refill it at the pump. But the next patch of cheatgrass mocked me. *We'll beat you yet,* it seemed to say. I'd go in soon for a break and some water. I breathed deeply, stretched, and bent down again, ignoring the thumping under my skull.

My bonnet was a feeble shield against this sun. Haloes of light glowed at the edges of my vision, and my hands began to shake. I breathed again to clear my head. Perhaps I should go back for a bit. Yes. Back to the house. Out of the sun. I staggered forward. My house wavered like a mirage across the field. Was I really headed toward it? My legs buckled, and I fell face first in a row of flax.

"Miss Brooks?" a male voice called from far away. "Hattie?" I felt a cool cloth being placed on my forehead.

"I'm . . . all right." If I kept my eyes closed and lay perfectly still, that is.

"Sip this." Strong arms tilted my head upward, and cool water slipped down my aching throat. I opened my eyes. And looked into Traft Martin's face.

"How . . ." I scrambled to sit up, but another wave of bile forced me down.

"I saw you fall." He set the cup down. "Must have been heatstroke."

I shook my head. Ouch. That hurt. "No. Stubbornness."

He smiled. His nice smile. "I've made up some vinegar water here. It'll take the heat out of that burn."

I looked at my arms, took the cloth he offered to me, and dabbed at my arms. "Thank you," I said.

"I'm glad I saw you," he said. "Hate to think of you passed out there all night."

A shiver ran through me at the thought. "I'm glad you saw me, too."

"Are you feeling better?"

I nodded.

"Can I fix you something to eat before I go?" He looked around the room. "Or some tea?"

"Tea would be nice," I said, closing my eyes. Wait till Leafie and Perilee heard who had played nursemaid for me.

Traft let me rest—I may have dozed off—while the water boiled and he made tea. "Here you go." I shifted up in the bed, leaned my back against the wall, and took the mug.

"Hope you don't mind me fixing a cup for myself," he said.

"Of course not." I was surprised. Not many of the men I knew drank tea. They mostly guzzled coffee. "What brought you out here, anyway?" I sipped the tea.

He smiled that movie star smile of his. "Besides rescuing damsels in distress?" he asked.

I felt my face color. It was no doubt as red as my arms.

"I was actually riding out to see you. With a business proposition." He blew on his tea. "This is probably not the time. . . ."

I rested the cup in my lap. "No time like the present, they say."

He nodded, then took a careful sip of tea. "I'll get to the point." He stared ahead with glazed eyes, as if looking out into the future. "I plan to grow the Tipped M Ranch into something big. Bigger than the Circle Ranch ever was." He turned back to face me. "Maybe even bigger than that ranch they always talk about in Texas."

His eyes did glow with some kind of vision of the future. "That sounds quite ambitious," I said.

There must have been a question in my voice. "And you

wonder why in tarnation I'm going on about this to you," he said.

"Not in those words exactly."

"Here's my proposition. Your three hundred twenty acres butt up against the southwest corner of the Triple M. Even if you get something out of your crops this year"—he jerked his head in indication of the parched fields outside—"what will it be like next year? And the year after?"

"I—" Truth was, I'd been so focused on making it to November, I hadn't allowed myself to think down the road much farther than that.

"I'm prepared to loan you eight hundred dollars so you can be done with the whole homestead headache." He leaned toward me. "You take that eight hundred dollars and commute your claim. No more fences. No more backbreaking work."

"I'm not much for borrowing money," I said.

"Here's the beauty of it." He set his cup down. "You don't have to! You take four hundred dollars to Ebgard and pay off the claim. It's yours, right and proper. Then you come back and I forgive the loan."

"I don't understand." I shook my head. The numbers were flying too fast and furious. "Why would you do that?"

"Because you'd turn over the land to me." His eyes shone brightly. "You'd be free of this millstone around your neck and ahead four hundred bucks to boot."

"I'd give you my land?"

"No, you'd sell it."

"Why?" This was hard to follow with a throbbing head. "I mean, why do you want this land?"

190

"I told you." He sounded impatient. "So I can run cattle here."

"But my farm, my house . . ."

"For four hundred dollars, you could buy yourself a sweet little house in town. Any town, for that matter. You wouldn't have to work like a railroad man anymore."

"Move off my claim?" The words were finally sinking in. "You'd run cattle over my land?"

"Well, not to put too fine a point on it . . ." He cleared his throat. "It would be my land. The Tipped M's land."

I fought down the hot anger boiling up in my stomach. There was something to consider in his offer, after all. This farm was hard work; I was whittled down at least two sizes what with all the chores and hauling and carrying. And not even the rosiest glasses could make my crop situation look good. There were harvest expenses staring me in the face, along with trying to finish repaying Uncle Chester's IOU. With Traft's offer, I could be done with it all and find somewhere else to live. A real house with curtains and proper shelves for my books and actual chairs to sit on, not old lard buckets. I could work for a newspaper, maybe even travel. Or I could settle down somewhere friendly, with neighbors close by on either side, and never move anywhere again. I'd been working so hard to prove up, I'd never even let myself dream about the kind of life I might really want to live. Traft's offer was fair, even generous. It made a lot of sense. "Your offer is reasonable," I said.

"I think so." He ran a hand through his wavy hair.

"But I must say no."

"Why on earth?"

"I doubt I could explain it to you." I shook my head. "I can barely explain it to myself." A hot breeze carried the sweet scent of prairie grass through the open door. "But I do appreciate the offer." I stuck out my hand to shake.

Traft stood up so fast the chair tipped over. He grabbed his hat and clomped it back on his head. "Hattie, you're making a very bad decision. Exactly like your decision to be so friendly with people you shouldn't." A muscle twitched under his jawbone on the left side of his face. He was angry. How angry, I hoped I'd never find out. "Perhaps you will change your mind after harvest."

I softened my voice. "Perhaps."

He moved to the door.

"Thank you," I said.

"What?"

"For bringing me inside." I held up my burnt arms. "For taking care of me."

He stormed out the door. I could hear the saddle squeak as he swung up onto Trouble and rode off.

I hugged my knees to my chest, praying I'd done the right thing. Praying I hadn't bitten off far more than I could chew.

CHAPTER 16

THE ARLINGTON NEWS

Honyocker's Homily ~
A Stitch in Time

My high school teacher, Miss Simpson, would approve of the lessons this new life is teaching me, even if very few of them are from a book. My domestic skills are much improved—out of necessity. While I will never give my neighbor Perilee any competition in the baking department, my cooking is downright edible. And, if I may say so without boasting, I can handle a quilting needle with the best of them. The quiet nights here give a person space to think. And I love to think about new quilt patterns. When I first arrived, I thought this country flat and dull. Now, I see each roll and dip, each cutbank and coulee, through fond eyes. This landscape cries out to be captured in a quilt.

Before I tackle a new project, however, I must finish the quilt started for a soon-to-arrive new resident. Back home, in Arlington, women relied on Dr. Tupper; here they rely on Leafie Purvis.

"Did you read the paper?" I'd reached the end of my thread so took a few locking stitches. Aunt Ivy would finally be proud of me. No sloppy work here. No relying on knots to fasten my tiny quilt stitches into place. "What do you make of Wheatless June?" I trimmed off the excess thread.

Perilee took another stitch. "As if it hasn't been hard enough already, with all the other food rules." She sighed. "Never thought I'd miss plain old bread."

"You have such a knack with substitutions." I paused to take a bite of the corn muffin on my plate. "I could eat these forever."

Perilee looked up from the quilt and scrunched her face. "Ugh. I can't hardly stand the smell of cornbread anymore."

I snipped a length of quilting thread from the spool. Perilee did look a little green. Talking about food probably wasn't the wisest. Leafie had taken me aside and told me about what it'd be like for Perilee right before the baby was born: "She'll be like a hen, wanting to nest but not much interested in food or drink." I was to encourage Perilee to eat to keep up her strength. Leafie had also given me a few tips on what to do when the baby came, but I didn't listen very carefully. Didn't need to. Karl was going to go for Leafie at the first sign of a baby. I knew to put newspapers under the sheet and to tie off the cord with string. "No more lessons," I'd finally begged Leafie. "Or I'll never want to go through this myself." Leafie had clucked at me, sounding like Rose.

I decided to change the subject. "So, here I am working my fingers to the bone for this baby." At that, Perilee patted her rounded belly. "Are you ever going to tell me what you're thinking about naming him?"

"Or her," said Perilee with a smile.

"Or her," I said.

Perilee shook her head. "We keep going back and forth. If it's a boy, I want to name it after Karl, and if it's a girl, after his mother, Charlotta."

I nodded and rethreaded my needle.

"But she'd be Lottie for short," added Perilee.

"That's real sweet." I went back to quilting. Prick the fabric, tug the needle and thread through, and pull. Prick, tug, pull.

"Karl won't have it." Perilee bit the thread between her teeth. "Says such names are asking for trouble these days."

I thought about it. Folks were wound tighter than a roll of

chicken wire lately. Besides the fuss with Elmer and others, Traft and his pals were going around pressing folks to join the Montana Loyalty League. "Good way to hunt the Huns right here at home," I'd overheard Traft badgering Pa Schillinger. He didn't say anything to me, though. He knew I'd already received an invitation to join, delivered to me personally.

"Karl might have a point." I tried to keep my voice even. "But maybe for middle names?"

"I suggested that, too. Karl still says no." Perilee leaned back in the chair, hands rubbing the small of her back. "Oof. Too much sitting." She reached for an old hat on the shelf over the stove. "So here's my solution. Everyone gets to put a name in the hat. The one we pull out is what we'll name the baby!"

"That's mighty brave of you," I said.

She grinned. "Don't tell, but I've burned the ones I don't like." She rolled her eyes. "Mattie suggested Mulie and Princess. Chase voted for Long John Silver." She held the hat out to me. "You can put a name in, too," she said.

"For you to toss in the stove?" I teased. "No, thanks." I stretched too. "I better call it a day. I've still got some chores to do at home."

Perilee held up the quilt. We'd bordered the squares with yellow calico. "It sure is pretty. Let's call it our Twinkle Star Quilt," she said, running her hand over the pieced front. "I can't wait till this baby gets here."

"Oh, no," I said. "It can't come till this quilt's done. And I figure we've got a few more weeks."

"Oh, all right." Perilee pretended to pout. "If you say so, I'll wait a few more weeks."

A Perilee promise is usually as solid as an oak, but this turned out to be one she couldn't keep.

I was sound asleep a few nights later when I heard someone banging around in my yard.

"Hattie!" Karl was calling. "Baby coming."

I threw on some clothes. "Don't waste time here. Go get Leafie." Karl nodded and urged Star on. Plug was cranky about taking a late night ride, but once we'd established that there was no going back to the barn, he trotted smartly toward Perilee's place.

Chase met me. "Mama's calling for you," he said. I gave him the reins. Chase's elfin face was pinched with worry. A job might distract him. "How about if you fill up the chip bucket? That would be a help for Leafie, I'm sure." He nodded at my suggestion and went solemnly about his work.

I hurried inside. Fern and Mattie—and Mulie, of course—were snuggled sound asleep in the little bed by the stove. No need to tiptoe around them. Those girls were blessed with the ability to sleep through the stormiest of sidewinders.

Perilee was abed in the back room.

"So, this baby couldn't wait for his quilt to be finished?" I'd brought in a damp cloth and wiped Perilee's brow with it. She took my hand in hers.

"It's coming so fast." Pain crumpled her face, and she moaned softly. She waved for me to close the bedroom door.

"You'll be fine," I assured her. "Leafie will be here pronto." She shook her head. "It's not like the other times."

"I'm right here." I stroked her hair.

"Karl wants this baby so bad." A tear coursed down her cheek.

"And he'll spoil him rotten, we both know that." At my words, she managed a weak smile. Then her smile twisted into a grimace.

"What do you want me to do?" I asked. Perilee struggled to a sitting position and pointed to the small of her back.

"It feels like someone's hammering away back there," she said. "Could you rub it for a while?"

With one knee on the bed, I knelt close and began to knead her back through her flannel nightgown. "Does this help?" She answered with a nod. I rubbed till my arms burned with pain. Finally she said, "Gotta lay down again." I helped her get situated.

"Leafie will want lots of hot water." I paused, my hand on the doorknob. "I'll be right back as soon as I get the kettle filled."

Chase had filled not one but two buckets with chips and had the stove fire roaring. "That's better than I could do," I told him. "Now, can you do one more thing?" I handed him an empty lard bucket. "I need to fill the kettle. I figure it'll take three or four buckets." Before I'd even finished, he was out the door. Soon, the kettle was filled and warming quickly on the stove. When he emptied out the last bucket of water, Chase looked around.

"Now what should I do?" he asked.

I pointed toward the basket I'd brought. "You look in there. I bet you'll find something to keep you busy."

I didn't stay to see his reaction to the copy of *David Copperfield*. Perilee was waiting. One look at her told me things were starting to happen. *Hurry up, Leafie,* I thought.

"Leafie—not coming," Perilee panted out.

"Oh, yes. She's on her way right now." I prayed my words were true.

"Won't . . . make . . . it." Perilee looked up at me. "Get . . . newspapers."

Right then my knees turned to jelly. I eased Perilee off the mattress and slipped several layers of newspapers under the sheets.

What next? Get ready for the baby. There was no fancy bassinet here on the homestead, like the girls fussed over back home in Iowa. I grabbed the willow laundry basket and lined it with some clean blankets. This baby's mattress would be an old feather pillow.

"Hattie!" Perilee cried out. "The baby!"

I ran to Perilee's side. She was panting and pushing, her face chalk white and drenched in sweat.

"Baby!" she repeated.

I had no choice. I stepped to the end of the bed and did the best I could. With a slickery swoosh, a tiny human being slid right into my arms.

"It's a girl!" I cried. Perilee closed her eyes and fell back against the pillows.

With the quilting thread, I tied off the cord and snipped. I knew babies sometimes needed a little whack to get them breathing, but I didn't think I could bring myself to thump this precious little life. Were newborns always this small? She must have been aware that I was all too new at this game, thank goodness.

"Waaah!"

"What a noise for such a tiny thing," I exclaimed. Perilee's eyes were still closed, but she smiled. I wiped the baby down and handed her to her mother. While she and the baby studied each other for the first time, I cleaned up the bed and tended to Perilee as best I could, trying not to be alarmed at the amount of blood. I hoped Leafie would come soon and assure me it was normal.

Despite her size, the baby knew what to do when placed at her mother's breast. She looked even smaller there, next to Perilee.

The bedroom door shot open, and Leafie breezed in. She whacked me on the back. "Looks like you managed fine." She shooed me out of the room and ministered to Perilee. A few minutes later, she called me and Karl back in.

She handed Karl the baby, all expertly swaddled in flannel blankets.

He held her tenderly, bringing her face close to his. *"Mein süsses Kind,"* he murmured. He kissed her gently on the forehead.

"Isn't she a sweet little thing?" Leafie's voice was light, but I saw worry behind her eyes.

"What should I do?" I asked.

"Well, first thing," said Leafie, "you could give new baby Charlotta a big kiss."

I turned to Perilee. "I thought you were going to draw a name out of the hat."

She smiled.

Karl handed the baby to me and went to Perilee.

"Hello, Lottie." I kissed her waxy cheek.

Leafie leaned over the baby and gave me some quiet instructions. "We need to keep this angel warm. Put her in one of the bread pans. Pad it with a blanket first. Then set it on the oven door."

I looked at Leafie. "Do you really mean it?"

She nodded. "I've kept more than one child alive that way."

I followed instructions and kept vigil the whole night. As soon as baby Lottie awoke with her kitten cries, I hurried her in to Perilee. After nursing and a good burping, I'd hurry her right back to the oven. We followed this routine for one solid week. I'd run over after morning chores, then back before dusk. God bless Rooster Jim; he kept my garden weeded and chickens happy that whole week. Finally, Leafie's worried look faded completely.

"I think we're past the worst of it," she said. "Little Miss Lottie seems to be doing just fine."

Perilee perked up, too. "I'm sorry I was such a worrywart," she said one day as I was doing her baking. "I was so frightened something would go wrong." She patted the baby's back as she slept against her shoulder. "I know it's silly, but I thought, well, with the war and everything . . ." She held my gaze. "That Karl wouldn't be allowed his baby."

My arms wearied as I worked the flour into the stiff dough. My heart wearied, too, that Perilee couldn't enjoy the good in her life after so much sorrow. "If God really was in the punishing game, why doesn't he send lightning down on the whole danged County Council of Defense?" My words brought a small smile to Perilee's worried face.

"Or the Kaiser?" she joined in.

"Or Mrs. Martin for wearing that awful yellow silk every other Sunday?" We both began to laugh.

Perilee shifted Lottie to her other shoulder. "Hattie, you are a caution. You'd better watch out for lightning bolts yourself!"

"I know, I know." Pleased to have lifted Perilee's spirits, I shaped the dough into two loaves and a dozen rolls. "Now, what else shall I do?"

"Oh, Hattie, not one thing more." Perilee finished braiding Mattie's hair. "You've done more than a sister would."

I slipped off my apron and hung it by the stove. "If you think you can manage, I might head home for a few days. I've got an installment to write and some weeding to attend to." Truth was, even with Rooster Jim's help, I was swamped under with chores, but I didn't want Perilee to feel bad.

It was too quiet at home, even with Mr. Whiskers' cranky meowing to let me know he didn't appreciate my being gone so long. I felt achy as I weeded my fields and carried water to the garden and fed the chickens, and mucked out Plug's stall. At first, I thought I might be coming down with a summer cold. As I sat to a silent supper all by myself the second night home, I figured out what was wrong. It was not illness but loneliness gnawing at my bones. I missed Mattie's songs, Fern's giggles, the baby's sweet smell, reading to Chase at bedtime, and sitting squashed round the supper table.

I missed my family.

June 18, 1918
Three miles north and west of Vida, Montana

Dear Charlie,

I do understand what you mean when you say you have changed since going to France. You only mention physical changes—and no, I don't believe you've gained twenty pounds! But I can read between the lines and know you've gone through others as well.

I told you that Perilee was going to have a baby. Well, she did, on June 11—a little girl, Charlotta, and I helped deliver her! That may give you some small clue as to the changes I've undergone. When I came out here, I thought only of having a piece of property to call my own. But this hardscrabble place has brought me so much more than that.

I hear from your mother that she is sending you copies of my silly installments for the Arlington News. *Though light in tone, they will help you see that my heart is now planted here, like Rooster Jim's cherry tree.*

Your friend always,
Hattie

CHAPTER 17

June 22, 1918
Three miles north and west of Vida, Montana

Dear Uncle Holt,

You know how Aunt Ivy always says a watched pot never boils? Well, here in Montana, a watched sky never rains. Wayne Robbins and Mr. Gorley talk about the rains of '16 that produced beets the size of basketballs and corn tall enough to tickle a giraffe's chin. No one will break any crop records this year. A favorite farmer expression in these parts is "Next year it will be better." This "next year country" makes for many sleepless nights for this particular farmer.

Rooster Jim brought my mail and paper out to me on Thursday. It'd been awhile since we'd had a game of chess.

"Hey there, Rose," he called out to the hen. "Lucky for you it's been drier than a Baptist saloon." He chuckled at his joke.

"She's taken to wearing water wings when it rains," I said. That made him laugh all the more.

"Hattie, that wit of yours and a nickel would get us a fine cup of coffee."

"Speaking of which, I've got some. Or maybe you'd rather have something cool." I stopped on the steps to my house. "There are oatmeal biscuits to round it out."

"Coffee, then," said Jim. He followed me in and helped me carry the coffee things. It was too hot to sit inside. "This is the life," he said after a vigorous slurp. He nibbled at the biscuit. "Why, Hattie, I believe you've learned to take the lead out of your baking."

I made a face at him. He did love to tease. Even more than Charlie.

"So, you fixing to go to the big meeting over to the school?" He reached for another biscuit.

"What meeting?"

"Oh, tells all about it in your paper there." He nodded toward the house. I'd set my mail inside.

I got up, brought the paper back, and found the article. "June 28, National War Savings Day," I read. "Every man and woman in the United States will be asked to purchase war savings stamps," I set the paper down. "But I already bought a Liberty Bond."

Jim shrugged. "War's an expensive proposition. Don't think the Huns much care about the finances of us folks here on the prairie."

I looked at the paper again. " 'No farmer in ordinary circumstances should be allowed to sign for less than one hundred dollars,' " I read aloud. "Surely we won't be expected to pledge that much. Why, we haven't even got enough money for gasoline for the tractors as it is!"

Rooster Jim shook his head. "With Traft running things, won't none of us have anything in our pockets but moths."

On War Savings Day, the inside of the schoolhouse was hot enough to bake bread. Folks' nerves and wallets were spread thin. But Traft had a group of toughs lining the back of the room. "I'm only following the instructions of the proclamation," he said to the grumbles about waiting afternoon chores. "These pledges don't total up to our allotment yet."

I signed my card, underlining the words "conditioned on crop" in the lower left-hand corner. I handed it to one of Traft's crew seated behind the teacher's desk. He handed it right back to me.

"Pledge is to be no less than a hundred dollars," he said.

I turned the card over in my hand. "Even if I have a good crop, that wouldn't leave me enough to pay all my bills."

The man shifted the wad of chaw in his cheek. "By order of county director Frank L. Houston, each farmer's share is to be one hundred dollars."

My hands trembled as I set the pledge card back down on the desk. "Be that as it may, this is my pledge."

"Everybody's got to make a sacrifice," he pressed.

I would not let myself cry. "This pledge does represent a sacrifice. I am already committed to a fifty-dollar Liberty Bond."

"Seems you need a lesson in patriotism," he sneered. "Maybe you need to be hauled before the judge."

I thought of Elmer Ren and Karl's barn fire and broken fence and bit back any more arguments. I snatched up the pen, made a cross-out, and wrote "$100."

He pretended to tip his hat. "Why, that's mighty generous of you, ma'am." His voice was as slick as lard on a skillet. I gathered up my skirts, pushed through Traft's rowdies and hurried outside. My stomach churned—and so did my temper. I needed some fresh air.

"Hattie! Wait." Leafie came up behind me. "I'm headed to Wolf Point tomorrow. Is there anything you need from the big town?"

"A miracle," I answered.

She smiled. "And what store carries those?"

"Leafie, I don't see how I'm going to make it." I ticked off months on my fingers. "July, August, September, October. Four months to finish the proving-up requirements." I waved my hands apart. "Yes sirree, I'll be a regular land baron as long as I get my crop harvested—"

"Barring hailstorms and grasshoppers," she interjected.

"—sell it for a profit—"

"As long as Congress don't fix the price too low."

"—and have thirty-eight dollars cash in hand to pay the closing fee on my claim," I finished.

"Thirty-seven seventy-five." She grinned. "You've heard

what they say about us homesteaders, haven't you? Most of us are still walking around 'cause we haven't got the money for a funeral."

I smirked. "Very funny." She could afford to joke about this. She owned her land outright. And as long as she could break horses, she'd never worry about money. Not in this horse-crazy country.

She patted my arm. "It'll all work out, Hattie. Don't you worry. Maybe not the way you think it's going to, but it will work out."

"I sure hope you're right."

"Listen, I'm taking Perilee's kids with me to Wolf Point. For the parade. Why don't you come with us?"

"Oh, I'm not in the mood." I brushed a mosquito away from my head.

She tucked her arm through mine. "Come on. It'll do you good." She raised one hand skyward. "Fussing won't make rain, you know."

I pressed my lips together.

"We'll come by early. You can take a turn driving Joey and Star." She nodded. "Nothing like a parade to take your mind off your troubles."

Wolf Point was buzzing. There was little I wanted to celebrate about National War Savings Day, but Fern, Mattie, and Chase didn't need to know that. Let them be children, excited by the prospects of music, marching, and folderol.

We passed by the Glacier Theater as we hunted for the best parade-watching spot. The current feature was *The Kaiser, the Beast of Berlin.* I expected they'd sell plenty of tickets to that one. The streets were lined with people. The children were dressed in their Sunday best, and I, in a flight of patriotism, had tied a red, white, and blue ribbon to my best hat.

Leafie gave Chase fifteen cents to buy three paper flags. Holding a toddling Fern with my right hand and a giddy Mattie with my left, I found a prime viewing spot on the boardwalk in front of Hanson's Cash Grocery.

"Here, girls." Chase handed his sisters their flags.

The Citizens National Bank of Wolf Point passed out fans with a slogan printed on one side: *Come across or the Kaiser will.* I was given one and used it, gladly. Each day seemed hotter and drier than the day before. Though I didn't own a thermometer, Karl had kept me apprised of the temperature. "Five days, ninety-five degrees," he said with a worried shake of the head. Even Mr. Gorley was gloomy: "Wheat's going to roast right on the stalk."

The heat was a standard topic of conversation.

"Hot enough for you?" asked Leafie, her red face peeking out from under a battered old bonnet.

"Got any eggs?" asked Rooster Jim, all spruced up in mostly clean clothes. "We could fry 'em right here on the steps."

"I've got some ice-cold sarsaparilla inside," said Mr. Hanson. "Come on in after the parade and help yourself. My treat." He tickled Fern under the chin and patted Mattie's curls. Then he handed me three crepe paper flowers, one red, one white, one blue.

"Look!" Chase tugged on my skirt. "Here comes the first band!"

Though they kicked up more dust than proper notes, the Circle town band was warmly welcomed by the crowd. A ripple of applause turned to a roar as they began to play "God Bless America."

I caught Leafie wiping her eyes, and I felt mine well up, too. It wasn't only the majestic music that tripped up my emotions. My mind filled up like a pretty girl's dance card. There was Charlie—whose last letter had been too long ago—sticking his sweet neck out on my behalf. Then there were Perilee and Karl. I could never have found better friends—a better family—than them. But what would Charlie think of my being friends with them? Did being born in Germany make Karl any less my friend? This puzzle made my head spin. Actually, it was no puzzle to me anymore. But thinking how to explain it to Charlie—that was the tangle.

The wind picked up around me, whirling my thoughts even faster. As if war worries weren't enough, what about money? I'd gone over and over my ledger. Even if I had a bumper crop, I didn't see how I was going to squeeze by. And that was before I pledged for those darn war stamps. I wouldn't even let myself think about not making it, about failing to prove up. My stomach churned with the worry, the heat, the uncertainty. Maybe it was too much to ask to have a place of my own; maybe I was always going to be Hattie Here-and-There.

Mattie reached for my hand and squeezed it, *one-two-*

three. As I squeezed back, those worries slipped right out of my fingertips. Would I trade any of my troubles to be back in Iowa, never having known this sweet little girl and her family? That was one answer I was certain of.

The hot, dry wind swept away the last notes of the song. Men replaced their hats as the band launched into their next number. They marched on, followed by the Fort Peck Livery and Sale Barn wagon, all decked out in red, white, and blue bunting. Mrs. Martin sat in the back of the wagon, a tribute to Mother Liberty. Next came two automobiles wearing bunting for Pipal's Garage and Service Station.

"Those are Luvernes," exclaimed Chase. "The newest thing." Not to be outdone, the Fuller Motor Company entered a fancy rig. "Touring car," said Chase in a dismissive tone. Touring cars were evidently old hat.

Behind the autos came the County Council of Defense, all mounted on Tipped M horses. Traft touched the brim of his hat as he passed me. I didn't acknowledge the gesture. Behind the riders, the Methodist church staged a patriotic tableau, and then the children of the Wolf Creek School—minus their star pupil, Chase—marched, adorned with blue sashes and singing "Over There." As my charges waved their flags in approval, a gust of wind snaked down the street.

Fern's flag flew out of her hand. "Fwag!" she cried, toddling toward the steps.

"Oh, careful, honey." I pulled her back. "You might get trampled!"

"Fwag! Fwag!" Plump tears rolled down her plumper cheeks.

"There, there," said Mr. Hanson. "None of that." He reached into his pocket and pulled out three pieces of ribbon-striped stick candy. "Hold on to this for a while," he told Fern. He gave a stick apiece to Chase and Mattie and then unwrapped the last one for Fern.

"What do you children say?" I asked.

"Thank you, Mr. Hanson!" Mattie and Chase chimed together. Fern flashed a juicy baby smile around her treat. Mr. Hanson laughed. "A sweet helps any hurt, don't it, Fern?" She kept working on her stick candy.

At the very tag end of the parade came Mr. Cogswell's delivery wagon, its sides adorned with hand-painted signs proclaiming "National War Savings Day Parade." Unable to resist this ripe opportunity for promotion, Mr. Cogswell had also tacked a smaller banner across the back of the wagon, advertising "Fresh Cherries at Cogswell's. Best price in town."

Mr. Hanson catcalled good-naturedly when he saw that. "Come on, children." He took Mattie by the hand. "Let's get something cool in you." Chase followed, and some of the other children from around town did, too.

"Go on ahead," I said to the children, handing Fern to Leafie. "Now that the parade's over, I can retrieve her flag."

"Better hurry," said Leafie, smashing her hat tight to her head. "With this wind, it'll be blown clear over to North Dakota in no time."

I scampered down the stairs from the sidewalk to the street. Fern's little flag had not escaped being trampled by the parade's participants. I picked up the sad, tattered souvenir, hearing her wails in my head. I didn't want her day to end on

212

tears, so I walked back over to the *Herald* office to buy another flag. What was a nickel, anyway?

A wrangle of male voices caught my attention. Down the way, from where the parade had ended, another parade of sorts was beginning. The leader appeared to be Traft Martin.

The crush stopped next to the land office. Several hulking men shouldered their way inside. Soon they were back, pushing a slim man with glasses out ahead of them. It was Mr. Ebgard.

"Word has it, Ebgard, that you haven't been doing your share to support the war effort," growled a man I didn't know.

"Seems mighty unpatriotic of you," said someone else. "Maybe with a name like Ebgard, you're hoping the Kaiser wins."

A tall man stepped forward, towering over the much smaller Mr. Ebgard. "Perhaps you forgot how many boys from Wolf Point are over there—"

"And Circle and Vida," called other voices in the ever-growing crowd.

"From all over around here, boys we grew up with . . ." The tall man's next words were nearly drowned out in cries and shouts. "Seems you'd be thinking of them instead of some foreigners."

I pressed up against a storefront, close enough to Mr. Ebgard to see sweat beaded up on his nose and forehead. His glasses were askew. He straightened them. "I have done nothing wrong," he said quietly.

"Nothing wrong?" Traft Martin spoke up, looking at the

213

gathered men. "Why weren't you watching the parade? And what about writing that letter to the governor? In support of that preacher over to Brockway?"

"His church is mostly immigrants. They can't understand him if he preaches in English." Mr. Ebgard's voice was calm.

"That's the language of loyal Americans." Traft took one step closer to Mr. Ebgard. I could see veins popping out on either side of Traft's neck. Rivulets of sweat rolled in icy streams down my spine.

"Tell you what we'll do, Ebgard." Traft spat out the name. "You can prove your loyalty here and now. Fred?"

The tall man—Fred—pulled out a small American flag. He waved it under Mr. Ebgard's nose.

"You love this country?" asked Traft.

"You know I do." Mr. Ebgard's chin quivered slightly, but his voice was strong and clear.

Fred backed up the street, almost to Erickson's Hotel. Traft pointed toward him. "Then prove it. You get down on your hands and knees and crawl before your flag." He stepped closer to Mr. Ebgard. "And when you get there, you kiss it. You hear me?"

The crush of men closed in on him. I wobbled like a newly dropped calf, overcome with the smell of sweat. And fear. And pure meanness.

Step forward, I told myself. *Make them stop.*

The men continued with their vicious prank. Someone pushed Mr. Ebgard, hard. He fell to his knees. His glasses flew toward me.

"Start crawling," Traft ordered.

Dread and disbelief turned me into a statue. I watched Mr. Ebgard struggle to his feet. His jacket sleeve was torn out of the shoulder seam, and his pants were filthy with horse droppings.

Do something! My brain cried out the orders, but my legs refused. I couldn't take my eyes from the horrifying scene.

Someone kicked Mr. Ebgard. He fell to the ground face first. Blood trickled from his nose.

I glanced around. Why wasn't anyone stopping this? A wave of nausea swept over me as it had that day I fainted in the field. There was no "anyone" at a time like this. There was only me.

"Traft." I could hardly get the name past my trembling lips. I tried again. "Traft!"

Startled, he turned.

"Go on home, missy," one of the men called.

I took a baby step forward. Thank God my legs held. "I— I—" What could I say to these men? "I have business with Mr. Ebgard." Another baby step forward. And another. I bent to pick Mr. Ebgard's glasses up out of the dust. "A legal matter." With trembling hands, I returned his glasses to him. "I'm sorry I'm late."

Mr. Ebgard rose and slipped them back on his face. "Won't you step into my office?" I took his arm—to steady myself.

A hand grabbed my shoulder. "What do you think you're doing?" I didn't recognize the voice, but I refused to turn. My

215

stomach churned; I could taste bile in my throat. I steeled myself against the blows that were sure to come.

"We've nothing against her." That voice I did recognize. It was Traft's. "Let her be," he said.

The stranger released me with a jerk, spinning me away from Mr. Ebgard.

"You're all a bunch of traitors," the stranger said. But most of the men began to ease away, as if they'd suddenly found other business in town. Fred and his flag were nowhere to be seen. Traft stared at me, then opened his mouth as if to say something more. He shook his head and walked away.

I made it into Mr. Ebgard's office before I collapsed, slumping into the nearest chair. "I feel . . ." I swallowed hard. "Sick."

Mr. Ebgard rummaged in the cabinet behind his desk. He pulled out a bottle and two glasses. He poured something into each one. "Drink this."

The liquid burned down my throat. After one sip, I set the glass on the desk. "That was horrible," I said. "Those men—"

Mr. Ebgard set his glass down, too. His hand trembled as he dabbed at his mouth with a handkerchief.

"They all look so normal." I couldn't express what was roiling around inside me. "Like neighbors."

He poured himself another shot. "Some of them were. My neighbors."

"I don't understand." My arms, legs, head, everything was heavy. Too heavy to move.

He lifted his glass to his lips, started to sip, then put the glass down. "It's the war."

I placed my palms on the desk, breathing deeply. "Did the war burn Karl's barn?" I said slowly. "Break little Elmer's arm? Change you into a criminal?"

"No." He sat heavily in a chair. "No. But this evil is so big. The fight has spread far beyond the battlefield. It's to the point that anything—even writing a letter on behalf of a pastor and his flock—can be seen as treason."

Mr. Ebgard's voice was calmer; I noticed my hands had stopped shaking. "I'd better get back to Leafie and the children. They'll wonder." I stood slowly, testing my legs. They wobbled as they had that day on the train, during the fat man's tirade. But they held.

"You are a brave girl." Mr. Ebgard patted my arm. "A brave girl."

I looked at his scraped and bruised face. "You might want to clean up before you head home," I said. "Good day, Mr. Ebgard."

"Good day, Miss Brooks." He opened the door and glanced outside. "All quiet," he said.

I stepped through the open door, pausing on the walkway to take another deep breath. I paused again before going over to Hanson's Cash Grocery. I tried to clear my mind of what had happened. Clear my mind so it wouldn't show on my face. My legs were barely shaking as I went inside.

"Here." Mr. Hanson handed me a sarsaparilla. "You look like you could stand to wet your whistle."

"Fwag?" asked Fern. Absently I handed her the trampled one.

"Hattie?" Leafie looked at me. I shook my head to keep her from saying anything else.

"Dirty." Fern threw the flag down.

I thought about Traft and the men with him, swarming like enraged wasps. I wiped my eyes. "Yes, it is," I said.

CHAPTER 18

THE ARLINGTON NEWS

Honyocker's Homily ~ Independence Day

Don't think, because we have no fancy bandstands or city parks, that we can't celebrate Independence Day with as much verve as you do in the big city. Folks from all around will gather on the banks of Wolf Creek to picnic, play baseball, and commiserate about the dreadfully dry weather. Though the tone will be light, we will stop at noon to honor our servicemen. And each of us, this writer especially, will pray that the current Allied success at the Battle

"And there'll be vanilla ice cream." Chase had gone on for a full five minutes about the upcoming Fourth of July picnic. "Oh, and the baseball game!"

"It sounds wonderful." I filled another kettle with water from my well and lugged it over to the struggling garden. Thank the Lord for the deep well Uncle Chester had dug. After carrying countless kettlefuls to the green beans that morning, my arms felt as if they would fall right out of my shoulder sockets.

Chase filled a smaller pot and carefully measured the water out over my sunflower. "Mama did this last year," he said. "Planted flowers in coffee cans. She said this year, she planted a baby instead." We both laughed.

As we carried water to my onions and beets and melons and carrots, I thought back to all the gallons of water I'd wasted in my life. Not here! Every drop was put to good use: even my Saturday night bathwater was stretched out, first washing me, then washing the cabin floor, and then washing the dust off the tiny flower garden by the front steps.

I stood and tried to stretch the kinks out of my aching back. "Oof."

"Karl says it's thirty-two days without rain. Mr. Nefzger says it's thirty-one." Chase dipped his hand in the pot, wetted his fingers, and sprinkled his red face with a few drops of water. "I think Karl's right."

220

"I'd bet on Karl, too." I tousled Chase's hair. "If I was the gambling kind."

With Chase's help, my chores were soon done. I sent him home. "We'll be by for you tomorrow, early!" he called over his shoulder. I bustled myself inside, and soon there were four chokecherry pies cooling on the kitchen table—if it were possible to cool in this blamed heat. I'd taken to sleeping on my mattress out in front of the cabin in the last week. There wasn't a breath of air inside at night, even with the door open.

The first night I'd slept outside there was a lot of outside and not much sleeping. It's amazing what you can hear when you're stretched out on the prairie grass. Once the chickens settled, the night birds got to talking. Then there was the rustling grass all night long. I could only wish that rustle was caused by a breeze. But the air was as thick as corn syrup. No, these rustles belonged to the prairie night—pack rats and prairie dogs and who knew what else. Perilee had seen a skunk not long back. The only animal I didn't much worry about was Violet's wolf. There'd been no sign of it since that one winter's day; bounty hunters no doubt had dispatched it, as they had most of the wolves in this part of the country.

The second night I dragged my mattress outside, I was done in from lack of sleep, the heat, and pulling weeds all day. Sleep snatched me up as fast as the hawk I'd seen snatch up a field mouse that day. Though the mattress did little to smooth out the lumps on the ground, it was better than sleeping inside that oven of a house.

Independence Day morning, Mr. Whiskers tickled me awake with a lick of his sandpaper tongue. I patted him, then stretched.

."Ouch." Every night I'd slept out, I'd found some new crick in my neck or back the next morning. I bent stiffly to pick up my mattress, took it back inside, and got myself organized for the day at Wolf Creek. In with the pies and the blanket and the fan from the National War Savings Day parade was something that would no doubt surprise everyone at the picnic.

When I was ready, I added to the letter I'd started to Charlie: *Here Leafie and I were worried about Lottie at first, being so small, but that child is now solid as a tin of lard. I wondered if the other children might have their noses out of joint a bit about the baby, but they all adore her. Mattie nearly mothers her to death! She got it into her head to make Lottie a quilt—"a sister quilt"—so I am helping her. The stitches are uneven but full of love.*

The jingle of harnesses made me set aside the letter, grab my hat, and take one last look around. If I'd forgotten anything, it would have to stay forgotten. I hefted my basket of goodies and stepped out to greet the Muellers.

"Don't you look the picture?" said Perilee. I smiled, noting with approval that there were some cherries in her cheeks. She'd been slow coming back from giving birth to Lottie.

"A picture of a cooked goose, you mean." I climbed up next to her and began to fan myself. "Do you think we'll ever get a breath of breeze again?"

"It'll be cool by the creek," she promised. "Nice and cool." We rode along in companionable silence. It was too hot even to visit.

"Hello there!" Rooster Jim helped the children out of the wagon when we reached the picnic grounds. Mattie ran straight to Leafie to show off Mulie's new sunbonnet. Chase helped Karl settle the horses, then took off with Elmer junior and some of the boys from the Lutheran church to bob for critters at the creek.

"Saved you a spot in the shade." Leafie waved us over. We set out blankets and an apple box for Lottie's bed.

I served up sweet tea, and we chatted with some of the women from church. "Is this everyone?" I asked.

"Nefzgers will be out after they close up the store at noon." Leafie rolled her cool glass against her forehead. "They never miss a baseball game, not even Bub."

I smiled into my iced tea glass. Wait till they saw what Arlington, Iowa, had to offer!

"Grace and Wayne will be along, too," she continued, ticking our neighbors off on her fingers. "The Martins rarely come."

That would suit me fine.

True to Leafie's prediction, the Nefzgers arrived in the early afternoon.

"Ready to play?" Bub called as he drove up in his wagon.

Though there were some good-natured grumbles about the heat, soon enough a field was laid out and players divvied themselves up. It had been a long time since I'd been on a baseball field. Though none of my neighbors knew it, baseball was something I could do. And do well, thanks to Charlie's patient instruction.

I reached into my basket and brought out my surprise.

"Can anyone play?" I asked, slipping my baseball mitt on my right hand.

"What's this?" Gust Trishalt spat juicily in my direction. He'd grumbled a bit earlier about the German folks from the Lutheran church playing. When Wayne pointed out that the name Trishalt sounded German, Gust shook his head. "It's Swiss," he said. "Swiss." I figured he'd fume more about me playing than the Lutherans.

"A willing player," I told him.

Gust hooted at that. " 'Spect you'd better play, then." He thumbed toward young Paul Schillinger. "On t'other team."

I nodded and went to join Paul's team. We would have first ups. Hitting was not my strength, but I managed a serviceable single after Paul's own single. Henry Henshaw hit Paul in with a powerful double. Then Chase came up to bat.

"Bunt!" I hollered. Even in this heat, I was pretty sure I could beat out a bunt and make it home.

But boys will be boys. With two outs, Chase swung for heaven, three times.

"You're out!" called Reverend Tweed.

Chase dropped his bat dejectedly. "I almost had it," he said.

Reverend Tweed patted him on the shoulder. "Better luck next time," he said. "Now, get on out in the field with your team."

Chase took his position in left field. We put all the young ones in the field, figuring they had the energy to actually run

224

after any ball that might find its way out there. Paul took the ball and headed for the pitcher's mound. The first batter he faced was Wayne Robbins.

"See if you can hit this," boasted Paul.

Wayne had a good eye. He connected sweetly and sent the ball sailing. So did the next five batters.

"None away," called Reverend Tweed as yet another batter came to the plate. "Score's five to one."

"Hey, Paul," I called out from third base. "Come here." Paul looked puzzled but came over to see what I had to say. I wish I'd had a camera to capture the expression on his face when I suggested we trade spots.

"But I always pitch," he said.

I pointed to the loaded bases. "This well?"

He shook his head but handed me the ball. I hurried out to the pitcher's mound.

"Now wait a minute," called Gust.

"Mow 'em down, Hattie," Leafie hollered.

Reverend Tweed wiped his face. "Play ball!"

Charlie would've been so tickled to see me strike out the first two batters. Six pitches was all it took.

Then Wayne stepped up to bat again. "Show me your best stuff," he called.

"It's so fast, you won't even be able to see it." Bragging wasn't ladylike, but it was part of the fun of baseball.

"Fast for a girl, maybe," he egged.

That did it! He was getting a snake ball.

I wound up and delivered. The ball spun toward the plate. And Wayne smacked it a good one. It soared over my head and far out into the field. The runners emptied the bases and the game was over. We'd been royally beaten.

"I'm sorry, Paul." I handed the ball back to our captain.

"It's only a game," he said. Then he winked. "I bet you'll get him next time." We shook on it.

"Next time," I said.

"Ice cream's ready," Pa Schillinger announced. It was just the thing atop a slice of my chokecherry pie, even if I do say so myself.

We visited and ate. Perilee and I walked down by the creek, shedding shoes and stockings to cool our feet. We filled our lunch baskets with wild plums from a tree at the creek bank, then rejoined the others and visited some more. Pa Schillinger was the first to pack up. "Evening chores," he explained.

"We best be going, too," said Perilee. I helped her carry the picnic things and tired, dirty children to the wagon.

Mattie screeched when Perilee tried to set her in the back of the wagon. "I wanna sit with Hattie!"

"Okay, sweetie." I took her from her mother and we settled on the wagon seat. Within a few minutes, she was sound asleep, her little body a hot water bottle on my lap. The front of my dress was drenched in perspiration.

As we neared the trail to my place, I eased Mattie onto Perilee's lap. "Drop me here," I told Karl. "I'll cool off as I walk." I kissed the top of Mattie's head, fetched my basket from the back, and strolled the rest of the way home. My dress front was nearly dry by the time my house came into view. I sat on the front step, drinking in the sweet scent of the wild plums in the basket on my lap, first enjoying the memory of the lovely day and then thinking about how to end this month's "Honyocker's Homily."

The sound of riders nudged me out of my reverie. Cowboys often rode my way, chasing down the odd Tipped M cow or two. These riders, three of them, appeared to be headed east, toward the Martins'. One rider broke off from the others. He turned his horse—a very large horse—my way.

"Evening, Hattie." I could smell whiskey from where I stood. "You have a nice time at the picnic?"

"I did, Mr. Martin." I stood up and turned to go in. There'd be no sleeping out tonight.

"Hot, isn't it?" He flicked the end of the reins at a mosquito. "Even worse than last summer."

"Yes, it is hot." Surely he hadn't ridden over simply to discuss the weather.

"Of course, last year we had the grasshoppers, too." Traft shifted in the saddle. "One minute the sky was as clear as Wolf Creek." He paused to look up, studying the twilight sky. "Next it was dark as night and thick with grasshoppers."

I shivered.

"Gorley's wheat was gone in minutes." Traft shook his head in an exaggerated display of sympathy. "Robbins' too. The flax was next. They didn't have enough of a crop left to cover seed money." He snorted a rough laugh. "Course, it wasn't only crops they got. I left my good jacket hanging on the fence post. Danged if those hoppers didn't munch their way through that, too."

"What is your point, Mr. Martin?" There was a point, of course. And tingles down my spine made me certain it wasn't a good point.

"Trying to get your attention," he said. He slipped off his horse. "That's all."

Crackling prairie noises carried softly on the air. I strained my ears over them to listen for the clicking of grasshopper legs and wings.

"Well, you have it."

He took a few steps toward me. "This is a hard life," he said in a gentler voice.

I had to laugh. "Stop the presses!"

"Hattie." He paused for a moment. "We got off on the wrong foot somehow."

"Wrong foot?" The levity was short-lived. "You call setting a man's barn on fire the wrong foot? Leading a mob against Mr. Ebgard the wrong foot?" I slapped my palms against my skirt in anger.

He reached me in one stride, grabbed my arm, and shook it so hard, plums went flying from my basket. "I want you to listen to me. To finish what I started to say once."

Was I getting used to his bullying ways? My legs didn't wobble one bit. I eyed his hand, and he turned me loose.

"I didn't set the fire at Karl's. By the time I heard about it, it was too late to stop them. And don't ask me who it was." He turned his hands up in a gesture of surrender. "But I was able to drag the burning bundle away from your barn before it went, too."

"What?" He'd been trying to save my barn, not burn it?

"And that thing with Ebgard. It did get out of hand, I admit." He shook his head, then cursed. "There's laws that say we got to support this country, this war. And when folks like Ebgard dodge their duty—"

"You have a nerve," I snapped. "Dodging his duty? What about yours? There you stand safe and sound while people like Elmer and—and—" I wouldn't even mention Charlie's name to this man. "Countless others go off to fight."

Traft reacted as if I'd whipped him. "You're right. That's what they all think. That I'm shirking my real duty." He rubbed his forehead. "I didn't wait to get drafted like some. I enlisted."

"Then why are you still here?"

"Same thing I wondered a dozen times over." He reached down and picked up one of the wild plums he'd jarred from my basket. "Then I found out. Mother finagled the governor to appoint me to the Council of Defense. The draft board said that could be my service." He rolled the plum in his hand, then cocked back his arm and fired the fruit off into the night.

The look on Traft's face was all too familiar. I'd seen it on my own face countless times while I lived with Aunt Ivy. I felt as if the final piece of a crazy quilt had just been stitched in place. This was one angry man. Angry at his mother, yes. But no doubt angrier at himself for letting someone else run his life. A thought presented itself to me— an understanding thought. Traft and I had that in common. Before coming out here, I hadn't much say in my own life either.

I couldn't help myself; in that moment, I granted Traft forgiveness for the ugly actions his bitterness had led him to. "I am sorry," I said, "for your troubles." *Do this unto the least of these,* the Bible taught. I could almost feel the star being added to my heavenly crown for this gesture.

He turned to face me. "You see, then, why I need your land."

"What?" My crown slipped. "No, I mean, I'm sorry for your troubles, but that doesn't mean—"

"Is it that fellow you write all them letters to?" Traft's eyes bored into me. "Are you working the place for him?"

"Charlie?" This conversation zigged and zagged like the rickrack on Mattie's dress. "Traft, I do thank you for saving my barn. And for attempting to save Karl's. But this conversation is over."

"You won't sell?" It was dark enough now that I couldn't see his face clearly, but the tone of his voice oozed barely controlled anger.

For some strange reason, Aunt Ivy's voice came to me at that moment. *A proper young woman turns down at least two proposals before accepting one,* she'd told me once. She'd been speaking of marriage proposals, of course, but I decided to take her advice anyway. "No," I said, turning down his offer to buy my land for a second time. "Good night, Traft." I strode up my two rickety steps with as much pride as I could summon. I turned as I opened the door, but he was already astride Trouble, wheeling the big horse around. They thundered out of my yard.

That wasn't the only thunder I heard that night. The skies

opened up and rain—glorious rain—quenched the dust-dry prairie.

Listening to the patter on my roof, I sat myself down and wrote the conclusion to my July "Honyocker's Homily":

> My uncle's hero is Abraham Lincoln, surely the ultimate symbol of independence. One of the stories I love best about Lincoln is that after his election to office, he appointed some of his bitterest enemies to his cabinet. It seems then, as now, the greatest freedom is found in forgiveness. Let us embrace that element of liberty as we forgive our enemies as we forgive ourselves.

June 15, 1918
Somewhere in France

Dear Hattie,

I've thought of you often lately. How you used to make me laugh, how you used to wind up like a windmill before you threw a ball, how you used to blow at the hair falling across your forehead. A fellow needs to think of pleasant things like that.

I came here thinking I was going to win this war and come on home in no time at all. Now I think I'll never leave this mud and cold and misery.

I know you expect your old pal to be full of humor, but my best buddy died this morning. I was not twenty

231

yards from him. In all the training, they never told us about the smell of death.

For the first time, I was not so confident of coming home. Not so confident of anything. I always bragged about killing some Germans. Killing is nothing to brag about. Nothing at all.

Yours,
Charlie

§ CHAPTER 19 §

THE ARLINGTON NEWS

Honyocker's Homily ~
Reaping What Was Sown

I could now give demonstrations at the state agricultural college on cutting and threshing grain. Plug was joined by his pals Joey and Star, as well as Wayne Robbins' horse, Sage. The foursome was hitched to the binder (by these very hands, after no small effort) and off they went through my wheat field. The flax had already been cut. That had been hard, as I hadn't been ready to give up my own little ocean. For that's what a field of flax in bloom looks like: acres and acres of sea-blue flowers, rippling in the August winds like waves.

Now the horse-pulled machine cut a swathe—literally—through the wheat. A reel feeds the standing grain into the sickle, where it is cut. I do not know for certain what magic is worked inside the binder, but the final product is a tied bundle of grain. These bundles—*shocks* to us farmers—are left standing on the cut end to dry. After my first day of binding, I surveyed my kingdom with no less pleasure than any royal personage. In a few weeks' time, my neighbors will come to help thresh my grain. My grain. Are there any lovelier words in creation? You longtime farmers may laugh at my enthusiasm, but I ask you to think back to your first harvest. I believe you will have to admit to such feelings yourself.

The first weeks of August brought rejuvenating rain. Then the weather turned even hotter. Thanks to help from Karl and Wayne Robbins, we were done binding my fields in a few days. I helped them as they helped me and thus passed the weeks while my grain dried, standing in proud shocks in the field.

The weather may have been good for the grain, but it did nothing for anyone's temper. Even my solid Plug balked when I tried to hitch him up to help at the Robbinses'.

That same night, I went in to fix supper. I set a plate on the table while I tried to think of something to make without cooking. In the few short minutes it took to scrounge up some food, the plate on the table had grown hot to the touch.

After eating, I took the letter I was writing to Uncle Holt and sat on the stoop to finish it. Mr. Whiskers was stretched across the doorjamb, spread out as long as he could be, trying to catch every possible breath of air to cool off. I reached down to scratch his belly, and he didn't even move. *Karl says that with this heat,* I wrote to my uncle, *my grain will be ready to thresh in about two weeks. I'm glad I'm not growing corn—it would pop before I could harvest it!*

Outside, puffs of dust rose up above the coulee. Someone was coming on horseback. Maybe it was Wayne on his way home from hunting; last week, he'd brought me two sage hens.

But it wasn't Sage who trotted into view. This horse bore the Tipped M brand. Sitting atop the range horse was Traft Martin.

"May I get some water for my horse?" he called out, pulling up by the well.

"Certainly." I had no squabble with Trouble, no matter what my feelings might be about his rider.

He pumped some water into the trough. "Things are looking mighty dry around here." He pushed his hat back on his head. "Mighty dry."

"Uh-huh." Hadn't I been lying awake nights, fretting over the very same thing? Once the grain was shocked and standing, there was always the fear of fire.

"You'll be threshing soon?"

"In a few days."

He nodded. "Hear the harvest over to Glendive was a disappointment."

I could see where this was going. "That's Glendive."

He gave a grudging smile. "And not here."

Now I nodded.

He swiped the back of his hand across his forehead and resituated his hat. "It's not too late," he said.

"Too late?" I parroted. "For what?"

"My offer." He hung the cup back up by the pump.

"I really am not interested." I tried to keep my tone even. Why was he pushing this point again? "For the last time, I can't accept your offer."

"That's a big mistake on your part." His green eyes turned gray.

I matched his stare with one of my own. I'd stood up to bullies before. "Perhaps. But it's my mistake to make."

He jerked at Trouble's reins. "So you think." He rode out of the yard. My yard.

For now.

Two days after Traft's visit, Karl and some other neighbors rumbled onto my place to start threshing. In the morning, I worked with the men in the fields. Then Leafie and Perilee came to help me bake for noon dinner. I suspect it was the promise of Perilee's pies—raisin and chokecherry and plum—that kept the crews working steadily. But my biscuits were respectable; Karl ate a half dozen himself.

"Oh, hon, that's only 'cause he needs some way to sop up Leafie's good buffalo berry jelly!" Perilee teased.

The children played around our feet as we washed another stack of plates. Chase was impatient. At eight, he thought himself old enough to help with the harvest.

"No sirree bob." Perilee put her foot down. "Those machines are no place for children." Chase had to content himself with running cold drinks out to the field. He carried water in crockery jugs, wrapped in burlap, and stashed them in shocks to keep them cool. He marked the shocks with a bundle of straw laid crossways on top so the workers could easily find them. Once, after he made a trip out with refilled jugs, I spotted a tiny figure standing on top of the thresher with Karl. I didn't say a word to Perilee.

"Let's sit a minute before we do one more thing." Perilee sat down, fanning herself with her apron. "Besides, Lottie's hungry."

"Oof. It feels like an oven." I poured lemonade for the three of us, and we sat. Leafie had slipped her shoes and stockings off; I did the same.

"What would the Ladies' Aid Society think?" Perilee asked, arching her eyebrows. Then she took off her own footgear and wiggled her bare toes. "Who cares—this is heaven."

We sat quietly, the only sounds the occasional cry of the curlew and Lottie's contented nursing.

"Saw Traft Martin riding this way the other day," Leafie said.

"Well, at least this time he left our fence line alone," said Perilee. She shifted Lottie to her other breast.

"He came by a few weeks ago, too." I rolled the cool glass against my neck. "And it wasn't a social call."

"He try to buy your claim?" asked Leafie. "He had the nerve to ask me to sell awhile back."

I nodded. "He wants to build the Tipped M into something even bigger than the Circle Ranch."

Leafie exhaled hard. "What did you tell him?"

I held up my hands, swollen from the heat, cracked by water and hard work. "I said this life was much too glamorous to ever give up."

Perilee laughed. "Sugar, you are a caution."

Leafie's face grew serious. "You be careful. It's one thing for me to tell him no. He wouldn't mess with me. But—"

"I know. I know." I held up my hand to stop her words from feeding an imagination that had already conjured up what an angry Traft might do. "I'm going to hang on until November."

"You need any help with that hanging on," said Perilee, "you say the word."

"Same on this side of the street," said Leafie. She tipped her head upward. "Lord, look at that sky."

Black clouds rolled over the plains. I recalled my conversation with Traft. "That's not grasshoppers, is it?" My heart throbbed in my throat.

"Don't think so." Leafie pushed herself out of the chair.

"Rain!" Perilee hopped up, too, and began to gather things together. "We better get everything inside. Mattie!" She waved her apron. "You and Fern come on in now."

We got everything—and all the children except Chase—inside just as the sky opened up.

"That's not rain." I had my forehead pressed to my one

238

window. With all the damp bodies, the room was as steamy as if it was wash day.

"Oh, Lord." Leafie's hand flew to her chest. "Hail."

The hard pea-sized pellets quickly turned to stones the size of eggs.

"Chase!" Perilee ran to the door, jerked it open, and screamed his name.

"Don't fret." Leafie pulled her back. "Karl and them have taken cover. Karl wouldn't let anything happen to that boy."

The sky hurled hailstone after hailstone onto my field. Like a pitcher on fire, throwing fastball after fastball, heaven struck me out and good. The cut flax, all neatly windrowed, was the first to be mowed down. Then the wheat, trampled to the ground as if a giant had stomped through. And stomped all over my dreams. I could do nothing but watch and feel my heart break in two. After what felt like hours, the clattering against the roof slowed.

"Looks like it's over," said Leafie.

The door slammed open. Karl, Wayne Robbins, and Chase burst inside.

"Karl!" Perilee rushed to him. Blood dribbled down his forehead.

"Blasted things the size of oranges," said Wayne. "And hard as coal."

While Perilee tended to Karl, I set about making some tea. "Nice and sweet," I said, handing a mug to the shivering Chase. "This will help." I closed my eyes. The tea could warm a frozen boy, but what could help me?

Chase took a shaky sip. "Karl threw me under the trac-tor. All he and Wayne could do was cover their heads with their arms."

The quiet was as powerful as the drum of hail had been moments before. I looked out through the open doorway. My kitchen garden was in shambles. Part of the chicken coop roof slumped against the well pump. Albert and the girls huddled, no worse for the wear, under the coop. The sunflower I'd been nursing along was broken in half, the yellow petals pummeled into the dirt.

I forced myself out the door and toward the fields. Wayne Robbins followed me, shaking his head.

"White reaper, my dad called it," he said as we took in the destruction. "The flax is done, Hattie. But you can save some of the wheat." His voice went down at the end, as if he was trying to convince himself of his own words. "Sell it for feed."

"Feed?" During all my months of ciphering, I had counted on selling my grain to the miller at grain prices, not to the odd farmer as cattle feed.

"You won't be the only one, Hattie." Wayne no doubt meant his words to comfort, but they only added to my wor-ries. How many other fields were destroyed by this hailstorm? There could be dozens of us trying to salvage what we could. How many farmers were there who needed to buy feed? Not as many as would need to sell it, that was certain. Tears burned at my eyes, but I would not let them fall. What good would they be, anyway?

I bucked up and we salvaged. Karl drove the hay wagon, pulled stoically by Joey, Star, Sage, and Plug, through the rav-aged fields. One small section of wheat, on a little dogleg of my land, had escaped the storm. Wayne, Chase, and I wielded pitchforks to lift the bundles there—not nearly enough—onto the wagon. Leafie patiently fed small loads into the thresher. I had laid in a huge store of gunnysacks, hoping to fill them all with the threshed grain. Normally, Karl had said, it would take three men to keep up with the thresher's output, filling the gunnysacks and stitching them with exactly seven stitches before tossing them onto the grain wagon. Today, thanks to the white reaper, Wayne Robbins alone could keep up with the task.

Later, I wrote about it to Charlie: *As I thanked my neighbors at the end of the day, I felt as if I was at a funeral. And in a way it was. A funeral for a dream. How could months of work be destroyed in a few minutes?*

After I finished the letter, I got out the ledger and turned to this month's entry. I had been so smug with Traft the other day. When the hope of a harvest was in sight. Now I totted up numbers this way and that. No matter which way I did the math, I owed more than I'd make. Even with my newspaper money, I'd be in the hole. How was I going to repay the binders? The threshers? Mr. Nefzger for the fence IOU? And the seed? The only bright spot in the whole mess was that I wouldn't have to make payment on the $100 war stamps pledge. And that only made me feel ashamed, not relieved.

I brewed myself a cup of tea. Mr. Whiskers must've sensed how low I was feeling. He hopped up in my lap, purring his comfort and encouragement.

"There's a way." I ran over the numbers one more time. "Besides Traft." I scratched Mr. Whiskers behind the ears. I prayed. I quilted. And prayed some more. No answer came.

As much as I wanted to throw myself a pity party, I couldn't. I did my chores—tried to revive my sad little garden, cleaned the chicken coop, put a pot of beans on to simmer for supper. Mucking out the barn, I saw Uncle Chester's chest. I put down the pitchfork and knelt in front of it, stroking the initials on the front. I leaned over, resting my cheek on the top of the chest, trying to draw comfort from it. Uncle Chester had believed in me. I'd believed in myself.

"I need to know what to do." I fiddled with the latches. "It'd break my heart—and yours—to sell out to Traft." Wiping my eyes, I sat up and opened the trunk. Maybe I'd missed something the first time I'd gone through it. Maybe there was a stash of money in the linings for a time like this. Hadn't he called himself a scoundrel? Didn't scoundrels usually have ill-gotten gains lying around somewhere?

This time I carefully inspected every inch of that chest. I took each item out, one by one, and set it next to me. When everything was out, I felt the lining, hoping to brush a secret trigger as I probed.

There were no secret compartments, no secret stashes, to be found.

It had been foolish even to hope, but desperation will make you believe almost anything. Carefully I replaced the contents in the trunk. As I set an old copy of *The Last of the Mohicans* back inside, I noticed something edged out, beyond the pages. I flipped the book open.

"Oh!" I sat back on my haunches and stared into the photo in my hands. It was of my mother and my father. Mother held a baby in her lap—me. Another man stood back of Mother. I turned the photo over for an explanation. *Me, Katherine, and Raymond with baby Hattie, January 1902.* I stared into the face of that three-month-old infant. So sweet. So happy. So hopeful.

Then I gazed into the faces of my parents. I could almost hear my mother singing to me and feel the tickle of my father's beard against my cheek. I pressed my lips to the picture and held it there for several seconds.

Then I looked at the other man. I knew, from the tight and slanted script on the back, who it was. Uncle Chester.

I studied his face. Was there any hint of disappointment there? Blame? All I could see was a warm and encouraging smile. Maybe even an understanding smile. I carefully tucked the photograph back in the book. The remaining items were returned to the trunk. I closed it up and did the latches.

"Thank you, Uncle Chester," I whispered. Finding that photo today, on my lowest of days, was another one of Uncle Chester's gifts.

I only wish I knew what it meant.

❧ CHAPTER 20 ❧

SEPTEMBER 1918

THE ARLINGTON NEWS

Honyocker's Homily ~
Matters of Age

So much fuss about age! Men can enlist in the service at eighteen but cannot vote until age twenty-one. Women are thought old maids at twenty-four. My time on the prairie has shown me that age has very little to do with one's mental acuity or physical ability. My "old hen" neighbor—her own label for herself—is sought after like a debutante at a grand ball for her horse-training skills. Rooster Jim claims to be "near to sixty" and he puts in days that

would send a younger man straight
to his bed. And the youngsters! Twelve-
year-old girls drive wagons, and
sixteen-year-old boys are left in charge
of farms while their fathers go east
for work. I myself have been under
the able tutelage of a boy just turned
nine; without Chase's wisdom, I might
not have made it through even my
first day as a honyocker. It seems un-
fair not to give credit where credit is
due simply because one lacks a certain
number of candles on one's birthday cake.

Every woman in the county—in the country—probably
spent the same sleepless night I did on September 11. I finally
gave up, got up, and made coffee. Too early even to do my
chores, I drank the coffee black, sitting on my steps, watching
the sky blush the palest pink.

In a few hours, at 7 a.m., Registration Day would start, the
third of the war. President Wilson was calling for thirteen
million men, ages eighteen to forty-five, to enroll. "Let's Finish What We Have Begun," trumpeted the *Herald*. I sipped
my coffee and thought about Mabel Ren. Elmer had already
registered; would he be drafted, leaving her all alone with
those six kids and that big farm? At least their crops were in.

Mrs. Martin had asked for prayers on Sunday for those
about to enlist. Sounded like she couldn't hold Traft back any
longer; he'd probably be the first in line.

My mind brought up a picture of all the men from Vida

who would be registering. I said a prayer for each of them by name, asking that if any of them got drafted, they would all come back to their homes and families. I thought of Charlie's last letter. Perhaps he'd meant it to be light, but the story he related only added to my worries: *I had a job a little out of the ordinary today. Was detailed to guard the target range. That is the target that the aeroplanes practice shooting at. One of the English chaps asked me if I had stood sentry before. On my reply in the negative he said, "Don't worry. The safest place is at the target." Guess he doesn't think much of the pilots' aim!* But at the end of the letter, he had drawn fifteen stars. I knew that meant he'd lost fifteen more comrades.

I had tried to write about my conflicted feelings in the last *Arlington News* installment. Mr. Miltenberger sent it back to me. "Our readers want homestead stories," he wrote, "not philosophy." I'd quickly written up a piece about harvest and dutifully sent that in. The check arrived, so I guessed it passed muster.

I leaned against the door frame. If I was this fatigued from one night's loss of sleep, how did Charlie and the other soldiers feel, wakeful night after night after night?

Fingers of deeper pink stretched across the sky. I couldn't help but watch it turn from rose to red to purple to blue. Etched against that changing and endless sky, I saw an eagle. Its wings spread strong and wide, it flew lazy loops above the prairie. Suddenly it dived down, down, down. Then it rose sharply. Something—a sage hen?—was trapped in its talons. The eagle screamed to announce his success, then flew toward a distant butte. I strained to watch and finally lost it in the rising sun. A Sunday school verse came back to me: *They will soar on wings like eagles, they will run and not grow weary; they will walk and not be faint.* I stood up. Even though I was both weary and faint, I still had a horse to turn out to pasture and morning chores to do. And I would do them on two tired legs, not on eagle's wings.

I was restaking my green beans when I heard a rider approaching. I glanced up, shielding my eyes from the sun with my vine-stained right hand. It was Rooster Jim.

"Come on in and have some coffee." I dropped my hoe and stepped toward him as he trotted Ash into the yard.

He wore an odd expression, one I couldn't read. "This isn't a social visit, Hattie." After he swung down off Ash, he seemed to spend an inordinate amount of time brushing prairie dust from his pants.

"Is something wrong? Is it Perilee?" I wiped my hands on my grimy apron. "The baby?"

"No, no, they're all right." He wrapped Ash's reins around the saddle horn. The silky gray horse nibbled at some clover that was taking over my onions. "Mr. Ebgard wanted me to tell you. Wanted you to know right away."

I edged toward him. "Jim, you'd best tell me right out. And be done with it."

He tugged off his hat. "It's Martin," he said, working his hands around its brim. "He's contested your claim."

"What?" I exhaled hard. "I don't understand. What's that mean?"

"It happens. A couple months ago, Lisa Edwards, over by Cow Creek, got her claim contested by a neighbor. Said she wasn't really living on the place, wasn't fulfilling the residency requirement."

"But I live here," I sputtered. "Have since I came out."

"Well, it's not your living here that Traft's challenging." Rooster Jim ducked his head and spoke to his shoe tops. "It's your age."

A warmth crept up from my chest over my neck to the top of my head. "Age?"

Jim lifted his head. "See, unless you're the head of household, you've gotta be twenty-one to file a claim."

"But Uncle Chester filed—"

"Traft says he had no right to leave you something he didn't really own."

"Is that true?" I rubbed my forehead. "About leaving it to me?"

Jim cleared his throat. "Technically, probably."

My head felt so light, I thought I might faint. "But why?" I asked. Don't know why I did—I knew the answer. Traft couldn't grow the biggest ranch around hemmed in by honyockers like me. He'd probably been cooking this up since I turned him down that first day. Oh, why had I been so smart to him? Maybe if I'd been a little more civil—

"What do I do?"

"Here's how it works. Mr. Ebgard hears the case because he's the closest land official. Traft tried to get him to make a ruling today, but Ebgard said you had the right to be heard, too."

Uncle Chester's letter came back to me: *I trust you've*

248

enough of your mother's backbone. Did I have enough for another fight? "So I have to go to Wolf Point?"

Jim nodded.

"When?"

"Tomorrow."

"But that's no time to—" I stopped myself. To do what? Age five years? I couldn't change the fact that I was sixteen. Well, almost seventeen, come October 28.

"Do you want me to go with you?" Jim asked.

I thought it over. I did. I wanted him and Karl and Perilee and Leafie. All my friends. I wasn't sure I did have enough backbone to face Traft one more time. But I couldn't bear the thought of having my friends watch me lose my claim. And to Traft Martin! "Thanks. But I'll go on in myself."

Rooster Jim patted my shoulder as he left. "However it comes out, you should be real proud of yourself, Hattie. Real proud."

I thought about that as I got ready for bed. What good was being proud when you didn't have a roof of your own to be proud under?

The bell jingled as I entered Mr. Ebgard's office. He hopped right up and found me a chair.

"Afternoon, Mr. Ebgard." I kept my chin up. Helped to hold back the tears.

"I'm real sorry about all this, Hattie." He fussed with some papers on his desk. "Part of the job."

"I know." I lifted my chin another inch. "Shall we get started?"

He sighed. "I expect we'd better."

The bell jingled again. Traft Martin swaggered inside. He made a big show of tipping his hat to me. "Good afternoon, Miss Brooks."

A curt nod was all I would give him.

Mr. Ebgard reached behind him and flipped through his files. He fumbled around so long that Traft began to rock on his feet. "Come on, Ebgard. Can't be that many *B*'s."

A few more moments and Mr. Ebgard pulled out a file. "Let me review my notes."

Traft slammed down on an empty chair. "What's to review?" He jerked his thumb toward me. "She isn't twenty-one. Plain and simple. She admitted as much to witnesses."

I opened my mouth to answer, but Mr. Ebgard interrupted. "When is your next birthday, Miss Brooks?"

"Coming up. End of October. October twenty-eighth."

"Hmmm." Mr. Ebgard scribbled something down.

"Now you can bake her a cake." Traft leaned forward on the chair. "Her birthday isn't the question here. It's her age. Ask her how old she is."

"I'm in charge of this hearing," said Mr. Ebgard. "And you'd best let me run it my way, Mr. Martin, or I will reschedule this hearing for October twenty-ninth."

I couldn't stop my smile. I still wouldn't be old enough on October 29, but I saw what Mr. Ebgard was trying to do.

"Now, Miss Brooks. Will you please tell me where you were born?"

"Oh, for crying out—" Traft slapped his hand on his thigh.

"Your birthplace?" Mr. Ebgard continued calmly. "And year?"

"Arlington, Iowa," I answered. "October twenty-eighth, 1901."

"See!" Traft closed his eyes to do the math. "That makes her sixteen. Nowhere near old enough."

"Who are your parents?" Mr. Ebgard asked.

"Raymond and Katherine Brooks," I answered.

He nodded and made a note.

"But they are no longer living." I touched Mother's watch, pinned to my blouse.

"Oh?" Mr. Ebgard scribbled something else. "So who is your guardian?"

I chewed on my lower lip. "No one, sir. I mean, different folks took me in, but I didn't have anyone official like that."

"No guardian?" Mr. Ebgard's pencil poised above the paper.

"No."

"Would you say your upbringing was different from most girls your age?" he asked.

"Cut this tea party talk and get down to business!"

Mr. Ebgard raised his eyebrow at Traft. "Your upbringing?" he prompted.

I thought about it for a minute. Mr. Ebgard's questions were even beginning to puzzle me. What *did* any of this have to do with my homestead claim? "Well, I guess it was fine. I mean, I didn't have folks to fuss over me like some girls I know." Mildred Powell, for one. If she even got one sniffle, her mother put her to bed and waited on her hand on foot. "I guess I learned to do for myself sooner."

"How much sooner, would you say?"

"How much?" I wrinkled my forehead. Then I smiled. I

251

saw exactly where Mr. Ebgard was headed. I decided to play along. "Oh, five or six years, I'd say." I nodded. "Yes, definitely five or six years."

"Ebgard!" Traft looked ready to explode.

"Five or six years. Hmmm." Mr. Ebgard scribbled furiously on his paper. "Very interesting." He scribbled some more. I glanced over at Traft. He was rolling a cigarette, dropping tobacco on Mr. Ebgard's office floor. The cigarette was finished by the time Mr. Ebgard spoke again.

"Mr. Martin," he began.

Traft shifted in his chair, dropped the cigarette in his pocket and smirked at me.

"Mr. Martin, while the law does specify an age of majority in order to file a homestead claim—"

"Yes, and it's not sixteen!"

"It also provides for the ability for a single woman, head of household, to file. Some might infer that the majority age applies in such a case—"

"Which it does!" Traft jumped up. It looked as if he'd figured out where Mr. Ebgard was going, too.

"I am going to rule that the head-of-household status takes precedence over the age requirement. And, as Miss Brooks has herself explained, her sixteen years are the equivalent of twenty-one years for other girls raised under more fortuitous circumstances." Mr. Ebgard scribbled one final time on the paper. "I find this contestation has no merit."

I fought the urge to throw my arms around Mr. Ebgard's neck. I was so happy, I probably would've squeezed the life out of him. "I get to keep my claim!"

"Well, to be accurate, you may continue to work to prove up on it." He smiled.

"Ebgard, don't be a fool." Traft ran his hand over his face. "We'll see what the Council of Defense has to say about this. You know, she's awful friendly with Karl Mueller. And I've seen her out at the Ren place and—"

"And I know that Miss Brooks has loyally purchased Liberty Bonds and war stamps." Mr. Ebgard was standing now. "At great personal sacrifice. I would be very careful about making any accusations along those lines about her." He leaned forward across the desk.

I thought there might be blows, so I jumped up. "No hard feelings, Mr. Martin?" I stuck out my hand. Traft looked as if he might spit in it. He turned on his heel and slammed out the door.

I held my breath as the window glass in the door rattled, then stilled. I turned to Mr. Ebgard. "I can't thank you enough."

"Nor I you," he said. "Now you go home and do what you need to so I can give you that final certificate come November."

"Give?" I teased. "For thirty-seven seventy-five, you mean."

"I'll take great personal pleasure in taking your cash and in signing my name to your deed." He reached for his hat. "Would you do me the honor of joining me for dinner? My treat."

Where I couldn't have eaten a bite before coming in, I was suddenly starving! "I'd love to." I took his arm and we strolled over to Erickson's Hotel and ate the biggest dinner they served.

❧ CHAPTER 21 ❧

OCTOBER 1918

THE ARLINGTON NEWS

Honyocker's Homily ~
An Ill Wind

The Spanish influenza epidemic has become more than a news item for us here. I will confess that until now, though I have prayed for the many stricken by this plague, the situation only touched me in a superficial way. After all, I don't know those Bostonians or San Franciscans or Kansans who have taken ill; the numbers, though alarming, held no personal arithmetic. But when I learned that Mr. Ballagh, a

baker at Hanson's Cash Grocery and
Bakery, had taken ill and died, my
heart ached. It seems the misfortune of
one can plow a deeper furrow in the
heart than the misfortune of millions.

Rooster Jim brought the news back from one of his trips to
Wolf Point. "The Spanish influenza," he said. "Mr. Hanson
and his whole family are sick with it. Same for the Ebgards."
And I'd heard that Mrs. Martin hadn't left Sarah's bedside in
three days.

Leafie got busy and whipped up huge batches of sagebrush
tea. "This is disgusting!" I spit out my first sip.

"Most stuff that's good for you is," she answered. She set a
big glass jar of the murky tea on my kitchen table. "I want
you to drink every drop of that," she ordered. "I don't know
much about this influenza, but I know sagebrush tea's good
for most of what ails." We shared supper together and then
she left, headed for Perilee's to deliver a jar of tea there.

The next morning, I had two visitors, bright and early.

"Hey, Hattie!" Chase called out. "Guess where we're going?"

"To New York City?"

Chase laughed. "Even better. Karl's letting me ride along
to Richey to pick up the part for the tractor." He hopped out
of the wagon and handed me a strudel Perilee had sent over.
"And don't tell Mama, but we're going to buy her a sideboard
while we're there," he confided. "Karl put some money down
on it last time he was to town." Chase smiled. "Now she'll
have a proper place to put her silver and such."

After I saw them off, I did my chores, then walked over for supper with Perilee and the girls. We quilted awhile on a Flying Geese quilt we'd pieced. It was one of the nicest things we'd done; we planned to enter it in the Dawson County fair next year.

"My eyes are starting to get blurry." I finished up the last of my thread. "I've got to quit. I'll come back tomorrow and we can finish."

Perilee yawned. "I'm bushed myself. What with all the excitement of getting those men off, I think I've worn myself pure out." I kissed Mattie, Fern, and Lottie and walked home.

Plug was stubborn the next morning. I wondered aloud at his behavior. "What is galling you?" Finally I got him fed and turned out. But by the time my chores were done, it was well after noon dinner that I started off for Perilee's. Fall nipped at the air, sending a little shiver through me. I remembered all those days this past summer when I'd craved a fresh breeze. I wasn't going to fuss about a little chill now!

As I walked, I thought about a quilt I'd been wanting to make. *I want to create a new pattern,* I'd written to Charlie, after he wrote to thank me for the Charlie's Propeller quilt. *Something no one has ever done before. One that captures this Montana country.* I had my eye on a piece of soft blue chambray at Mr. Dye's store for the sky and I'd been saving scraps of brown gingham for the prairie. What would I call it? Montana Muddle? I smiled. That would've been a good name for some of the first quilts I made. But my stitching was getting surer and my eye for color stronger. All the Red Cross ladies were asking my opinion now for color combinations for the patchworks they were making to send to the soldiers. Big Sky Star? That sounded real nice. Then it came to me: Hattie's Heartland. I smiled. That was it. I couldn't wait to tell Perilee what I'd cooked up.

As I crested the coulee by Perilee's, I glanced across the prairie. Something didn't look right. It only took a moment to realize what it was. There was no smoke coming out of Perilee's chimney. On this cool day. With a new baby.

My feet flew down the hill.

"Perilee? Mattie?" I pounded on the door. "It's me." There was no answer but a weak mewl, as if from a newborn kitten. I lifted the latch and stepped inside.

"Oh, sweet Jesus." My legs buckled beneath me. Perilee lay on her bed, the baby across her chest. Mattie and Fern were ashen heaps, feverish on the floor. I tossed my shawl aside and moved to the stove, talking all the while.

"I'm here, Perilee. It's Hattie. Everything's going to be all right." I got a fire lit and set a kettle on to boil. They were all burning up with fever, so there was no point in boiling water, but it gave me time to gather my thoughts to figure out what to do. No time to go for Leafie. I was afraid of what might happen while I was gone.

"Baby." Perilee whispered the word and handed Lottie to me. She couldn't have felt hotter if I'd picked her up out of the oven.

"We better get her cooled down," I said. Perilee nodded weakly. She started to say something else, but the effort launched her into a coughing fit. She turned away, but not before I saw she was coughing up awful stuff.

While I drew water for Lottie's bath, I saw the still-full jar of sagebrush tea. "Darn you, Perilee," I said under my breath. It was wretched, but it might have helped. No use fussing now. I poured the tea into a saucepan and set it to warm over the stove.

I stripped the baby out of her sweat-soaked dress and diaper. She cried—hers was the little mewl I'd heard from outside the door. Her tongue was coated white, and her eyelids drooped. "There, there," I cooed, and gently bathed her with the cool well water. It seemed to ease her some. After the bath, I diapered her but left her otherwise bare. I broke some bread into a bowl, poured milk mixed with sagebrush tea over it, and fed her tiny bits. Then I laid her in her bed and ministered to Mattie and Fern.

Fern seemed to perk up some after her bath and nourishment, but not Mattie. A wave of nausea swept over me at the sight of her head lolling this way and that when I put her back to bed.

Perilee fought with me when it was her turn for the treatment. "The girls," she protested hoarsely.

"They've had their turn and now it's yours." I bathed her face and arms and legs with the cool water. Only three small bites of food passed between her lips before she fell into a fitful sleep. She woke only to cough, a miserable gut-wrenching cough, as if she was trying to turn herself inside out. In the kitchen, I took two onions and sliced them thin and began to fry them on the stove. When they were soft and transparent, I mixed them with flour to make a poultice and put the whole mess on Perilee's chest. Aunt Ivy had always said onions were the best thing for drawing out the bad vapors of a cough. I didn't know what else to do.

That poultice brought some quiet. Perilee seemed to sleep, truly sleep, for several hours. During that time, I kept bathing the girls, forcing tea or water or graveyard stew into them.

Fern whimpered at my every ministration, but Mattie didn't say a word. It was as if it took all of her strength to draw in breath after grating breath. No matter how many times I bathed her, her face was hot and flushed.

This was my pattern all through the day and the night and into the next morning. I moved from one to the next, bathing, coaxing, petting, soothing. I was too busy to even pray.

I had finished bathing Mattie once again. She was as limp as Mulie when I nestled her back in her bed.

"Sleep well, Mattie." I stroked her damp hair. "When you get to feeling perkier, I promise to buy you any flavor soda you want!"

A tiny smile flickered across her gray face. I squeezed her hand *one-two-three* in our secret code. She didn't squeeze back.

"Hattie," Perilee called softly from the bedroom. I dragged myself in and helped her use the chamber pot. It was getting harder and harder to keep my eyes open. But it was time to change Lottie and Fern and bathe them again. This time, Fern ate ten bites of toast and milk.

"Good girl!" Funny how such a small thing can cause complete elation. Yawning, I rinsed out the bowl. I had to sit. Just for a minute. The rocker was right there. Oh, it was heaven to be off my feet. For a minute.

I jerked awake. Heart pounding, I flew to check on my charges. Lottie was cooler and sleeping quietly. Fern's color seemed improved, and Perilee was still sound asleep. When I got to Mattie, her lips were as purple as the spring crocus, her skin the color of wet ashes. She was mumbling, calling for Mulie.

"Here she is, sweet, right here." I placed the rag doll in her arms. But she didn't seem to see it. She kept reaching, kept crying out.

"Mama!" she said. And then she was quiet. I picked her up to rock her, her hot tiny body spooned next to mine. I rocked her for several minutes before I realized the awful grating sound had stopped.

"Mattie?" No response. I took her warm hand and squeezed it, *one-two-three.* Nothing.

"Mattie, honey. Wake up." I held her close. *Oh God, don't take this child. Please don't take this child.*

I kept rocking for quite some time. If I kept rocking, it wouldn't be real. Mattie would wake up from this sleep, calling for Mulie and chattering away about the wonderful dreams she'd had. She'd wiggle off my lap and want to play nurse to Mulie, as I'd played nurse to her. She'd sing a warbly lullaby to Fern and Lottie. She'd pat her mother's cheek. She'd do all those things and more if only I kept rocking. Then she'd wake up.

Fern stirred. "Mama," she moaned.

"Shh, shh," I quieted her. "I'm with Mattie now."

Fern's voice woke Lottie and she began to cry. I slowed the rocker. The others needed me. I had to get up again.

Even though she could no longer feel it, I stroked Mattie's forehead. My heart unraveled as I bent to kiss her. Why this sweet child? Oh, why? I stopped the rocker and sat for several minutes more, tears pooling in my eyes, holding that precious body.

"Mama," Fern whimpered.

I stood up and carried Mattie to the parlor. I gently laid our little magpie down on the sofa, Mulie across her chest. Slowly I slid a quilt up over her pudgy toes, over those hands I'd held in mine so many times, and lastly over the top of her brown curls.

"Hattie?" Perilee's weak voice straggled out of the bedroom.

"Coming." I wiped my eyes with my apron. As much as I wanted to have someone share this pain, I knew I could not tell Perilee. Not yet. Not till she was out of the woods herself.

The day passed in a blur of bathing, cleaning, feeding, and forcing that vile tea into Fern, Lottie, and Perilee. I didn't dare sleep. I would not sleep. Only by staying awake could I keep death from visiting this house again.

At breakfast the third day, Leafie came. "I was by your place and the chickens were cussing up a storm to be fed," she said. "Figured you were here."

"It's bad, Leafie." I wanted to fall into her arms and be comforted, as I hadn't been able to comfort Perilee.

Leafie took in the quilt-shrouded body I had placed in the parlor.

"Ah, no. Not our magpie. Our Mattie." She knelt by the sofa for several minutes. "Does Perilee know?"

I nodded, aching with the rawness of that memory. Perilee had been so strangely quiet when I'd told her the bad news. It was as if she'd known it all along, even in her fevered state.

Leafie closed her eyes. I handed her a handkerchief and we stood together, arms around each other's waist, weeping for the senseless loss.

She dabbed her eyes. "We need to bathe her. Dress her." Her voice caught. "What does Perilee want her to wear?" That question started a fresh new flood of tears. But we composed ourselves, and Leafie went to talk with Perilee. She brought back Mattie's Sunday school dress. Then we bathed and dressed her one last time.

As we were finishing, I heard horses. Karl and Chase! I stopped them at the door. "Don't come in. This house is full of the influenza." I could not meet Karl's eyes. "You'd best stay at my place for a while."

Karl nodded. He sent Chase on a pointless errand to the barn. "There is bad news," he said.

I pulled my shawl tighter. "Mattie." It was all I could manage.

Karl covered his eyes with his hands. Then he nodded again and turned away.

The next day, Karl came back with a small, sound coffin he had built himself. October 28, the day I turned seventeen, was now a funeral day.

Perilee was still too ill to move, so Karl, Leafie, Chase, and I would bury our girl.

I had asked Karl to bring my navy dress. And something else. "My flowers are all withered," I said. "Go to Uncle Chester's trunk in the barn. Bring me the crepe paper flowers you'll find there."

The morning of the funeral, I melted paraffin on the stove and then carefully dipped each crepe paper flower. I carried the waxy bouquet carefully as I joined the others. Before Karl closed the coffin lid, I took one last look, pleased to see Mulie tucked by Mattie's side.

"I did that," said Chase. "I didn't want her to be lonely."

I pressed my fingertips to my lips, not wanting to cry in front of Chase. After a moment, I felt composed enough to put my arm through his and we followed Leafie and Karl out beyond the house.

"Perilee wants her here," said Karl.

Karl, Chase, Leafie, and I stood by the freshly dug grave, on the top of the coulee east of the house. "She can see the sunrise each morning," said Karl.

"You gonna say some words?" asked Leafie.

"Me?"

Leafie gave me a look. I took a deep breath and counted to ten. I didn't know what words to say. I began anyway.

"Lord, it may take you some time to get used to our Mattie. She can talk your ear off."

Chase and Karl both nodded.

"But you'll soon come to see that knowing her is like having sunshine and strawberries every day. We ask you to take very good care of our little magpie. And help us, Lord . . ." Here my voice wobbled. "Help us get used to the quiet spaces she used to fill up."

Leafie blew her nose. "Amen."

Chase wrapped his arms around my waist, and I held him close. Karl lifted shovel- after shovelful of dirt onto the fine wooden box he'd built. We stayed until the hole was filled. Then I planted the three waxed flowers I'd brought. I felt as if I might crack in two as we all carried our sorrow back to the house.

Ours was not the only loss on that prairie. The Nefzgers lost their Leta, Mr. Ebgard his wife. Not even the wealth of the Martins could save them from grief: the youngest boy, Lon, survived his bout, as did Sarah, but their mother, who was a faithful nurse to both, did not.

Mr. Dye sold far too many black armbands for mourning and kept selling them right into November.

CHAPTER 22

NOVEMBER 1918

THE ARLINGTON NEWS

Honyocker's Homily ~ Quilting Lessons

In my year on the prairie, I have learned to quilt. At the beginning, my fingertips bled from needle pricks that caught skin rather than the fabric. My eyes crossed from picking out stitches when I tried to pair up two acrimonious fabrics. My neck ached from crooking over the quilting frame.

Slowly my skills improved. Calluses formed on my fingertips, my eye grew skilled at selecting friendlier fabrics to piece into the same block, and my neck is now accustomed to hunching over my work. And I can turn the saddest rag of a shirt to find the one good spot that can be snipped out and turned into a quilt patch. As much as I have improved, however, I have learned neither how to piece together a ledger book when the money isn't there nor how to take a bitter loss and turn it this way or that to find a "good side."

I took a cup of coffee and sat on my front steps, staring at that great expanse of Montana sky. A few short months ago, I'd seen it as a magic carpet, carrying me to my dreams. Now this sky held no promise.

I thought back to finding that photo of my family in Uncle Chester's trunk. I thought maybe it meant to keep going, that all would work out. But nothing short of a miracle would allow me to finish proving up on the claim. Last evening, after supper, I'd gone over my ledger half a dozen times. Each time I got the same answer. And it wasn't good. They were the kind of numbers Uncle Holt would have written in red ink. And though I had prayed and figured and thought and schemed, I could not come up with a way to make those numbers look any better. This was beyond being short the $37.75 for the filing fee. This was debt. Owing folks. Something I'd come out here to avoid. There were still a few bushels of grain to sell for feed but that wouldn't make a dent in my empty money pot.

My stomach felt as if I'd eaten a bushel of green apples.

Doing what I needed to do to prove up my claim had left me more beholden to the folks who meant something to me—Karl and Wayne Robbins and Mr. Nefzger—than I'd ever been to all those relatives I'd lived with.

Maybe I could've rallied myself. Before. But Mattie's death had upended me; I couldn't get my footing. It was enough of an accomplishment to write my final installment for the *Arlington News*. I had no idea how to settle my accounts. And no heart for it, either.

I sat, quiet and alone. No tears. No shaking my fist at God. Nothing but a heavy stone in my chest that used to be a heart filled with dreams and possibilities. There should be fireworks, at least, when a dream dies. But no, this one had blown apart as easily as a dandelion gone to seed.

Perhaps there was no escaping my role of Hattie Here-and-There. Perhaps that was my fate in life. My call. Trouble was, while I might be able to talk my head into such a thought, my heart wasn't buying any of it. My heart wanted a place to belong. A home of my own.

A cloud of dust from the northeast clued me in to company coming. Over the coulee burst Rooster Jim, jouncing astride his new Indian motorcycle. It appeared he had a better handle on this vehicle than he did on the bicycle.

"Hattie, didja hear?" He roared into the yard. "The war's over. The boys will be coming home." He parked his motorcycle and then himself on the step next to me. "You don't look very happy about the news."

"Oh, it's wonderful, Jim." Charlie would be coming home, safe and sound. And all the Vida men I'd gotten to know. There'd be no more gold stars in anyone's windows.

And maybe things would go easier for folks like Karl and Elmer Ren and all the others. "Wonderful news, really."

Rooster Jim reached over and put his hand on mine. "I hope you don't plan a career on the stage," he said. "I love you, child, but you can't act worth beans."

That won him a weak smile. I showed him my ledger. "I guess you'll have to find a new chess partner," I told him.

Rooster Jim shook his shaggy head. We sat in silence for a long time. I have no idea what he was thinking, but I thought back to all our chess games. And his wild bicycle ride. And nearly drowning Rose trying to get her to be a good hen. Funny memories like that should make you laugh. Not cry.

"You worked like a trouper to make it go, Hattie. Nothing to be ashamed of."

I thought about that. I wasn't ashamed, but I was heart-broken. "I did give it a good shot, didn't I?" I sniffled.

"That you did." Jim reached in his pocket for pipe and to-bacco. He filled his pipe and lit it, puffing noisily. "You know, my mama used to say the Lord works in mysterious ways—"

I held up my hand to stop him. "That was Aunt Ivy's fa-vorite saying, too. Well, letting me lose the claim is more than mysterious. It's downright mean."

"Now, I know my mama's still fussing about me up there." Jim pointed heavenward and gave a wink. "But she'd be proud to know I believe it."

"What?"

"That things have a way of working themselves out. That there's reasons for our valleys and for our peaks."

"Well, I'm ready for a peak. And soon." I stood up and brushed off my skirt.

"Maybe you should trust in that Lord of yours. I suspect He's got a grand plan for someone like you." He pushed himself up, too, then moved toward his motorcycle.

I felt bad to have been so short with him. He certainly had done his share to help me out. "Jim, I'm so down. I didn't mean to drive you off."

He laughed. "Takes more than a cranky word to drive me away. I want to spread the good news about the armistice before it gets dark." He straddled the motorcycle and started it up. I watched his dust trail for a good long while.

The past few months played through my mind. I shook my head at my own foolishness. I had been so determined to do everything on my own when I first arrived. Chase had had to rescue me from my own stupidity on my very first homestead day. There were so many people who'd helped me. I pressed my fingers against my lips to keep from crying. It sure seemed like this was where I belonged. There was Leafie, with her blustery talk and gentle ways. And Jim. Of course, I couldn't even let myself think about Perilee and the children. And Mattie.

I resumed my list: Grace at church, Bub Nefzger, Mr. Ebgard. Oh, he had been my white knight that day with Traft.

My white knight! He'd rescued me once before. Maybe he could help me again. He might know some way around this, something I could do. I freshened myself up, mounted Plug, and headed to Wolf Point.

269

I launched into my story as soon as I burst in Mr. Ebgard's door.

"Slow down, Hattie," he said. "And sit down."

I did both, then finished my thought. "I was wondering . . ." I had come up with this idea on my ride into Wolf Point. "Could I reapply? Start over?" I leaned forward. "I have some debts to pay off first."

"Oh, Hattie." He pulled off his glasses and rubbed his eyes. "I'd loan the money myself—"

"I'm not asking that." I sat up straighter. "Just a chance to start again. You know. Like Chester did."

He chewed on his moustache. "I wish you could. But . . ." He shuffled some papers on his desk. "There's no such provision. The three-year deadline is firm."

My heart, which had been so full of hope on the whole long ride to town, slumped like a fallen layer cake. "I had to try . . ." I stood up. "I do thank you, Mr. Ebgard. For everything."

His mouth dipped down at the corners, as if he might cry, too. "This is no comfort, I'm sure, but you aren't the only one." He rearranged the papers on his desk. "Mabel and Elmer Ren, the Saboes, and . . ." His voice drifted off. "It was a bad year. Nobody's fault. Next year we'll shake these hard times."

"Next year," I echoed. Who had told me some folks called this next-year country? Well, next year wouldn't be better for me. Not here, anyway. I shook his hand and stepped outside. The November wind came up behind me and knocked me off balance. As if it was telling me to leave, too.

"Miss Brooks."

I turned. Could the day get any worse? "Mr. Martin." Something in his face caught at me. The confidence was diminished; there was actually a softness behind those eyes. Of course. "I am sorry about your mother," I said.

"Thank you." He smiled ruefully. "She got her wish, didn't she? The war ended before I could fight."

There didn't seem to be an appropriate response.

"I'm looking forward to being done with the Council of Defense, too," he said. "Get back to being a rancher. That's what I know best."

Being a rancher. It was an opening, and I was desperate enough to take it. "Mr. Martin." I put my hand on his arm. "Traft. Could I buy you a cup of coffee?" There was no way around it. I'd have to sell to Traft. But it would leave me with enough money to buy a house. Maybe in Wolf Point. Or even in Vida.

"I don't—"

I cleared my throat. "I'm ready to sell."

He shook his head. "I'm not buying." As hurtful as the words were, they were said without anger.

My stomach looped itself into a knot. "Not buying? But you wanted to expand the Tipped M. You wanted pasture land—"

He turned to face me. "I'm a businessman. Why should I buy your claim now?"

"I'd take four hundred," I said. "That's half of what you offered before."

He exhaled loudly. "Hattie, I can get it for next to nothing. At the end of the month, when the county takes it back." Was there a twinge of sadness in his eyes? A touch of pity for my loss? "I pay the back taxes and it's mine." He gently removed my hand from his arm—I hadn't even realized it was still there—and strode off.

Perilee opened her front door to me the next morning. How many times had I climbed those steps since January? I couldn't begin to count. "Coffee's on and I've got strudel, fresh from the oven." She pulled me into a hug as I stepped over the threshold and held me there extra long. When we stepped apart, she quickly ducked her head, but not before I saw the weary pain in her brown eyes.

I waved at Karl, out by the new barn with Wayne Robbins. They were poking around Karl's tractor. "Hey there, Hattie," Wayne called out. Karl simply returned my wave.

"Something wrong with the tractor?" I asked. Wayne was a whiz with persnickety engines.

Perilee poured two mugs of coffee. "Sit you down. I've got something to tell you."

Settled with a cup of Perilee's coffee and a slice of apple heaven on the plate in front of me, I nearly lost my nerve to tell her my story. Maybe if I didn't say it out loud, it wouldn't be true.

"I do, too. I went into Wolf Point yesterday," I began. "Saw Mr. Ebgard."

"And?" Perilee's fork paused over her slice of strudel.

"I—" My head bowed and the tears I'd so fiercely held back in front of Traft fell fast and furious. I lifted my face to meet my good friend's. "I've lost it, Perilee. Uncle Chester's claim." I fumbled in my skirt pocket for a handkerchief to wipe my drippy nose. "My claim."

"Oh, sugar!" Perilee jumped up, skimmed around the table, and put her hand on my shoulder.

"I thought I'd have a home of my own," I blubbered. "B-b-but now I've got nothing."

"You've got something better than any old claim shack." Perilee lifted my chin. "You've got people who love you to pieces."

I sniffled. I'd lain awake all last night thinking about that very thing. That's when I'd come up with my plan. "I was hoping . . ." I blew my nose. Perilee pulled a chair around and sat so we were knee to knee. "I thought maybe I could stay here with you for a bit. I could teach Chase and help Karl and—" The look on Perilee's face stopped me cold. She sighed and shook her head. "I know it's a lot to ask," I added.

"I would've been sick if you hadn't asked." She took my hand. "I can't think of worse timing to tell you, but . . ." Her eyes darted around the room. "I'd give anything to have you stay with us. But this house . . ." She waved her hands. "Everywhere I turn, there's something that says Mattie. For some folks that might be a comfort. But not for me."

"What are you saying?"

She pressed her lips tight together, then blew out a breath. "We're going to sell. Move." She jerked her head toward the window. "Wayne's going to buy our tractor and one of the calves. Karl's picking up an automobile in Wolf Point tomorrow. Brand-new Dodge touring car!" She gave a half smile. "Anything that doesn't fit in, we'll sell at auction."

I folded my hands across my chest, as if to keep my broken heart from falling clean out of my body. "No!" But even as she spoke the words, I knew this was what they should do. Had to do.

"It's for the best." Now Perilee's face was wet with tears. "Karl's cousin has a machine shop in Seattle. After Mattie . . . after everything, Karl wrote and asked if there were any jobs. His cousin wrote right back and told us to come. He's even found us a house to rent."

"You've known for a while?" I asked. "And you didn't even tell me?"

Perilee looked at her hands. I could barely hear her whispered answer. "I couldn't. Couldn't say good-bye. Not to you."

I leaned hard against the chair back. "When are you leaving?"

Lottie began to cry from the bedroom. Perilee rose to get her. "Soon," she said. "Real soon." She came back carrying Lottie. I held my arms out and took her, cuddling her close, breathing in the sweet baby smell of her. "I've got to make this last," I said.

Perilee stepped close and wrapped her arm around my waist. "You are my sister of the heart," she said. "Geography can't change that."

I leaned in to her. "I know, I know." But I would've given anything to change the geography separating Seattle from Montana.

At the end of the week, Leafie badgered me into going into Wolf Point for the Armistice Day pageant. The whole town

274

had turned out. One of the Ebgard girls dressed up as Victory, a huge flag wrapped around her like a toga. On top of her dark curls she wore a crown bearing the word *Peace*. Traft Martin and the rest of the Dawson County Council of Defense led the crowd in patriotic songs. I couldn't help think about how, a short time ago, Mr. Ebgard had been seen by some as a traitor. But he had been successful in lobbying for federal aid for farmers so that they could buy spring seed. That was a sight more than any of Traft's crew had done.

Leafie nudged me. "Look at that!"

Rooster Jim came roaring up on his motorcycle, flags flying everywhere. There was even one stuck in his battered hat.

Leafie slipped her arm through mine. "Let me buy you a cold drink."

We walked toward the O.K. Café.

"So, the sale is all settled?" Leafie asked. She sipped her cherry phosphate.

I nodded. "The papers were signed yesterday." I twirled my straw through my chocolate soda.

"It won't be the same around here." Leafie pushed her glass away.

I couldn't answer. If I'd tried, I would've broken down for certain.

"Go see them in Seattle. That'd be a nice adventure for a young girl." Leafie fished in her pocketbook for some coins to pay for our drinks. She made a great show of it, but I knew she was giving me time to pull myself together. "There we are. Thirty-five cents. Just right." She laid the coins on the counter.

Leafie finding the correct change was the only thing that was "just right" about life right now.

Back home again, I went through my things to find the perfect going-away presents for Perilee and her family. Not that I had much to give but, after some last-minute quilting, I was satisfied.

The gifts in a basket over my arm, I stood at the bottom of Perilee's steps.

"I believe there's something in here for you," I teased Chase. "Maybe an apron or frilly handkerchief?" Tentatively, he took the proffered package.

He tore off the wrapper. "Oh! Your books!" He cradled my Stevensons to his chest. "This will keep me company the whole way to Seattle. Thanks, Hattie. Thank you." He patted the books. "I hear there's not just one library in Seattle, but three. Won't that be something?"

"Looks like you got your wish," I said. "The one you made the day of the big storm." I reached out to shake his hand. After all, he was now a young man of nine. But he slipped in close and gave me a hug. I hugged back. Hard.

I handed a small packet to Perilee. "For the girls, when they're a bit older." Inside, I'd wrapped my mother's tortoise-shell combs, one for Fern and one for Lottie.

"They'll treasure these, you can be sure." Perilee placed them in her pocketbook.

"Karl, this isn't much, but I hope you enjoy it."

Karl smiled when he opened his package. "*Danke.* Thank you, Hattie." I figured he could use Uncle Chester's Zane Grey collection to help him learn to read English.

"Sugar, this is too much." Perilee shook her head.

"Wait a second." I pulled out one more package. "There's something in here for you."

Perilee tore off the brown paper. Her eyes lit up like starbursts when she saw what was inside. "Your quilt!" She stroked the fabric.

"A brand-new pattern." I blinked back tears. "Mattie's Magic."

She studied each and every inch of it. I didn't mind the scrutiny; this was my best effort. Every stitch was tiny and true. The center of each block was a square of chambray, for Montana's never-ending sky. That square was bordered with sawtoothed triangles, forming smaller squares. There I'd used some of the brown gingham to capture this broad prairie. Opposite each brown triangle was a splash of color, something that reminded me of our little magpie, all bright and full of life.

"Why, here's your dancing dress." Perilee smoothed her fingers over the quilt top. "And Chester's work shirt, and that calico I gave you." She opened her mouth as if to say something else, then crumpled the quilt close to her heart and rocked in place for a moment.

Karl sounded the horn on their new automobile. "Time to go!" he called.

Perilee stepped toward the car. I threw my arms around her and hugged for all I was worth. She stroked my back for a while, then gently pushed me away.

"Hon, when someone's a true friend, there's no need to miss 'em." She patted her chest. " 'Cause they're always right here."

We both wiped our eyes.

277

"You'll come," said Karl. It was more order than invitation.

"Yes, sir!" I laughed.

"I'll drive him crazy if you don't," said Perilee. "You might even find a good job out there. You know there'll always be room for you with us."

"Maybe after the new year," I said. I had wrestled and wrestled with this. Something kept me from saying yes to going with them. Something unfinished that I couldn't name.

"No piecrust promises, now." She shook her finger at me.

"No, ma'am." I hugged her again. "Perilee—"

"I know. I know." Perilee took Lottie from Karl, grabbed Fern's hand, then closed her eyes briefly. I wondered if she was thinking of a sweet little magpie then; I was.

She straightened her shoulders. "Karl's going to leave without me," she said. She climbed in and closed the door, and off they drove, without one backward glance.

I packed my things in Uncle Chester's trunk. Thanks to the auction and the things I was leaving behind, most of my belongings—except what was left of my books—fit inside. I closed the lid with a satisfying whump and did up the latches and straps. Rooster Jim had offered to cart it to the train station in Wolf Point for me. I'd answered an ad, after all, and would be starting in two weeks as a chambermaid at Brown's Rooming House in Great Falls. I had to laugh. Here I was heading off to the very same kind of job I'd left Iowa to avoid. The Lord certainly does move in mysterious ways. This time I was thankful for the job. In six months I'd have my debts paid off and could make a fresh start. I didn't know yet where that would be.

Uncle Holt sent me money for the train fare. *It's enough to come east again,* he'd written, *but I suspect your future is not here in Arlington. Use this to head as far west as you care to go. I am thankful the ocean will stop you from traveling too far from us.*

When Jim came for my trunk, he also brought my mail. There were three letters from Charlie. I read each one slowly. I didn't realize until I was finished with the last letter that I'd been holding my breath.

> *Looks like I made it. There are far too many that weren't so lucky. I ship out in a few weeks. Uncle Sam's been good enough to let me save up a few bucks. Thought I might come see what's so great about that sky you're always bragging on. Write me in care of Mother's to let me know if you are up for a visitor.*
>
> > *Your Charlie*
>
> *P.S. Mildred Powell got herself engaged to Frank Little. Mother hesitated to write me of it, for fear a broken heart might lead me to some front-line heroics. I don't know why everyone thought I was sweet on her. Anyone with two eyes could tell I was sweet on a southpaw pitcher with big dreams. Is she sweet on me?*

I picked up a pen to answer Charlie's letter.

❧ CHAPTER 23 ❧

December 12, 1918

Dear Charlie,

When you get to Wolf Point, stop in and see Mr. Ebgard. He has offered to drive you down to that spot I wrote you from so often—three miles north and west of Vida, Montana. He has the most stylish new Luverne automobile, so I would accept his offer if I were you. I wish you could've seen my acres in the spring, all green fuzz creeping along the prairie, or in late summer, when the flax turned the fields deep sea blue.

Maybe, just maybe, if you stand on the steps of my home—if Traft hasn't carted it away so that his Tipped M cows can run free—you will catch loose memories on the breeze. Listen—do you hear Chase rescuing me from the

*pump handle? Mattie scolding Mulie for tearing her new
dress? Leafie nursing this neighbor or that? Do you hear
Rose and June cackling in Rooster Jim's yard? Perilee's
angel voice soaring above the mishmash of voices at the
Vida church? It won't take you long, standing there, to
understand what I mean about that sky, the endless and
aloof Montana sky.*

*I have to laugh at myself, already looking at that time
through rose-colored glasses. Don't think I could ever
forget the smutchy odor of a burned barn, or the vinegary
scent of fear of folks born in the wrong country, or the
achingly clean perfume of paraffin-dipped crepe paper
flowers. The blessing is that these heartbreaks are but a
few of the patches in my prairie year quilt.*

*You asked me an important question. One I can't
answer yet. Perhaps you could step off the train at Great
Falls. I can't say that I'd be disappointed to have dinner
together. That would be nice. My only plans now are to
work at Brown's until my debts are repaid. Though I
should feel a total failure, my time on the prairie has
branded this hope on my heart: next year it will be better.*

My new job didn't allow pets, but there were no com-
plaints from Mr. Whiskers about that. He'd made it clear he
was in Vida to stay. At least one of us had found a home. And
Leafie was pleased as punch for the company.

"It's going to be lonely around here, what with both you
and Perilee gone." She shook her head. "I'll be able to slice up
the quiet and serve it on toast!"

I handed over Mr. Whiskers' travel case. "Not that he'll need it anymore," I said. "But he likes to curl up in it once in a while on a cold night." I tried not to think about all the nights he'd kept me warm.

Rooster Jim welcomed Albert, June, and Rose back to the fold. Martha had quit laying; she'd been the main dish at my farewell party. Though I'd auctioned off most everything else, I gave Plug to Elmer Ren Jr.

I didn't want anyone to see me off at the station. I'd arrived alone and wanted to leave that way. Settling myself on the train seat, I couldn't help but smile. My traveling companions could've passed for the twins of those with whom I'd ridden out to Montana. Now, the rough ways and clothes seemed cozy and familiar. And, I had to admit, that fat man had been right. There was too much promised of eastern Montana. She gave all she could, but she couldn't support so many home-steaders. Honyockers! That's what he'd called us, and that's what we were.

The train left the station with a jolt. A letter crinkled in my skirt pocket. I'd nearly memorized it. *The Boeing Airplane Company is looking for mechanics, and I happen to know a good one—me!* Charlie had written. *Maybe we will both end up in Seattle.*

I leaned my head back against the seat and closed my eyes. So much had happened in one year's time! Now here I was, headed to Great Falls. What next, I didn't know. I wanted to keep writing. Perilee's last letter had noted that there was already one woman reporter at the *Seattle Times* newspaper. Maybe there was room for two.

The train lurched over a patch of rough tracks, jarring me out of my woolgathering. Outside, the blue Montana sky stretched forever. Come to think of it, Montana had kept her promise. I *did* find a home in my year on the prairie. I found one in my own skin. And in the hearts of the people I met.

Leafie had been amazed at all that I packed up to take with me. "Do you need *all* them books?" she'd asked. But there was one thing I'd left behind: Hattie Here-and-There. I wasn't going to miss her. Not one bit.

I settled myself in and faced west.

Perilee's Wartime Spice Cake

1 cup brown sugar, firmly packed
1½ cups water
⅓ cup shortening or lard
⅔ cup raisins
½ teaspoon each ground cloves and nutmeg
2 teaspoons cinnamon
1 teaspoon baking soda
1 teaspoon salt
2 cups flour
1 teaspoon baking powder

Boil brown sugar, water, shortening, raisins, and spices together for 3 minutes. Cool. Dissolve baking soda in 2 teaspoons water and add with salt to raisin mixture. Stir together flour and baking powder and add to raisin mixture one cup at a time, beating well after each addition. Pour into a greased and floured 8-inch square pan and bake at 325 °F for about 50 minutes.

(Adapted from Butterless, Eggless, Milkless Cake, in *Recipes and Stories of Early Day Settlers;* and from Depression Cake, described in *Whistleberries, Stirabout and Depression Cake: Food Customs and Concoctions of the Frontier West.*)

Hattie's Lighter-than-Lead Biscuits

¾ cup cooked oatmeal, cooled
1½ cups wheat or rye flour
4 teaspoons baking powder
¾ teaspoon salt
2 tablespoons lard, shortening, or butter
¼ cup milk

Mix oatmeal with sifted flour, baking powder, and salt. Cut in lard, shortening, or butter. Add milk and mix, forming a soft dough. Do not overmix. Roll out on lightly floured surface to ¼ to ½ inch thick. Cut with floured biscuit cutter (or drinking glass) and bake on an ungreased cookie sheet at 425 °F for 12 to 15 minutes.

(These are what Hattie served to Rooster Jim in Chapter 17.)

Author's Note

When I heard that my great-grandmother Hattie Inez Brooks Wright had homesteaded in eastern Montana by herself as a young woman, I found it hard to believe. Tiny and unprepossessing, she was the last person I'd associate with the pioneer spirit. But I was intrigued and played detective for several weeks, without much luck, trying to find out more. One day I stumbled onto the Montana Bureau of Land Management records. The thrill I felt when I discovered a claim number with her name attached! A query to the National Archives soon put into my hands a copy of her homestead application paperwork. I was hooked.

Though my great-grandmother didn't keep diaries or journals, other "honyockers" did. I ordered them up through interlibrary loan (God bless our librarians and our library systems), reading them by the dozen. The reasons for heading west were as varied as the homesteaders themselves. But common themes stitched their way through these stories: endless work, heartache, loss, and, incredibly, fond memories of those hardscrabble homestead days.

287

Before I even realized what was happening, I had a book started, thinking it would be "just" a story about homesteading in the days of Model Ts rather than covered wagons. My research quickly showed me I could not set a story in 1918 without speaking to the issue of anti-German sentiment. Many of the incidents in *Hattie Big Sky* were based on actual events, including the mob scene with Mr. Ebgard.

This book and the Iraq war started at nearly the same time. On the very day that I read of merchants renaming "sauerkraut" and calling it "liberty cabbage" in 1918, I heard of restaurants changing "french fries" to "freedom fries" in 2003. The more I studied life in 1918, the more I saw its parallels in the present.

After all is said and done, however, I wrote this book to share a woman's homesteading story. What dreams did the real Hattie hope to fulfill in leaving Arlington, Iowa, for a homestead claim shack near Vida, Montana? I wish I knew. But I was ten years old when she died; at ten, I couldn't imagine that frail white-haired ladies had lives beyond baking snickerdoodles for their great-grandchildren.

My great-grandmother proved up on her claim, but I couldn't let "my" Hattie keep hers. Most honyockers went bust; the railroad men *did* promise too much of eastern Montana, as the fat man on the train complained. Though one succeeded and one failed, both Hatties found something priceless during their time on the Montana prairie: family. And what happier ending could there be than that?

Further Reading

For those interested in reading more about the Montana of Hattie's story, here are several favorites from my research:

Bad Land: An American Romance, by Jonathan Raban, Pantheon Books, 1996.

The Generous Years: Remembrances of a Frontier Boyhood, by Chet Huntley, Random House, 1968.

Homesteading, by Percy Wollaston, Penguin, 1997.

Photographing Montana 1894–1928: The Life and Work of Evelyn Cameron, edited by Donna Lucey, Mountain Press Publishing, 2001.

Riders of the Purple Sage, by Zane Grey, Grosset and Dunlap, 1912.

The Stump Farm, by Hilda Rose, Little, Brown, 1928.

A Traveler's Companion to Montana History, by Carroll Van West, Montana Historical Society Press, 1986.

When You and I Were Young, Whitefish, by Dorothy M. Johnson, Montana Historical Society Press, 1982.

Wolf Point: A City of Destiny, by Marvin W. Presser, M Press, Billings, Montana, 1997.

Learn more about World War I at www.firstworldwar.com.

Learn more about your own family and state history at www.usgenweb.com.

About the Author

Thanks to her eighth-grade teacher, Kirby Larson maintained a healthy lack of interest in history until she heard a snippet of a story about her great-grandmother homesteading by herself in eastern Montana. Efforts to learn more about Hattie Wright's homestead times felt like detective work; why hadn't anyone told Kirby research could be this much fun? Her three years' work on *Hattie Big Sky*, winner of a Newbery Honor, involved several trips to Montana, one by train, as well as countless hours in wonderfully dusty courthouse records rooms and newspaper morgues.

Kirby Larson lives with her husband, Neil, in Kenmore, Washington, where they are both active in the community. Their son works in the film industry in New York; their daughter is an interior designer. When she's not reading or writing, Kirby is teaching, gardening, traveling, or drinking lattes with friends.

HATTIE BIG SKY

Kirby Larson

A READERS GUIDE

★ "Larson creates a masterful picture
of the homesteading experience
and the people who persevered."
—*School Library Journal*, Starred

1. In the first chapter, Hattie is given a "wonderful opportunity." What do you learn about her as a person when she says yes to going to Vida?

2. When Hattie arrives in Wolf Point, she meets with Mr. Ebgard (page 25), who explains more fully the requirements of proving up on a claim. One requirement is to build a house, but fortunately for Hattie, Uncle Chester has already done that. The other tasks include setting 480 rods of fence (which is 7,920 feet; picture 587 VW Beetles in a very, very long row) and planting crops on one-eighth of the claim, or in Hattie's case, 40 acres (picture an area nearly as big as 40 football fields). How would you have reacted to this if you had been in Hattie's shoes?

3. On page 50, Hattie copies out a humorous poem about the trials and tribulations of rationing and other wartime deprivations. She sends it to Charlie to give him a laugh. How do you think people really felt about being deprived of such essentials as flour and sugar? How might people today respond if a war or other events necessitated rationing?

4. After Violet's tail becomes a snack for the wolf, Hattie goes to visit with Perilee and learns that Karl is being required to register as a "resident alien." What is Hattie's response to this? How does her reaction compare to Perilee's?

5. Charlie's letters to Hattie start out full of bravado. She says he is "full of spit and vinegar" when he's issued his bayonet (page 30). Over the course of the story, the tone of his letters changes. Near the end, he writes, "I always bragged about killing some Germans. Killing is nothing to brag about. Nothing at all" (page 232). What might have contributed to Charlie's changed perceptions of the war?

6. At one point in the story (page 119), Hattie realizes that she and Traft may have more in common than she'd like to admit. What traits does she think they share? Do you agree with her assessment?

7. In her May "Honyocker's Homily" (pages 161 and 162), Hattie writes about the lessons she's learning on the prairie and how they "pertain more to caring than to crops, more to Golden Rule than gold, more to the proper choice than to the popular choice." Discuss what she might mean by this.

8. Even though homesteaders worked long, hard hours, they still made time to write to friends and family back home. Hattie's letters to Uncle Holt become the basis for her column, "Honyocker's Homily," in which she shares her story of life on the prairie. Letter writing isn't as common today, but people still reach out to one another through the written word. Can you think of other, contemporary equivalents of letter writing? Why do you think it's so important for us to tell our individual stories?

9. One nickname for eastern Montana is "next year country," as Hattie tells Uncle Holt in her letter to him dated June 22, 1918 (page 204). Based on the story of *Hattie Big Sky,* does this seem like a fitting nickname? Why or why not?

10. When Hattie stumbles upon the men harassing Mr. Ebgard, she wonders why no one comes forward to stop them. Then she realizes: "There was no 'anyone' at a time like this. There was only me" (page 215). What gives her the courage to step forward?

11. After Hattie fails to prove up on Uncle Chester's claim, Rooster Jim tells her "things have a way of working themselves out . . . there's reasons for our valleys and for our peaks" (page 268). What is he trying to tell her? Do you think things will work themselves out for Hattie?

In Her Own Words

A Conversation with
KIRBY LARSON

Q: Your great-grandmother's experience as a homesteader inspired *Hattie Big Sky*. Is this your great-grandmother's story?

A: I do know that my great-grandmother homesteaded near Vida, Montana, and that she proved up and later sold her claim. And I found a newspaper article that said she had dinner with a Vida family one Sunday—big news! But our family doesn't know much about her early life, before she married my great-grandfather when she was thirty-seven. This book is more a re-creation, based on reading and research, of what her time on the prairie and at the homestead might have been like.

Q: Have you always been interested in history?

A: Not at all! I detested memorizing dates and facts when I was in school; I thought that was what history was. When my daughter was in junior high, she introduced me to historical fiction and I became an avid reader, thoroughly enjoying books like *The Dreams of Mairhe Mehan* by Jennifer Armstrong, *Catherine, Called Birdy* and *Matilda Bone* by Karen Cushman, and *Our Only May Amelia* by Jennifer L. Holm. As much as I enjoyed reading those books, it never occurred to me that I could write historical fiction. It took two women who never went beyond eighth grade—my grandmother Lois Brown and my great-grandmother Hattie—to teach me to love history.

Q: How much of *Hattie Big Sky* is fact and how much fiction?

A: I spent three years researching *Hattie Big Sky* and worked hard to get enough information to accurately re-create another time and place. Many of the names, events, et cetera, are factual, but I've tweaked them so that they make a more engaging story. For example, I did read one journal entry where a woman reminisced about seeing a wolf bite off a calf's tail when she was a young girl. That was such a delicious incident, I knew I would have to include it in *Hattie Big Sky*.

Q: Which character is most like you?

A: My daughter says Hattie sounds exactly like me at times! And, truth be told, there's a lot of Violet in me, too.

Q: Hattie is based on a real person; are any of the other characters based on real people?

A: No doubt there is a touch of people I know in each of the characters I create. And I did use names of real people—the postmaster, August Nefzger, for example— to honor the Vida pioneers. I also used names of some of my family members. (They know who they are!) But the characters in the story are created solely out of my imagination. The Hattie in the story is not my great-grandmother. And though people want to believe Charlie is real, he, too, is a created character. The letters he writes to Hattie, however, were inspired by letters my husband's grandfather, Myron Hawley, sent home when he was a young man fighting in World War I.

Q: Why does Mattie have to die?

A: More people died from the Spanish influenza than died in the battles of World War I. Because of this, I felt that I couldn't write a story set in 1918 without an influenza death. To be completely honest, I had planned for another character to be the one to die. When I wrote the scene where Hattie comes to the cabin and Perilee and the girls are all sick, I suddenly realized that it wasn't going to be that other character but Mattie. I cried the whole time I wrote the scene; in fact, I still get teary about it. But it was the right thing to do for this book.

Q: There are a lot of parallels between this story and current events. Did you write it to get a message across about war?

A: I'm a quote collector, and one of my favorite quotes is from Samuel Goldwyn, about making movies. To paraphrase Mr. Goldwyn: If you want to send a message, call Western Union. I don't think I can write a good story if my sole motivation is to get a message across. I tried to tell this story as best I could from Hattie's point of view. My hope is that I left enough room for readers to figure out for themselves what this story means to them.

Q: Does Hattie marry Charlie?

A: Everyone asks me that! To be honest, when I finished *Hattie Big Sky,* I thought I was finished with Hattie's story. But so many people have been writing to me asking what happens next that I've begun to think about writing a sequel. And I won't know until I write it—if I write it! —what happens between Hattie and Charlie.

Ashes of Roses
MARY JANE AUCH

978-0-440-23851-5

Sixteen-year-old Margaret Rose Nolan, newly arrived from Ireland, finds work at New York City's Triangle Shirtwaist Factory shortly before the 1911 fire in which 146 employees will die.

Nightjohn
GARY PAULSEN

978-0-440-21936-1

Sarny, a twelve-year-old slave on the Waller plantation, risks terrible punishment when a slave called Nightjohn teaches her to read.

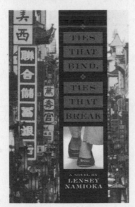

Ties That Bind, Ties That Break
LENSEY NAMIOKA

978-0-440-41599-2

The moving story of a young girl who refuses to follow the Chinese tradition of having her feet bound and pays a high price.

A Great and Terrible Beauty
LIBBA BRAY
978-0-385-73231-4

Sixteen-year-old Gemma Doyle is sent to the Spence
Academy in London after tragedy strikes her family in
India. Lonely, guilt-ridden, and prone to visions of the
future that have an uncomfortable habit of coming true,
Gemma finds her reception a chilly one. But at Spence,
Gemma's power to attract the supernatural unfolds; she
becomes entangled with the school's most powerful girls
and discovers her mother's connection to a shadowy
group called the Order. A curl-up-under-the-covers
Victorian gothic.

Rebel Angels
LIBBA BRAY
978-0-385-73341-0

Gemma Doyle is looking forward to a holiday from Spence
Academy—spending time with her friends in the city,
attending balls in fancy gowns with plunging necklines, and
dallying with the handsome Simon Middleton. Yet amid
these distractions, her visions intensify—visions of three
girls in white, to whom something horrific has happened
that only the realms can explain.

Colibrí
ANN CAMERON
978-0-440-42052-1

At age four, Colibrí was kidnapped from her parents in Guatemala City, and ever since then she's traveled with Uncle, who believes Colibrí will lead him to treasure. Danger mounts as Uncle grows desperate for his fortune—and as Colibrí grows daring in seeking her freedom.

Bucking the Sarge
CHRISTOPHER PAUL CURTIS
978-0-440-41331-8

Luther T. Farrell has got to get out of Flint, Michigan. His mother, aka the Sarge, has milked the system to build an empire of slum housing and group homes. Luther is just one of the many people trapped in the Sarge's Evil Empire—but he's about to bust out.

When Zachary Beaver Came to Town
KIMBERLY WILLIS HOLT
978-0-440-23841-6

Toby's small, sleepy Texas town is about to get a jolt with the arrival of Zachary Beaver, billed as the fattest boy in the world. Toby is in for a summer unlike any other—a summer sure to change his life.

I Am the Wallpaper

MARK PETER HUGHES

978-0-440-42046-0

Thirteen-year-old Floey Packer feels as if she's always blended into the background. After all, she's the frumpy younger sister of the Fabulous Lillian. But when Lillian suddenly gets married and heads off on a monthlong honeymoon, Floey decides it's her time to shine.

The Lightkeeper's Daughter

IAIN LAWRENCE

978-0-385-73127-0

Imagine growing up on a tiny island with no one but your family. For Squid McCrae, returning to the island after three years away unleashes a storm of bittersweet memories, revelations, and accusations surrounding her brother's death.

The Boyfriend List

E. LOCKHART

978-0-385-73207-9

Ruby Oliver is fifteen and has a shrink. She knows it's unusual, but she's had a rough ten days. She's lost her boyfriend, her best friend, and all her other friends; had a panic attack; failed a math test; done something suspicious with a boy; had an argument with a boy; and had graffiti written about her in the girls' bathroom. But Ruby lives to tell the tale (and make more lists).

A Brief Chapter in My Impossible Life
DANA REINHARDT

978-0-375-84691-5

Simone's starting her junior year in high school. She's got a terrific family and amazing friends. And she's got a secret crush on a really smart and funny guy. Then her birth mother contacts her. Simone's always known she was adopted, but she never wanted to know anything about it. Who is this woman? Why has she contacted Simone now? The answers lead Simone to question everything she once took for granted.

Stargirl
JERRY SPINELLI

978-0-440-41677-7

Stargirl. From the day she arrives at quiet Mica High in a burst of color and sound, the hallways hum with the murmur of "Stargirl, Stargirl." The students are enchanted. Then they turn on her.

The Book Thief
MARKUS ZUSAK

978-0-375-84220-7

Trying to make sense of the horrors of World War II, Death tells the story of Liesel Meminger—a German girl whose book-stealing and storytelling talents sustain her foster family and the Jewish man they are hiding in their basement, along with their neighbors. This is an unforgettable story about the power of words and the ability of books to feed the soul.